OPEN PRIMARY

AMERITOCRACY, BOOK 1

A.C. FULLER

To women everywhere fighting for political change.

[PART 1]

JULY, 2019

The first thing I ever did in life was swing the 1988 election. The simple fact of my existence—combined with my father's hypocrisy—destroyed any chance the Democrats had that year.

Maybe that explains why I avoided politics for the first couple decades of my life. Or maybe it was because I can't stand liars, and even the most virtuous politicians are liars from time to time. But I can't avoid politics anymore, and I don't want to.

Things have gone too far.

That's why I'm at Colton Industries in Santa Clarissa, California, just fifteen minutes from Stanford University. I'm sitting in the steel and marble lobby of Building 7, as team after team of Project X presenters stream out of the hall of doom. The hall where dreams go to die. The hall where I'll be spending the most important fifteen minutes of my life.

I should be refining my closing pitch and double-checking my spreadsheets, but I'm nervous, so I distract myself by peering

3

at the cute guy at the reception counter. He greeted me when I arrived, handed me a bottle of Colton Brand artesian spring water, and asked me to take a seat. For the last twenty minutes, I've been sitting in a leather armchair, watching his high-top fade peek out over the top of his iMac.

The back panel of the screen is covered with stickers, mostly pictures of turntables and digital equipment I don't recognize. One particular sticker piques my interest—*Willie Nelson for President*—and it's got me walking over to talk with him. I could use the excuse to do something other than second-guess myself some more.

I stand directly in front of his monitor, so he can't see me, as I read his nameplate. *Malcolm Rozier*. I'm trying to think of something witty to say about the fact that we have the same initials when Malcolm slides his chair around and says, "Can I help you, Ms. Rhodes?"

"It's Mia."

He smiles. "Can I help you, Mia?"

"I was just wondering, will they have a USB-C connector for my MacBook? In the presentation hall, I mean?"

He looks at me like he's not sure if I'm serious, then a wave of recognition passes over his face. "You didn't get the email?"

"Ummm...I..."

I pride myself on being prepared. Some say I *over*-prepare. Back at my day job running the Seattle offices of the online magazine, *The Barker*, my coworkers tell me I'm "a bit of a Monica." But I see from the way he looks at me, his dark brown eyes full of concern, that I've missed something.

"I emailed all presenters this morning." Malcolm's voice is deep and soothing, but his message isn't. "No PowerPoint presentations. The judges have reviewed your materials, including the PowerPoint, so they're limiting the final round to a five-minute opening statement followed by a ten-minute Q and A."

No PowerPoint? I stare at him, trying to play it cool, but inside, I'm panicking.

Stalling, I tap the Willie Nelson sticker on the back of his monitor and say, "Now *he's* a candidate we can all get behind."

Malcolm stands and leans forward across the counter, turning his head to see the sticker. "Oh yeah, that."

"Country music fan?"

"Sort of. I love Willie, Johnny Cash, Woody Guthrie, DeFord Bailey. All the old Americana. Not so much with the modern, 'Bro Country' stuff."

I'm vaguely familiar with all those names, but my country music knowledge doesn't extend much beyond early Taylor Swift.

Malcolm is tall, almost a foot taller than me, and I have to lean back a little to meet his eyes. I run my hand across the curved back of the monitor. "And what are these other stickers?"

"Equipment companies. I DJ in the evenings and on weekends, so..." He glances around the waiting area, then digs a business card out of the inner pocket of his blue blazer. "I'm on YouTube."

The card lists a website, a YouTube channel, and the name *Rozier Productions.*

"Cool," I manage, smiling despite the sinking realization that I'm about to bomb my presentation.

Malcolm cocks his head and squints. "You didn't get the email, did you?"

"I try not to check my email when I have a big event, which is, like, never. Too much stuff from work, too many things to...*throw me off my game.*" I say the last part like a total dork, and immediately regret it.

5

"Shouldn't be more than a few minutes. Can I get you another water, or some coffee, or anything?"

"Nah, I'm just gonna go and try to memorize a few things."

"I'm sure you'll do fine in there."

"Sure," I say, disagreeing in my head as I walk back toward my seat.

"You know, I follow your website," he calls after me.

I turn on the low heels of my cream and black T-straps, and shoot him a look. He's got a shy smile on his face, nerdy but handsome. It puts me at ease.

"Thanks." I'm genuinely surprised he's taken the time to research my site.

"What you're doing is awesome," he continues. "We need viable third-party candidates and independent candidates. I hope you win the money."

Ten minutes later, Malcolm leads me into the presentation room, which looks like a luxury movie theater—six rows of seats angled slightly so the rows in the back are higher than the ones in the front.

Malcolm walks down the light blue carpet and up the four steps to the stage in the front of the room. I follow and he gestures to a silver podium, puts a hand on my forearm, and says, "You're gonna kill it, Mia."

When he turns to leave, I lurch forward and grab his bicep, pulling him in closely. He smells like seaspray, like a male mermaid, and because I sometimes say ridiculous things when I'm nervous, I whisper, "Do you really think Willie Nelson could win?"

He pulls away slightly, like he's trying to decide whether I'm fun-crazy or stalker-crazy, then winks and strolls out of the hall.

Alone on the stage, I stand at the podium and look down at the seating area, which is lit with dark red LED lighting. Only eight of the seats are full, and I know all eight of my judges. Well, I don't *know* any of them, but I did my research on the flight down from Seattle. Five are board members of Project X, three men and two women. They don't carry much weight on the judging panel, so I'm not surprised that all five are seated in the second row.

About five feet below me, the three members of my *real* audience stare at me from the front row. To my left sits Alvin Chang, Chief Operating Officer of Colton Industries and co-founder of Project X. A tall, lean man, with short black hair, Chang wears round Harry Potter glasses and a bored look on his face, like he's seen one too many presentations today. Eleanor Ruff, an older woman with spiky, silver-grey hair and a piercing glare, sits to my right. She's the Executive Director of Project X and a well-known badass around Silicon Valley.

Directly in front of me, between Chang and Ruff, is Peter Colton himself. The boy wonder. Silicon Valley's most eligible bachelor and the man voted "Most Likely to Win an Antonio Banderas Look-alike Contest." Okay, I made the last part up, but he does look a bit like the actor with his shoulder-length black hair, olive skin, and custom-tailored black suit.

It's not his looks that make him such a rockstar of the tech and philanthropic worlds, though. Colton made his first billion dollars back in 2007 when he sold his cloud computing company to some other cloud computing company when he was just twenty-nine years old. In the years since, he's been the kind of billionaire we all tell ourselves we'll be when we finally become billionaires. He bought a soccer team, learned how to pilot his own private jet, summited Kilimanjaro, invested in revolutionary solar technology, and dated movie stars.

He also founded—and funded—Project X, a program that

chooses ten non-profits per year and gives each one $150,000 to support its mission. Each non-profit also gets access to Project X's network of entrepreneurs and tech gurus. And that's why I used a personal day to fly a thousand miles south. That's why I'm staring down at Peter Colton.

He stares back, his dark eyes fixed on mine, his smile both warm and serious, like he's concealing a secret I desperately want to know. On any other day, his look would have left me flustered. But today I'm locked in, ready to go.

After all, I'm trying to save democracy.

I wiggle my toes and rest my hands on the podium, not sure if I should speak first.

Thankfully, Chang breaks the silence. "Hello, Ms. Rhodes. I'm Alvin Chang. To my left, Peter Colton. To his left, Eleanor Ruff. Behind us, well, the other judges of Project X." He gestures toward the board members, but clearly doesn't want to take the time to introduce them. "We apologize for the late change to the structure of the presentation."

"No problem," I lie.

"You have five minutes," Chang continues, "followed by ten minutes of questions. We've reviewed your materials, so our goal is to get to know Mia Rhodes, your passions, and your reasons for applying to Project X."

This is the moment I've been waiting for. I stand as tall as I can at five foot two, throw my head back to get one of my misbehaving auburn curls out of my eye, roll up the sleeves of my white button-down, try in vain to smooth the creases on my black slacks, and say, as boldly as possible, "American democracy is broken."

I pause for effect, scanning the eyes of my three primary judges and casting occasional glances at the five judges behind them. "When we're young, we're taught that the American political system is a meritocracy, that the cream rises to the top, that our leaders and representatives are the best among us.

"That's a lie. What we saw in the last presidential election—and to varying degrees in state and even local elections—was a perverted popularity contest. The barriers to entry are so high that entrenched political power can and does retain its position. The state of campaign finance means that we live in a fundamentally corrupt democracy, where both parties are under enormous pressure to favor business interests over those of the people. We reward the best media manipulator, the biggest celebrity, or the candidate with the biggest ad buys, rather than the smartest, bravest, or kindest among us. Furthermore, technology is now moving at a rate at which politics and media *cannot* keep up.

"Barriers to entry. Perverse financial incentives. A broken media system ruled by technology it can't understand, let alone control. As these trends continue to affect our elections, America will careen down a path toward becoming a failed democracy. A failed state."

I step out from behind the podium and walk the stage, imagining that I'm the star of my own TED Talk. "America needs a new system for choosing a president. That's why I created Ameritocracy2020.org."

"Yes," Ruff interjects, "we've *read* the materials, but what, exactly, is it? Some sort of *website*?"

Her question throws me off, both because I'm only two minutes into my speech and because she says "website" like it's some newfangled fad. But Ruff is a technological wizard, so I assume she's speaking disdainfully about my concept, not the technology I'm using to bring it into the world.

"Ameritocracy2020.org—or just *Ameritocracy*—is a web-based platform designed to find the best independent presidential candidate in the country, and to fund that candidate to compete against the Democrats and Republicans in the 2020 election. If the presidential election is going to be a reality show, I want to create the fairest, most transparent reality show in history. If our political system is going to be ruled by money, I want independent candidates to be funded as well as the established parties. If—"

"Tell us how it *works*," Chang says, crossing his arms.

The interrogation has begun, but I'm gaining confidence, so I walk a little circle around the podium, my heels tapping loudly on the wooden stage.

"Think of Facebook," I reply. "Anyone can start a profile, write posts or upload photos or videos. Ameritocracy is like that. Any U.S. citizen can set up a profile on the site, as long as he or she will be thirty-five years of age by November 3, 2020—election day—and meets the other basic requirements to run for president. We have a brief form to fill out—name, background, and so on. Once you set up your profile, you are a candidate for president in 2020. From there, you can upload your issue platform, videos of yourself making your case to the voters, photos of yourself shaking hands and kissing babies, whatever. Essentially, it's a site on which anyone can run for president of the United States."

"How will your winner be chosen?" Chang asks.

"The final day to register is February 1, 2020. From there, we will have multiple elimination rounds, just like on The Voice or most other reality shows. Right now, we're using ranked-candidate voting. Registered users can rank their top ten candidates, and the votes are combined with a proprietary algorithm to determine our leaderboard. I've tied the key elimination rounds to the major party primaries. So, on Super Tuesday in March of 2020, we'll cut the field to twenty-five candidates. The Republican and Democratic fields will be narrowing around this time

—and media attention will be at its peak—so we'll narrow the field to allow our voters to focus.

"Through the spring and early summer of 2020, we'll have a series of debates and eliminations. Twenty five candidates to twenty, twenty to fifteen, and so on. On July 4, 2020, around the time of the Republican and Democratic Conventions, there will be a final debate, live on our website, featuring the final six candidates. We will then open the voting for twenty-four hours, and, at the end of that time, the top vote-getter wins our competition and all the money we've raised. At that point, we hope he or she will be in a position to compete in the general election against the Democratic and Republican nominees."

"How many candidates do you have right now?" Chang asks, a hint of condescension in his voice.

I planned for this question. Ever since I started the website in an espresso-fueled rage shortly after the 2016 election, Ameritocracy has floundered. Now, two and a half years later, I only have a few dozen candidates, and, frankly, most of them are too far outside the mainstream to have any chance of getting elected. I have no PR, no money, and no way to make the site seem credible. That's where I hope Project X will come in.

"Only a handful, at this point," I say, "but interest in the 2020 election is picking up and—"

"From the numbers you submitted," Ruff interrupts, "it appears no one is using the site."

"We've grown slowly so far, yes."

"We?" Ruff asks.

"Just me, actually. I plan to staff up if I'm selected as a Project X winner."

"When you crown a winner, they'll run as a third party candidate?" Chang asks.

"As an independent. One of the rules about entering is that

you cannot be an elected office holder from the Democratic or Republican party."

"A third party candidate is the future," Ruff says, smirking. "And *always* will be."

She and Chang laugh, and I glare at them. I've heard the joke before, and don't especially like being made fun of.

"So, are there other rules?" Ruff asks, still chuckling.

"Very few. We accept candidates of all backgrounds and political persuasions."

"What about hacking?" Chang asks.

"We haven't had any problems with—"

"What I mean is, if the site grows, what are the risks of hacking?"

"We will be developing solid layers of security." It's the first time I find myself sounding like the obfuscating politicians I loathe, but the truth is that I don't know what I'm talking about when it comes to cyber security. I *plan* to hire experts if the site grows, but it's not something I can speak about with any authority.

"Okay," Ruff sighs, looking at her watch. "But a presidential campaign requires the candidate to raise a couple hundred million dollars, and that's not counting support from the DNC, RNC, or Super PACs, which your winning candidate won't have. Assuming more people enter your competition and the site grows, and assuming you crown a winner by vote around July Fourth, why do you expect them to have any chance in the 2020 election?"

"Two reasons," I say. "Celebrity and money. As Ameritocracy grows, we expect the leading candidates to become well known, to attract mainstream media attention and massive social media followings. Their best posts and videos will go viral. If American politics must be a reality show, we will at least create one with a level playing field and a higher purpose."

I smile at Chang and Ruff, but they don't seem impressed. Peter Colton, who hasn't said a word, stares up at me with that mysterious smile, chin resting on his balled-up hands.

"The second reason we'll have a chance is that we're raising money. Registered users can make donations, and the unique thing about our platform is that the donations *aren't* made to your favorite candidate, they're made to our organization. The understanding is that, after we pay operating costs, we'll give one hundred percent of the remaining funds to our winning candidate in July. No matter who wins."

"Celebrity and money," Chang says. "Good thinking. How much have you raised so far?"

"We're still in the beginning stages and—"

"Seven thousand three hundred dollars and sixty-two cents," Ruff says, looking down at a stack of papers she seems to have pulled out of thin air.

"So far, but—"

"So, what you're really looking at is a long-term play here," Ruff interrupts. "You have no chance of impacting the 2020 election, even if we award you a Project X grant, so maybe 2024, 2028?"

I know she's probably right. Even if I win the money, it could take years to gain traction, given how little attention we've gotten so far.

Before I can respond, Chang says, "Tell me more about the candidates. You said there were a few dozen?"

"Thirty-eight, to be exact, mostly from the fringes. Far right and far left, plus a couple total crackpots. The idea is that, as the site grows and more Americans begin to pay attention and vote, more serious candidates will join. And if the idea gets some traction, and more credible candidates enter, more donations will come in, which will make more candidates want to enter because the idea itself will begin to seem viable."

We're running out of time and my audience is restless. Chang stares at his phone as Ruff puts papers into a briefcase on her lap. I wonder why Peter Colton hasn't spoken, but I prepped a closing statement, specifically geared toward Colton, so I may as well deliver it.

"If you don't have any more questions, I'll finish with an analogy I heard recently." I lean forward and lock eyes with Colton. "For decades, very few people climbed Mount Everest. Only the best trained, most professional climbers dared make the trip. Recently, new technologies have allowed amateur climbers to reach the summit at amazing rates. Smaller and more efficient oxygen tanks, better routes, well-trained assistants, fixed ropes and ladders. Technology allows people to do what, just two decades ago, would have been impossible. Technology *should* do the same for democracy. It should give voice to the voiceless, challenge entrenched power, and allow the best ideas—and the best *people*—to rise to the top. With your help, I hope Ameritocracy will play a small part in that."

There's a slight change in Colton's expression, something more like a regular smile. He stares right at me, and I hold his gaze, gathering all the courage I can muster. "I *know* this idea is just starting out. I *know* it may take some time. But I've spent the last six years managing the day-to-day operations of *The Barker*, an online magazine with seventy employees. If I'm lucky enough to win Project X, I know I can turn Ameritocracy into something that will make a dent in our broken political system. I hope you'll give me the opportunity to try."

～

Despite the interrogation, I closed strong, and I'm proud of myself as I wash my hands in the palatial bathroom outside the meeting hall. Pressing my palms against my neck, I allow the cool to spread through my body, which calms me.

I walk back into the lobby and nod at Malcolm as I pass his desk. "Nice to meet you. I'll check out your YouTube videos."

"I'll keep an eye on your website," he says, picking up his ringing phone.

Waiting for my Uber, I survey the Colton Industries campus. From where I stand, I see three other large buildings, all glass and silver and curves, surrounded by green grass and new sidewalks. Everything screams "new wealth."

When the Prius arrives, I slide in, pulling out my phone to make sure my flight is on time. I feel calm and accomplished, the way I always feel when I've done something hard, something I was afraid of. As the car pulls away from Building 7, I glance back wistfully, like people do in movies.

That's when I see Malcolm, running through the front door and waving at my driver to stop.

The driver doesn't see him.

"Stop," I say. "Stop for a sec."

I roll down my window as Malcolm rushes up.

"What?" I ask. "What is it?"

"I just realized something important," he says. "If Willie Nelson runs for president, they'll probably drag up his old tax scandals. It's never gonna work."

I blink for a moment, confused. "You're right," I say eventually. "The single flaw in an otherwise perfect candidate. Um...is that why you flagged down my car?"

"I wish," he says.

I raise an eyebrow, waiting for him to explain. Then he leans his head through the window slightly and, for one ridiculous moment, I think he's going to kiss me.

[2]

Instead, Malcolm does something even more surprising. "Mr. Colton would like to invite you to our Friday night staff party," he says. "And he's asked me to help you find a dress for the event."

"Why?" I ask, stunned. "I mean, what for?"

He looks down at my shirt and pants. "He just figured you wouldn't have packed for a formal party."

"I mean, why is he inviting *me*?"

"I'm just the messenger here, Mia. Will you go?"

I shoot him my best skeptical look, but I see from his stoic face that, even if he knows what's going on, he won't say. "Are *you* gonna be there?" I'm not flirting, though it may appear that way to Malcolm. I'm just nervous and like the idea of a friendly face.

"Sort of," he says. "I'll be DJing."

"Then sure. I'll go."

I apologize to the driver, hand him a twenty, and follow Malcolm back into the lobby of Building 7, trying to figure out what my first question will be.

He takes his seat behind the iMac and says, "The party is at

16

eight, so we've got a little over three hours. I need twenty minutes to finish some things, then my replacement comes. Like I said, Mr. Colton asked me to take you shopping for a dress, but only if you'd like one."

I lean on the reception counter casually, trying to pretend that there are circumstances under which I'd say no to shopping with the credit card of a billionaire. "A dress?"

"The Friday night parties tend to be more formal than you'd expect for a Silicon Valley company with no dress code. Let's just say that these aren't your typical staff parties."

"And he asked you to take me shopping? For real?"

"If you're more comfortable in what you're wearing, that's fine as well. Mr. Colton is a bit of a libertarian when it comes to his parties. All are encouraged to dress up, and most do, but there's no requirement. Individual choice and all."

He's right that I didn't pack for a formal party. I didn't pack at all. I flew down on the 10 a.m. out of Sea-Tac, planning to be home by midnight. I didn't even bring a toothbrush. Speaking of which, "Where will I stay?" I ask.

Malcolm is typing fast, and he looks up from his screen. "We can get you a hotel room, or you're welcome to stay in Building 12, the dorm for staff who spend the night. The rooms are individual, pod-type spaces, but they're nice."

With that, his eyes are back on his computer, and I shuffle back to the chair I sat in earlier. I pull out my iPhone to check my email, scroll past a couple dozen work-related non-emergencies, and open one from my mother.

Dearest Mia,

How did your presentation go? I can't wait to talk with you.

Love,

Mom

My mom is a waitress at the same Greek diner in Connecticut where she's worked since before I was born. Her calls on Saturday mornings are the only reason I don't sleep until noon, and I need to let her know that I won't be there when she calls my landline tomorrow.

Mom-

Not sure yet. Good, I think. Strange things are happening. Staying over in California a night, so you won't reach me on my home phone tomorrow.

Love you,

Mia

I scroll for a few minutes, ignoring work and deleting spam, then realize the email Malcolm mentioned—the one informing me of the change in presentation structure—isn't there. Not that it matters now, but I'm curious. I scroll again, look in my spam folder, then run a quick search. I have definitely not received an email from Malcolm or anyone at Colton Industries.

Malcolm is now standing behind his chair, updating a young woman who's taken his seat behind the iMac.

I step over, wait for him to finish and, when he nods toward the door, I ask, "Did you lie about the email to all the presenters, or just me?"

"It was a test," Malcolm says, breaking a long silence as we drive off the Colton Industries campus. "The committee wanted to see how you'd do under pressure."

"So, you lied?"

"I was *told* to lie. And you must have done just fine."

"I guess so, but can you tell me anything more about what Mr. Colton said?"

Malcolm takes a soft left onto a wide, two-lane road that heads straight into the small town of Santa Clarissa. "I can't," he says. "Not because I don't want to. I just don't know much else."

"Then tell me about the town."

"Isn't much to it," he says, and I can already see that. We enter a small commercial district, no more than eight blocks long because I can see where the buildings stop and the road continues its path toward the rolling brown hills in the distance. The town looks like it was dropped, all at once, onto a huge patch of flat farmland. When Malcolm explains the history, I learn this is basically what happened.

"In 2012, when Mr. Colton built the campus, he wanted to provide everything his employees would need on site. Free food. Gyms. Child care. Bus service to and from San Francisco, Oakland and all the cities within ninety minutes. By 2014, enough people had relocated to the surrounding area that a small town popped up almost overnight. Other than the old post office, and a bank building that's now a yoga studio, every structure you see was built in the last five years."

"Wasn't that the plot of a *Simpsons* episode?" I ask.

"Yes it was, and I can't promise that's not where he got the idea."

Most of these baby buildings are modern, square structures of wood and glass, all between two and four stories. On the ground floors are a mix of juice shops, boutique clothing stores, and restaurants. On the upper floors are apartments and offices, most of which have wide balconies covered in plants and small trees. Taken as a whole, Santa Clarissa looks like a new section of Disneyland designed for rich Californians. Main Street USA, Silicon Valley style.

Not that I have anything against the opulence. Most Friday evenings I'm arranging last-minute weekend travel for Alex Vane, my boss at *The Barker*, or arguing with our web host about why the site is running slowly. If I'm lucky, by eight o'clock I'm on my couch, eating macaroni and cheese out of a plastic container while watching Netflix. Spending an evening shopping on Peter Colton's dime is a notable improvement.

Malcolm parks and we pass a couple clothing stores and a boutique cellphone shop before stopping at the window of a store called *Mama Mia*, which displays a variety of heels and flats, and even the occasional pair of designer boots. In the back, they appear to have at least a dozen racks of dresses.

"This is the largest store in town," Malcolm says. "Good mix of stuff, from what I hear."

Before he can finish his sentence, I'm inside the store, practically salivating. I'm not a clothes-hound. Not exactly, anyway. Would I spend lots of money on clothes if I had lots of money? Maybe, and I hope to find out someday. But I do *love* nice clothes, even if I can't afford to wear them.

"Mr. Colton said that it's on us," Malcolm says, finding me at a rack of cocktail dresses.

"Thank you."

It takes a good twenty minutes, but I find three possible dresses and Malcolm follows me to the dressing rooms in the back, where I step behind a curtain and he takes a seat on a round velvet bench.

As I squeeze myself into an emerald green, A-line, princess-style dress, I call through the curtain, "So if you can't tell me anything more about what he said, tell me more about Peter Colton."

"You read the blogs, don't you?"

"And yet, I asked you anyway. What's *not* on the blogs?"

"I've only worked for him for two years and, honestly, I don't know him that well. I was just starting to make a living with my music when YouTube changed their advertising rates. Then the club gigs dried up. I took this job as a temporary thing and, well..."

He trails off, the way everyone does when they're talking about dreams deferred.

"So what are these parties like?" I ask, worried the dress I'm trying on makes me look like a teenager at a junior prom.

"Kinda crazy. We work hard all week, often twelve or fourteen-hour days. Well, *I* don't, but the engineers and coders and managers do. Every Friday, Mr. Colton throws a party with a different theme."

This is important data. "What's the theme tonight?"

"Western."

I poke my head out from behind the curtain. "Seriously?"

Malcolm looks away awkwardly, probably because he thinks I'm naked behind the curtain, or is at least imagining that I *could* be. "Western," he says again, eyes glued to the floor.

"Western? And formal?"

"We leave things pretty open to interpretation. Like I said, Mr. Colton is a libertarian about these things. I wear the same black slacks and blue blazer every day, just swapping out t-shirts. But some people go all-out for these parties."

"Can you elaborate?"

"It's a mix. Some go super formal, some get all kinds of crazy with their outfits, some just show up in their work clothes."

"So you really can't help me figure out what kind of outfit I should get?"

"Sorry."

Thinking quickly, I say, "There were a pair of red leather cowgirl boots up front. Can you ask if they have those in a seven and a half?"

I duck my head back behind the curtain as Malcolm heads to the front of the store. I try on a black crepe sheath dress that makes me feel like Jackie O, but it's too formal for a western theme. By the time Malcolm returns, I'm in a cream flare dress with three-quarter sleeves. It's not exactly a line-dancing dress, but it has a similar shape. It ends just above my knees and is the closest I'll come to a western look on short notice.

Malcolm hands me the boots, which are hand-stained and covered in fine decorative stitching. "Too informal?" I ask, doing a little twirl before sitting on the round bench and trying on the boots.

"You look great."

I walk a couple loops around the store, checking myself in the mirror as I pass. The boots are a little tight, but they accent my reddish-brown hair, and will break in over time. Also, they look *really* nice on me. I decide I can get through a night in them.

I gather my clothes and follow Malcolm to the counter. "If you can't tell me much more about Peter, tell me about you."

"Not much to tell. Grew up in Oakland. Still live there. All I ever loved was music, but I can type fast and be pretty organized when I need to be. Applied for this job when the music dried up and, for some reason, I got it. Now I take the Colton Industries electric bus out and back five days a week."

He pays for the dress and boots, the clerk bags up my business attire, and we step onto the sidewalk. It's past six now, but still hot since it's the middle of July, so we head straight to the car.

"What about you?" he asks as we drive back toward the campus. "What's your story?"

"I assume you Googled me."

"I did, but not much came up. I know you manage the offices at *The Barker*, and that you started Ameritocracy a couple years ago. Seems like such a cool idea. Why aren't more people signing up?"

"Why aren't *you* signing up?"

He goes quiet for a moment, and I think I've said something to offend him. Then he laughs. "I would be a *terrible* politician.

Plus, I'm only thirty-one."

"Maybe in 2024?"

"Maybe. But seriously, I'm so sick of politics."

We're bonding a little, and I turn to him as he eases into the long driveway that leads into the campus. When he shifts his eyes from the road to me, I ask, "Do you think Ameritocracy can work? I mean, get big?"

"With enough money behind it, over time, yeah."

"That's what I'm afraid of. I started on a whim, thinking I'd slowly build it into something. If I win the money, that'll...I don't know. I guess I never thought I'd win. Now I'm scared. Nervous. *Something*."

Malcolm slows the car and scans an ID card to open the entry gate. "Just because he invited you to the party doesn't mean you won."

"But you won't tell me what it *does* mean, so..."

"I won't," he says, pulling up alongside Building 7 and shutting off the car. "But I *will* tell you this. For the first five or six years, when I would DJ, I'd get hella nervous before *every* show. Every. Single. Show. Even when I knew I was prepared, knew I was gonna kill it. Then my mom told me something that helped. She said, 'Malcolm, nervousness is just excitement without the breathing.' It doesn't always work, but ever since then, when I'm feeling nervous, I take a few deep breaths. Turns out I'm usually just hyped."

"So you're saying I *should* be nervous?"

"I'm saying you should be *hyped*."

I laugh awkwardly, excited but not entirely sure what he's getting at. Before I can ask, his laugh fills the car and I hear it like I'm wearing fancy headphones—crisp and full of bass. But it's not just his laugh. The leaves on the trees are greener than they should be as they sway in the warm wind. I brush my hand on the leather seat and it feels softer and smoother than before.

I still don't know exactly what he's implying about Colton, but something about the moment feels significant.

Then, just like that, it's over.

"I gotta go finish some work things," Malcolm says, "but you can hang out in the lounge, just off Conference Room D, which is where the party is. Restrooms are there, snacks, whatever you need."

He opens the car door, but I grab his arm. "Can I ask you something?"

"No need for the preliminaries. Just ask."

"There's something that's been nagging at me. You said that Mr. Colton wanted to see how I'd do in an on-the-fly presentation, that he told you to lie about sending me an email. And you said you lied only to me."

"That's right."

"Why? I mean, if he wanted to test me—and *only* me—it means he'd already studied my proposal. Already knew about my project. One way or another, he'd already made up his mind, right?"

Malcolm smiles, and I meet his eyes, which are locked on mine with a slight look of concern. "He has."

An hour later, my face is washed, my makeup done with the touch-up kit I keep in my purse, and my hair tied up in a messy bun, a few stray curls dangling down to frame my round, freckled cheeks. I'm full of excitement, but as I walk into the party, I realize that I've misunderstood the western theme.

The hall is decked out in what I think of as traditional western items, but it also has a darker, dystopian feel. The walls are covered with wooden wagon wheels and even a few cowboy hats, but also old logic boards and antique keyboards. A mechanical bull sits in the center of the room, surrounded by a pit of foam balls. The bull itself is bright purple, modern-looking, and etched with the Colton Industries logo. To my right, hay bales surround a large bar area and emit a subtle blue glow, like they have tiny LED lights in them.

I expected music, but there is none. All I hear is the whizzing of the electronic bull and the chatter of a hundred people, most standing in small groups. A large group surrounds the bull, watching with rapt attention. Every so often, a shout of joy or terror fills the room as a rider flies off and lands in the ball pit.

Then everyone turns at once, stares for a moment, and returns to their conversations.

I don't see Malcolm, but it turns out he was right about the outfits. Around twenty percent of the people are wearing jeans and t-shirts or other informal workplace attire. The rest are decked out in all manner of costume.

One man wears a tuxedo and a giant cowboy hat that appears to be made from wearable computer screen material. As he walks past me, it lights up and black lettering appears as it would in a word processing program: *Hello, my name is Benjamin Singh. Can I buy you a drink?*

The message isn't for me, but for the two women to my left. One is dressed in a black leather mini skirt with fringe made from earbud ends and a belt made of old cellphones hinged together end to end. The other wears what looks like a standard Sexy Cowgirl Halloween costume, complete with a suede vest, knee-high suede boots, and a fake gun in her holster.

I shuffle past them toward the bar and see that it's not a fake gun, but a toy laser gun. She pulls it out and points it at me as I pass. "Pew, pew," she says, ignoring Benjamin Singh, who now stands about ten feet away.

I put my hands up in the universal sign of surrender and smile. "You got me."

Before I can ask her where to find Peter Colton, Ms. Cellphone Belt says, "I like your outfit."

"Thanks," I say. In addition to the cellphone belt, she's wearing a stenciled western shirt that—miraculously—matches the cellphones. "I like yours, too. Are you sure I didn't take the 'western' thing a bit too literally? You guys look fantastic."

"Nah," Ms. Sexy Cowgirl says. "This is a come-as-you-are-or-imagine-yourself-to-be kind of party. But we do like to incorporate a bit of a techy, post-apocalyptic vibe into all our events."

A dozen other costumes confirm this. "Very cool. Can you

tell me where Peter Colton is? I mean, do you know if he's here yet?"

Ms. Cellphone Belt looks around the room casually. "Haven't seen him. He usually comes late."

I nod toward Benjamin Singh, whose sign now reads: *If you won't let me buy you a drink, at least let me fix your laptop.* "What's his deal?"

The two women exchange glances.

"You wanna take this one?" Ms. Cellphone Belt says.

Ms. Sexy Cowgirl laughs. "He's a bit odd, but a genius, and basically harmless."

As we stare at him, his hat-screen runs through a series of increasingly-bad pickup lines.

Your name must be Google, because you have everything I've been searching for.

Your curves are like Windows Vista. They've got me feeling so unstable.

Is your name Server Maintenance? Because I'm not doing you, but I probably should be.

"Yuck," I say, turning my back to him.

Ms. Sexy Cowgirl pulls out her fake laser, points it at Benjamin, and scowls. He staggers back, pretending to be hit, then disappears into the crowd.

"I think you're new here," she says, placing the laser gun back in her holster. "I mean because I don't recognize you. Want a bit of free advice?"

"Sure."

"Benjamin's actually alright. One of Peter's top web architecture guys. He just plays a creepy stalker at parties. Around Silicon Valley, day-to-day sexism gets shrugged at, and creeps usually get away with a lot more than they should."

"As long as they're geniuses," Ms. Cellphone Belt adds.

"Right," Ms. Sexy Cowgirl says. "Benjamin doesn't talk much, and sometimes has a tough time discerning where the line is. But on the scale of Silicon Valley genius scumbags, he's like a *two*."

I offer up a weak smile. "On *that* note, I think I need a drink. Thanks for the tips."

"No problem," Ms. Sexy Cowgirl says.

"Have a good night," Ms. Cellphone Belt adds.

Across the room, I step into the hay bale bar and order the specialty cocktail, The Blade Runner Cowboy, watching in disbelief as the bartender pours a shot of top shelf tequila into a blue-tinted champagne flute, adds a splash of orange liqueur, then fills the glass with original Coors beer. He garnishes with orange rind and fresh mint, then hands it to me.

"What makes this drink Blade Runnery?" I ask.

"The glass," he says before turning to make a drink for someone behind me.

I sip the cocktail, which is a lot better than I expected, and scan the room. Dozens of interesting-looking people mill about, most in their twenties and thirties, some dressed up, some not. I'm about to take a seat on a blue-tinted hay bale and settle in for some serious people watching when Peter Colton walks through the door.

It's almost as though the crowd parts for him, too, because he moves easily from the door to the center of the hall, pauses at the mechanical bull, then glances at me as though he knew I'd be standing awkwardly near the hay bales.

Seconds later, he's at my side, his shoulder-length black hair parted in the center and tucked behind his ears. "Nice to see you again," he says.

Though he looks like he might have a captivating Spanish accent, he doesn't. He was born and raised in the U.S., and he speaks quickly and without as much charm as you might expect.

I take in his outfit, a vintage tuxedo the color of bone,

embroidered with elaborate brown stitching down the lapels. "You're late to your own party."

"Thanks for coming."

"Thanks for the dress."

"Love the boots."

"Thanks." I sip my drink and look around the room, trying to think of something else to say, and I feel his eyes following me. To break the awkward silence, I say, "Do you want one?"

He smiles at me with that same quizzical smile he had plastered across his face for most of my presentation. "I don't drink."

I expect him to continue speaking, to explain why I'm here, why he didn't say anything during my presentation, and maybe even why he had Malcolm lie about the canceled PowerPoint. But he doesn't.

We're both quiet, staring at each other as shouts near the mechanical bull fill the room. The look lasts long enough to be odd, but not long enough for my cheeks to get red, as they sometimes do when I'm out of my element. I can't tell whether he's trying to make this awkward, or if he just has an odd manner.

I can't take it anymore. "So, what did you want to talk to me about?"

Without answering, he takes my hand and pulls me gently toward the back of the hall to a raised platform covered in straw and surrounded by a worn wooden fence. The four tables on the platform are unoccupied, lit from above by the same blue and silver light that pervades the space, and covered in large artificial candles, their LED flames somehow flickering realistically. We take the table in the corner, sitting side by side and looking out so we can survey the room.

I talk a lot when I'm nervous, and right now my stomach is doing somersaults. "Is this the VIP area?" I ask, half-joking.

"Actually, yes."

"You didn't say anything at my presentation."

"No."

"And you told Malcolm to lie to me about canceling the PowerPoint?"

"Yes."

"And now...here we are."

"Yes."

He still wears that damn smile, and I sip my Blade Runner Cowboy to keep my annoyance from showing, the flavor of the cocktail growing on me as its contents take effect. "Why am I here?"

"I'll tell you, but first, tell me why you started Ameritocracy? And I don't mean the rehearsed answer for the board of directors at the presentation. Tell me about the moment the idea *struck*."

As he says the word "struck," he claps his hands together, shaking free a lock of hair from behind his ear. He tucks it back and smiles, more like a person this time.

As I contemplate my answer, I finish my drink and Peter gets the attention of a waiter standing in the corner of the VIP section, who I hadn't even noticed when we sat. "Another drink for Ms. Rhodes, and I'd like a Red Bull with lime."

"Right away, Peter," the waiter says.

Peter smiles at him, then turns back to me. "So, tell me."

"Your employees call you Peter?"

"Most of them, but let's not make this about me."

"Fine, fine." I'm not a big drinker, so the cocktail has me feeling loose enough to press through my insecurities. "The idea came to me about three years ago. Just a tiny kernel of a whiff of a notion during the 2016 election cycle. I was disgusted by the whole process. The negativity, the superficiality. I was already thinking about what I could do to change things. Then we got the result, and I kicked into high gear. The morning after the election, I pulled out a blank yellow legal pad and wrote a manifesto."

"What was the first thing you wrote?"

"It's embarrassing."

He shrugs. "Tell me anyway."

"I wrote, 'America perfected the reality show, then became one.'"

He leans in, the light from the LED candles dancing on his face. "Well, America does love slogans. And how'd you come up with the word Ameritocracy?"

"I did what people do in the twenty-first century. I hopped online and started looking at URLs. I considered *Third Party*, *America 2020*, and a million others."

"Tell me some of the others."

"Some of them are pretty corny."

"Try me."

"*President Freedom dot U.S.*, which I considered mostly because the domain name was available. Then there was...wait lemme think...there was *The 2020 Election Show*, *Pick 2020*, *Democracy 2.0*, *Democracy: The Website* and, my personal favorite: *Democracy: The Game Show*."

"Why didn't you go with that?"

"Too on the nose. And anyway, most of the URLs were taken. I needed something jazzier, something catchier. I liked the idea of implying America plus meritocracy. So I settled on *Ameritocracy*." I say the last word with a flourish, moving my hand through the air like Vanna White unveiling a new puzzle, a move I learned from my mom, who never misses an episode of *Wheel of Fortune*. "I thought Ameritocracy could be like 'Google.' A word no one knew before the search engine came along, and now it's a household word."

"It *is* catchy," Peter says as the drinks arrive. He squeezes a lime wedge into a champagne flute of Red Bull. "Tell me about the moment. Not just what you *did*, but how you *felt*. You wake up on Wednesday, November 9, 2016, and what do you *feel*?"

His smile is gone now, and I'm starting to feel the particular nature of his charm. It's an intensity of interest, a desire to know, and an impatience with superficialities. I consider myself a no-BS kind of person, so the moment I see this about him, I relax fully. And answer honestly.

"I cried. I'd been obsessed with the election for a year, following it on Twitter, listening to podcasts, occasionally checking in on cable news. By the end of it, I was emotionally worn out, then the big twist ending was like a kick in the stomach. I wouldn't have been thrilled with any outcome. The whole process was so screwed up and depressing, but riveting at the same time. It's the cliché of the car crash you can't look away from."

"And the car crash is America itself."

"Exactly. So I wake up Wednesday morning, check Twitter and CNN to make sure I hadn't dreamed it, then cried for thirty minutes. I wasn't just sad about what had happened. I was overwhelmed by the whole process. But mostly I was disappointed with how I'd handled it. I got wrapped up in the spectacle, in the horse race aspect of it. I felt like I hadn't *done* anything."

The lights dim throughout the hall, shifting from silver-blue to deep maroon. I look up, but Peter catches my eye. "Please continue."

"In those first moments, I hated the country. Hated the hypocrisy of generations of politicians. I wanted to firebomb the White House and the cable news stations and *The New York Times* and *The Washington Post* and all the podcasts and local papers and lying politicians and every goddamn congressman on earth, not to mention the lobbyists who line their pockets. The only person I hated more than all of them was myself. For

32

my gullibility. For quitting. For taking the road of cynicism and defeat and hopelessness."

"What do you mean, quitting? It sounds like you followed the election closely."

We are getting too close to a subject I'd rather avoid, so I gesture toward the center of the room, where the mechanical bull is being wheeled out. "Is something happening? I mean, in the room?"

Peter studies the room, then looks back at me. "Dancing starts soon."

"Oh, is Malcolm gonna play his stuff?"

"Not sure. I don't get into the details of the parties."

"Okay," I say, a little disappointed.

Peter takes my hand softly, then waits until I look up. "Please," he says, "I just want to understand. What did you mean by 'quitting'? You have a full-time job, and I'd bet that you know more about politics than anyone in the room. You—"

"I didn't vote," I say, emptying my second drink and studying him for a reaction.

"That's not what I was expecting."

"Well, everyone knew who was going to win Washington State. So it wasn't going to affect anything, at least not in the presidential race."

"True enough."

"I don't know. I followed the presidential race so closely that I stopped paying attention to local politics, to ballot measures, my congressional rep. Everything else fell away. I became a spectator. A spectator at a car crash."

"That's understandable."

"Understandable, but not *forgivable*."

I hope he'll tell me, "It *is* forgivable," but he doesn't.

"The voting part is just symbolic," I say. "And I would have voted if I'd been in a swing state. I guess the reason I cried was that I hadn't acted. I'd consumed more news than anyone I knew, and I hadn't turned it into *action*. Not nationally, not in my community, not even filling out a damn ballot. Nothing."

"So Ameritocracy is your way of atoning?"

"It's not *just* that, but yeah. Too many people didn't do enough in 2016. I want to do my part to make 2020 different. Better. And if not 2020, then 2024, 2028. I'm still angry, still disappointed. I have been for years. But I'm not willing to let others make these decisions without putting up a fight. Not anymore."

He stares at me for a long time, and his curious smile is back. "The reason I asked, the reason I was so insistent, is that I wondered if it had anything to do with your father."

I pull my hand away and lean back, throwing him a look that's half surprise, half angry glare. "We don't talk about my father."

"I'm sorry. I didn't know. I just—"

"No," I say firmly, waving at the waiter, who bolts to get me another drink.

Before the presentation, I assumed the Project X committee would look into my background, but now I know Peter has created a neat little theory about me. About how my father lost the 1988 Democratic nomination for president because of a tabloid scandal. About how the scandal erupted after his affair with my mother became public. And about how the affair never would have *been* public if I hadn't been born. Maybe Peter even knows that I don't have a relationship with my father, and assumes that Ameritocracy is some kind of Electra-complex payback.

I don't say any of this.

When Peter finally catches my eye, I just repeat, "Yeah. We *don't* talk about my father."

"I'm sorry I upset you," Peter says timidly after my new drink arrives. "Did Malcolm tell you why I wanted to see you?"

"Not exactly."

"He can keep a secret. That's important in an assistant. Would it surprise you to hear that you won Project X?"

In an instant, my agitation turns to excitement. I sit up a little. "Yes."

"Then this is gonna shock you." He pauses, clearing his throat. "Project X would like to donate five million dollars to Ameritocracy. We'd like to offer you technological help, office space, and connections with the people you need to turn your site into a major force in the 2020 election."

I study his face as the realization that he's serious spreads through my whole body. It's a tingling sensation, like my cells are infused with good champagne, but the feeling is immediately pushed to the side by a wave of trepidation.

My first thought is that he's just saying this so he can sleep with me. But that makes no sense. His life over the last ten years has been a parade of beautiful girlfriends, most of them richer and more successful than me, with an average height of five-foot-ten.

"What's the catch?" My tone is more accusatory than I intended. "I mean, thank you, of course. Oh my God, thank you. But—"

"But what's the catch?"

"Yeah, I guess I just don't...I mean...did you say five *million* dollars?"

He takes a small sip of Red Bull. "I did."

Like I mentioned, Peter Colton is known for giving away a lot of his money, so it isn't the money that has my head spinning. Well, obviously it *is* the money, but there's something else. It's...I don't know.

Something I can't place.

I'm thinking of how to respond when a slow and steady bass line fills the room, the opening notes of "I Walk the Line," followed by Johnny Cash's deep voice. Just as I start to get into the song, it changes, the word "line" playing on repeat like a broken record, faster and faster, higher and higher until it becomes a single screeching note like the high range of a police siren.

Malcolm stands in a raised DJ booth, wearing the same black slacks and blue blazer as before, but now with a white Golden State Warriors t-shirt underneath. He's toying with the crowd, which works itself into a frenzy as the single high note continues for at least ten seconds.

Then, he drops the beat.

A chunky hip-hop track below laser sounds, beeps, hisses, and layer after layer of wavy synth. The small crowd in the center of the dance floor goes nuts. Dozens of onlookers rush to the center to join in the dancing.

Peter touches my hand. "Mia?"

His eyes are fixed on mine. He's been watching me watch the scene.

"What do you say to my offer?"

It might be the mention of my father, or the shock of Peter's offer, or possibly just the fact that I've had two and a half Blade Runner Cowboys and Malcolm is shredding the room with his mix, but there is no way I'm going to talk anymore.

"Do you dance?" I ask.

Before he can respond, I grab his hand and drag him to the center of the crowd.

Peter is a better dancer than I expect, and, for the first time, he seems to be having fun. But he hasn't relaxed his intensity. In fact, he's krumping like a madman. Arm jabs, stomps, and chest pops have taken over his body in an energetic burst that, when combined with the maroon lighting, make him look like the star of an energy drink commercial.

The scene is made even stranger by the fact that, twelve hours earlier, I was on the train to the airport, eating oatmeal out of one of those paper tubs from Starbucks, trying to decide what show to binge-watch over the weekend. Now I'm cutting a rug with a hot billionaire who just offered me five million dollars. And he can *move*, too.

I, on the other hand, dance like a total dork. My style is all jumping and flailing and shaking, but I don't care. I'm overcome by the music, by the strangeness and newness of the scene, by the five million dollars dangling in front of me, and by the topsy-turvy drunkenness that comes from mixing great tequila and lousy beer.

When the music transitions into a slow, distorted version of Ella Fitzgerald's "Blue Skies" blended with sweeping strings, I spin and spin at the center of the dance floor, giggling like a fool and swelling with a feeling I haven't known in years.

Possibility.

[4]

I stretch my arms and legs and roll over, reaching for my spare pillow. My right arm and leg drop into space, but there's no pillow there—no *bed* there—and I struggle to keep myself on the bed.

Crash.

On the floor, I wonder where I am. I blink a few times as I take in the tiny room, which is flooded with sunlight. It's maybe ten by ten, with a small desk, a flat screen TV, and an uncommonly narrow bed, which I now stare up at from a sparkling hardwood floor.

Malcolm brought me back here last night, I recall, standing stiffly. I'm in the staff dorms of Colton Industries, and the night comes back to me in dreamlike waves.

Colton and I danced. I had another cocktail, he had another Red Bull, and we danced some more. Each time he tried to bring up the five million, I changed the subject.

When Malcolm's set ended and another DJ came on, Peter said goodnight, promised to check on me in the morning, and asked Malcolm to set me up a spare room. The details are hazy, but I remember how tall he was, leading me down the hall and opening the door for me. He didn't come into the room, just got me a bottle of water and stood in the doorway, making sure I was alright. And he said something funny, too. Something about the money and booze and music of California corrupting me.

And now, here I am. Not hungover, exactly, but groggy and disoriented.

I find my phone on the nightstand and, by some miracle, I have no new calls or texts. Though I don't remember bringing them back, my work clothes are folded neatly on a chair. Still in my dress, I grab a keycard from the small desk and head out to the shared common room and kitchenette, a large round room with six hallways leading into it.

I'm thankful it's empty.

I like to have some time to myself in the mornings, and today I have a lot to think about. Plus, I don't do human interaction before my first cup of coffee. At the counter, there is cold-brew coffee on tap. I pour myself a large glass with heavy cream and take a seat at a small table.

The elation of the previous night is still with me, but also an understanding that I have a decision to make. In general, I try not to make important decisions before noon, but the coffee is *exceptionally* good, and I begin to get that tingling, alert feeling that tells me I'll soon be human again.

Questions arise and circulate in my mind, giving way to others, then circle back in new forms. I wasn't just avoiding Peter's offer because I was overwhelmed. I have real concerns about taking his money. Halfway through my coffee, my mind is sharp and I've landed on three distinct issues.

First, is Peter trying to sleep with me? I dismissed that question last night, and now it seems even more unlikely. He limited his questions to my project, to my motivations. There were no cheesy lines, no sketchy advances. Even while we danced, the overwhelming feeling was of celebration. It's actually pretty cool that a boss can party in such a carefree way with his staff. The more I consider the idea that the five million is some elaborate plan to flirt with me, the more ridiculous it seems. I stomp down hard on the question of whether that's a letdown.

My second worry is more amorphous, but when I put words to it, those words are "ulterior motives." Despite being known as a philanthropist, Peter is a cutthroat businessman, and it's possible he wants to use my site to gather data on users, or for some other reason I'm not thinking of. When I think of it in those terms, it seems like a pretty big conclusion to jump to, but that doesn't dissipate my slight hesitation.

Third, even if his motives are pure, the money feels like too much, too fast. Though I've had all sorts of fantasies about revolutionizing democracy, deep down I expected 2020 to be a proof-of-concept year for Ameritocracy. In my wildest dreams, I'd win Project X, expand the site with the money, get a few serious candidates, maybe a little media play, and try to build it into something that could have real impact by 2024 or 2028.

Five million dollars would change everything. I could quit my job, hire a staff, and build out the Ameritocracy website to accommodate more web traffic. Five million dollars would allow me to make this real.

As I contemplate, my phone chirps with a text message from a 510 area code. A number that's not in my contacts.

It's Malcolm. Hope you got some sleep and you're not too sore from dancing. I'm off today, but Mr. Colton made me promise to check in with you first thing.

I read his message twice, refill my cold-brew, and reply.

Me: *Hey rockstar. Found coffee. Slowly coming back to life.*

I press send, then immediately start typing another message.

Me: *Can I ask you a question?*

Malcolm: *No preliminaries, remember?*

Me: *Sorry. Did you know Peter was going to offer me A LOT of money? That what you meant when you said I should be hyped?*

Malcolm: *Yes and yes.*

Me: *Canceling my PowerPoint was to see how I'd do under pressure?*

Malcolm: *Yes.*

Me: *Okay, bear with me...odd series of questions coming.*

Me: *Do you think he actually cares about my site?*

Me: *I mean...why me?*

Me: *Why this project? Why now?*

Me: *And why so much money?*

He's typing a new message, so I walk a slow lap around the room. I don't know why I'm asking Malcolm. He's Peter's assistant. Do I think he's going to tell me his boss is a scumbag? I know he'll lie to me if his boss tells him to, because that *literally* already happened. But dammit, I have to ask someone. And he gave me his DJ card. He can't be a villain's loyal henchman if he's working a side hustle, right?

His message pops up.

Malcolm: *He cares about politics and government. Dude's got a Twitter list he follows religiously. All the top journalists and commentators from the left and the right.*

This reassures me. Maybe it's solidarity between the assistants of handsome rich guys, but I want to believe Malcolm. I'm still hesitant, though.

Me: *Why me? Why my site?*

Malcolm: *Mr. Colton's a disruptor. Turned cloud computing on its head. He's trying to do the same with solar. Not a shock that he'd jump on an idea trying to do the same with politics. Your project is utterly badass. I'm guessing he just sees that.*

Me: *Thank you for the 'utterly badass' part.*

Malcolm: *What exactly did he offer, if you're cool with saying?*

Me: *Five million, office space, startup help, connections.*

Malcolm: *!!!!!!!!!!!!!!!!!!!!!*

Me: *That's word-for-word what I said.*

Malcolm: *Knew he was gonna do something big, but DAMN.*

Me: *So...*

Malcolm: *So I guess what you're asking is whether he'll interfere, take over.*

Me: *And?*

Malcolm: *I don't think so. He funds projects and lets them do what they do. Some succeed, some don't. Never heard of him being a micromanager, though.*

Me: *Thanks, but what I'm really asking is, can I trust him?*

Malcolm: *I think trust is something that only exists between two people, so I can't answer that for you.*

Me: *Do YOU trust him?*

Malcolm: *I do. He's never been anything but decent to me.*

Me: *Thanks.*

Malcolm: *Sure.*

I set my phone on the table, grab an apple from a bowl on the counter, and sit back down.

When I was a teenager, my mom taught me how to make decisions, and I still use her method. First, I figure out all the possibilities. In this case, I have three: 1) Take the money, 2) Don't take the money, 3) Try to negotiate something else.

Next, I let all the options hang in my head while I ask questions.

I've never been a journalist, but I've worked with some good ones, ones who get the facts before they write the story. I try to emulate that habit, getting my information straight while I'm still agnostic on a decision. Once I've gathered all the information, I check in with the options. Usually one of them just *feels* right at that point. I like the process because it keeps me from going with my first emotional reaction, but it also keeps me from being too indecisive.

While texting with Malcolm, this process has been taking place in the background, and I know where I'm headed.

Me: *I think I'm gonna do it.*

Malcolm: *Good. Wasn't going to tell you what to do, but I'm glad.*

I'm trying to figure out how to read that, and how to respond, when I'm interrupted by loud steps clacking down the hallway. A tall blonde woman and short brunette appear in the room, then stagger toward the coffee. After a moment, I realize that they're Ms. Sexy Cowgirl and Ms. Cellphone Belt from the party. Behind them, without the tuxedo or computer-screen cowboy hat, is Benjamin Singh.

I smile, but their eyes are on the floor. They seem to need coffee even more than I did, so I turn back to my phone.

Me: *Thanks for the help. Gotta run, but I hope to hear you DJ again soon.*

Malcolm: *Later, and congratulations!*

Back in the room, I sit on the bed, ready to make a final decision. I think about calling my mom, or my best friend Steph back in Seattle, but I don't. Instead, I stare out the single window at the Colton Industries campus. I'm three or four stories up, and I follow a footpath with my eyes, past sprawling lawns, modern buildings, and empty benches. The campus is sunny and quiet.

Then I see him.

Peter Colton walks toward the building I'm in, alongside two men and two women, none of whom I recognize. I wonder whether he's coming to see me, and I glance around the room. For some reason, I don't want to talk with him in here. Maybe because it's small and cramped, maybe because it's too personal, or maybe just because I want to get some of that California sunshine before I return to Seattle. Whatever the reason, I throw on my work clothes, tie my curls into a bun, and take the elevator to the ground floor.

Stepping out into the bright sun, I see the group about ten yards away.

Peter is dressed in dark blue jeans, a black V-neck t-shirt, and black boots. He looks better casual, more like a person I'd talk to in regular life. Which is good because this is certainly *not* regular life. He parts with the group and walks toward me.

As he approaches, he sees me and smiles widely, but doesn't say anything.

My plan is to play it cool. I'll ask about the timing of the donation, discuss board positions, the location of the offices, ask for an assurance of total independence, and talk through a dozen other questions and concerns.

But instead, I smile back at Peter, do a bad impression of the krump dance he displayed the night before, and blurt out, "I'll take the money. Can we get some breakfast?"

[5]

eter and I take a sunny sidewalk table at a bistro called Baker's Dozen in the small town of Santa Clarissa. I get the sense that, in Silicon Valley, extreme luxury often comes in down-home or even ironic packaging. He must be a regular, because a waiter sets down a champagne flute full of Red Bull within seconds of our arrival. As Peter pulls a silver laptop from his briefcase, I order orange juice instead of asking what kind of breakfast joint has champagne flutes.

On the ride over, I concealed my excitement. Emotionally, I was all-in, but I tried to be as professional as possible. So I loaded my "sober businesswoman" program and asked my questions. Peter assured me that he had no plans to interfere in the day-to-day management of the site, promised me the donation in full by Monday morning, and told me he'd put me in touch with his best lawyer to answer any questions that could arise in the process.

Now, we can move on to the fun part. The website itself.

After the waiter sets down my juice and we order breakfast, I slide my chair over to Peter's side of the table, where he's already logged onto the Wi-Fi and pulled up my homepage: Ameritocra-cy2020.org.

"First question," Peter says. "Why that URL?"

"I also bought Ameritocracy 2024, 2028, 2032, and so on," I say, sipping my juice, which is the coldest, freshest orange juice I've ever tasted. "I envision it as seasons of a show."

"Walk me through the site," he says.

I start with the main menu, which has six options.

1. Register

"Anyone can view any portion of the site," I explain. "They can read candidate profiles, watch videos, and so on, but only registered users can vote. Registering also allows users to sign up for email or text alerts, such as general news from the site, updates from their favorite candidates, or reminders to vote at key deadlines."

2. Search All Candidates

"This is where users find candidates who don't appear in the top twenty on the homepage. They can search by home state, key issues, age and gender, ethnicity, and a dozen other variables. The one thing they *can't* search for is Democratic or Republican party affiliation."

3. The Rules

I'd summarized many of the rules during the presentation, but I now explain that this is where the fine print lives. "This is where we keep the candidate rules, which, in addition to including the basics required by the Constitution, include two key provisions. First, candidates may not have held any elected position as a Democrat or a Republican in the last ten years. Second, candidates may not accept funding from PACs, Super PACs, or any other outside campaign contributions. Not even individual donors. This rule is crucial because it levels the playing field. I want candidates to have free access to the site, and I don't want candidates to be able to sway voting with money from outside sources."

4. The Schedule

"This is a more detailed version of the schedule I explained during the presentation, the key dates being February 1, the last day candidates can register, Super Tuesday in March, when we narrow the field to twenty-five, July 4, when we hold the final debate, and July 6, the final live show when we crown a winner and award the money."

5. Donate

"Because we're a non-profit, donations are tax-deductible. Users can choose whether to donate to Ameritocracy the company, which helps pay for operating expenses, or to the award fund, the money that will go to the winning candidate to finance their campaign in the 2020 election."

6. About Us/Contact

"This section gives a brief history of the project, and how to get in touch."

After I take Peter through the menu, we focus on the home-page, the bulk of which is taken up by the list of our top twenty candidates, and this is where I get embarrassed. "We haven't exactly attracted the best and the brightest."

"Do you mind?" Peter nudges my fingers off the track pad and scrolls through the list.

"What happened to Charles Blass?" he asks.

"Dropped out a couple days ago. Heart condition."

"Kinda liked him."

I'm surprised, and my face must show it because Peter says, "Not his politics, but he had *pizzazz*."

"Like I mentioned in the presentation, we need to attract more mainstream candidates if we want to be taken seriously."

"Blass *is* to the left of Karl Marx, but, you have to admit, dude has style."

I laugh because it's a rare bit of cleverness from Peter, but also because it's true. Blass is a seventy-year-old linguistics professor at San Francisco State University, and a self-described "warrior poet." A member of the Communist Party, he's a long, skinny scarecrow of a man who wears a Russian military *ushanka* hat year-round. He first chained himself to the UC Berkeley administration building in 1968 to protest the war in Vietnam, and has been doing it for various causes ever since. He attracted a following of devoted students and former students early on, and led the competition for a couple weeks earlier this summer.

At the moment, our top candidate is Destiny O'Neill, who bills herself as a "South Park Conservative." A few years ago, she blogged for *The Barker* for a short time before branching off to do her own thing. We were still Facebook friends when I launched the site, so she was one of the first to sign up. She's a camgirl, a YouTuber, and—as neutral as I promised myself I'd be about the results of Ameritocracy—someone I desperately hope will soon be replaced at the top of our leaderboard.

In addition to her number one ranking, the top-20 list shows her age, 35, and includes a picture and a candidate statement. In her photo, Destiny is dressed in a low-cut tank top and a bright orange trucker hat. Plus, she's holding a rifle. Her candidate statement reads, "Taxation is theft. Death to the EPA and FDA. Guns and beer. Anti-feminist MILF."

Peter has already clicked through to her Platform Page, and is scanning her answers to the standard candidate questions.

"In the 'Candidate Summary' section," Peter says, "she wrote—and I'm quoting here—'Individual freedom. Individual liberty. If people want to call me the MILF candidate, I don't have the right to tell them not to. That's *their* right. And get government out of our bedrooms. I should have the right to do whatever I want to do in bed, with *whoever* I want. And if I want to smoke a bowl beforehand, I should have that right.'"

He takes a long sip of Red Bull. "Is she serious?"

"She's the kind of person whose beliefs change based on the number of likes a particular post or video is getting. Does she believe the character she's playing? Like most politicians, maybe, maybe not. But, whether she believes it or not, it's what she's choosing to put out into the world."

"And she's ranked number one?"

"Well, *for now*. It fluctuates. She's probably just in it for the PR, though she actually brings us more attention than we bring her. She already had a huge following on YouTube, Reddit, and Tumblr who are now voting for her on Ameritocracy. Mostly perverts and MRAs, I'm guessing."

"MRAs?"

"Men's Rights Activists. Anti-feminist guys who...it's not important. Anyway, like I said in the presentation, most of the candidates now are from the fringes. The Charles Blass and Destiny O'Neill types. The key will be attracting more candidates from the left, right, and center. I'm hoping that'll happen as the site grows."

Peter navigates back to the top-20 list. "I see what you mean. Mostly oddballs, it looks like, which leads me to my big question. In your presentation, you said that the top-20 list is generated by a proprietary algorithm. How does it work?"

The food arrives, and I have an excuse to go quiet while I try to remember all I can about the algorithm, which I paid one of our web guys at *The Barker* to create. He's a former Google employee, and told me that what he was setting up was similar to the way Google decides which sites to display first in their search engine. Except ours is a million times simpler.

I bite into the best biscuit I can remember tasting, then slather it with jam and devour it. I finish my orange juice and, before I can set the glass on the table, the waiter is back, refilling it. "Free refills on fresh squeezed OJ?" I say. "This is one *classy* town."

Peter laughs. "I know the owner."

I take a quick bite of scrambled eggs, then do my best to explain our ranking process. "As I said in the presentation, for the early rounds we use ranked-candidate voting. Registered users pick their top ten candidates and a point value is applied to the candidates based on their choices."

"And how do you assign points? Ten for first, nine for second, like that?"

"No, we want to more closely mimic the one-person-one-vote system, while still retaining elements of ranked-candidate voting, so we use the Fibonacci series. One, two, three, five, eight, thirteen, twenty-one, and so on. So, if a user chooses ten candidates, their first place choice gets fifty-five points, their second place choice gets thirty-four, and so on down to one point for their tenth choice."

"And what if they only choose, say, their top five candidates?"

"We still use the Fibonacci, but it's a smaller series. One, two, three, five, eight."

"Got it," Peter says between bites of eggs Benedict. "And users can change their votes?"

"The rankings constantly change because users can change their votes every twenty-four hours." I finish my scrambled eggs before continuing. "But the algorithm also includes other metrics to generate the rankings. We track social media mentions as well as social media shares, memes, and so on. So, if someone shares a candidate's Ameritocracy Platform Page to Facebook, for example, that's a tenth of a point. Twitter mentions are a fiftieth of a point. We have bots cruising every website to get a sense of popularity."

"Why do you do that?"

"During the last election, I read something about how memes are allowing a kind of ground-up political conversation, which is both a blessing and a curse. Either way, it's a reality. Up until a few years ago, the mainstream media provided a filter, shielding people from the oddest or most hateful ideas, from the far left and the far right. But now, everything from mundane political quotes to hate-filled propaganda can spread from the dark swamps of the Internet in real time. By typing some text on an image and sharing it with friends, anyone can spread a message that affects the political conversation. We wanted to make social media part of the initial rounds of voting to reflect this new reality. And, of course, the more shares, the more people hear about us and the faster we grow. As we grow, we hope that key speeches or position papers will go viral."

"Smart idea. But in the final round it will be one person, one vote, right?"

"Right. To register for the site, you must be of voting age by November 3, 2020, and you must prove your U.S. Citizenship. Essentially, you have to register to vote, but with our site."

"Brilliant. The whole thing, I mean."

Then I say something I don't expect. "I'm actually proud of it."

"You should be."

"I mean, it's not perfect, but it gives me a feeling of hope. Like we can hear from actual Americans, in real time, in the most democratic way possible."

"Joining is free, right?"

"One hundred percent free. The site has no ads, as you can see. Of course, it favors those with Internet access, but that covers almost everyone these days when you count smartphones. We've even considered ways to let people vote who don't have them."

Peter pops a grape in his mouth. "You keep saying 'we,' but I thought you were the only staff member."

"Steph," I say. "My best friend Steph is back in Seattle and I always thought she'd be the first person I'd hire, if I ever had the money to hire someone. She and I talked through a lot of this together and, though she's *technically* not part of this, she's a big part of it."

"That raises the question," Peter says. "How will it be when you move down here?"

That catches me off guard, and I take a moment to reflect while sipping my juice. Peter mentioned that offices would be included with the money, but I assumed he meant offices in a general way. Like, he'd *pay* for office space back in Seattle. Now I see that he meant office space he already owns.

I'm still considering this when he says, "I'm sorry. I can tell I've surprised you. You were thinking you'd stay in Seattle?"

Relieved, I say, "Yeah, kinda. Um, I hadn't really thought it through, actually. I just assumed..."

After an awkward silence, he says, "It's up to you, of course, but I thought when I said office space—"

"You thought I knew you meant down here."

"Exactly."

Peter goes back to his breakfast as I think it through, again struck by a feeling that everything is moving too fast. Of course, I'd had the thought that I *could* quit my job. Who doesn't have that thought when someone offers them five million dollars? But I hadn't *decided* it. And I certainly hadn't considered moving. What about the lease on my apartment, and what about Steph?

The anxiety builds up in me, and I push a pile of homefries around my plate with my fork.

Peter notices my unease. "Would it help if I showed you what I have in mind?"

"I'm assuming it's back on the campus."

"Oh, no. You need to be separate, totally independent. When I said I'd throw in office space, my thought was that it would save money and you could be in the tech hub of the world. No offense to Seattle, of course."

I'm relieved because the campus *would* be too close for comfort, but I'm also confused. "Then where do you mean?"

"Here. Upstairs. When I said, 'I know the owner,' I meant I own this building."

～

We finish our breakfast, then walk up a set of stairs next to the front door of the restaurant. The building is only three floors, and I get the sense right away that Peter intends to loan me floors two and three.

The second floor space is beautiful: A wide open, loft-like common area with lots of windows, sleek silver and white office furniture, and a few glassed-in private office spaces. In the center of the room, a black spiral staircase leads up to the third floor, which is nearly identical.

"You'd need to get computers and some other equipment, but the basics are already here," Peter says. "The office is the former home of a virtual reality company I bought a few years back."

The sun streams through the tall windows, reflecting off the glimmering wood floors. I'm awed, but I try not to show it.

"Anyway," Peter continues, "it's up to you. This is your baby. I was just thinking that I could give you this space through the end of your competition. You'd be surrounded by elite tech help, and tech is going to be a major part of your next phase of development."

He's right about that and, honestly, it's one of my biggest concerns. I'm a bit of a generalist. I know a good amount about a lot of different things, but I'm not an expert in anything, and *certainly* not in the technology required to build out the Ameritocracy website. I'll need some heavy hitters from the web design and tech worlds to make sure the site can support what I hope will be a huge influx of users. Of course, I could find those people in Seattle, but Peter's help would be a load off my mind.

I wander through the space, inspecting the bathrooms and kitchenette like a picky real estate agent. I stare out a window to the street below, to the table where Peter and I ate breakfast. If I worked here, I'd probably eat a lot more of those incredible biscuits.

Everything is perfect, and that might be why I'm uneasy.

Then I remember what Malcolm told me yesterday, that anxiety is excitement without the breathing. Peter watches me with a kind smile, not at all bothered by our little misunderstanding about where I'd locate the offices.

I take three deep breaths and I'm immediately convinced that Malcolm's mother was right. My anxiety dissipates and I'm filled again with the feeling of possibility from last night. But not just possibility. I'm filled with gratitude, excitement, and a burning desire to get to work.

I meet his smile with one of my own. "How soon can I move in?"

[6]

It's nine a.m. Monday morning, and Alex Vane is staring at me like I'm the girlfriend who just admitted to cheating on him. We're sitting in his office at *The Barker*, and I've done the first thing on my list of five things to do before leaving Seattle: quit my job.

"When?" he asks.

"I'll give my two weeks, but the final debate is less than a year away and, honestly, every day counts. If we can find a way to get me out of here sooner, I would really appreciate it."

Alex does a lap around his desk, thinking hard.

He's around forty-five, tall, and good-looking in a superficial kind of way. Not the kind of way I've ever been attracted to.

Bird, Alex's number two, sits to the side of Alex's desk, trying hard not to look me in the eye.

Since the moment I decided to move to Santa Clarissa—high on fresh-squeezed orange juice and drunk on the light from the floor-to-ceiling windows—I've dreaded this conversation. Alex and Bird know as well as I do that I'm a crucial part of *The Barker*.

Technically, I'm not number three on the org chart. There

really isn't a number three. Just Alex, the CEO and major decision-maker, and Bird, the senior editor and social media master.

But I keep a hundred things off their plates every day, and they know it. I make it so they never hear about the broken printer, or our web host trying to raise prices, or the daily drama between employees. Even though I complain about the job from time to time, they've treated me well and offered consistent raises to acknowledge my value. I feel bad about leaving them, but not bad enough to stay.

Alex finishes a second lap around his desk. "And this isn't about money, right?"

"I told you, Alex, it's about my site."

"I didn't even know you were down in California." He turns to Bird. "Did *you* know about this?"

Bird doesn't respond.

I say, "I didn't tell anyone I'd even applied to Project X. I didn't think I'd win, and I *never* expected to get..."

I look back and forth between them, and I can tell they're in panic mode. They remind me of stereotypical sitcom dads, left alone with the kids for a day while mom is away. With no idea what to do, they feed the kids soda for breakfast, burn dinner before ordering a pizza, and destroy the house by the time their wives return. That's a crummy show, and it's even worse in person.

I'm the wife who holds *The Barker* together, but I'm not leaving for twenty-four hours. I'm leaving for good. This is what they're worried about. They don't know how the office runs, and they don't *want* to know.

I have a plan. "Gregory is ready to take over."

"Gregory?" Alex's voice is weak. "I barely *know* Gregory."

"He's been assistant office manager for a year. He already does half my job."

"He's good," Bird says. "Smart."

"But does it have to be *Gregory*? That takes so long to say. Why not just 'Greg'?

Bird and I let out simultaneous sighs, then Alex sits, and I relax. I'm not worried that he'll be mad. He's not the type to explode in anger or anything. I just don't like disappointing anyone. At the same time, I can't let that stand in the way of saying what I need to say.

With all the confidence I can muster, I say, "I'd like Friday to be my last day."

Bird responds before Alex has a chance. "*This* Friday?"

"That's what I want, but I don't want to leave you high and dry. I'd be willing to chat with Gregory over the following week, talk him through any crises that might arise."

Alex glances at Bird, who nods. "Okay," they say at the same time.

After a long, awkward pause, Bird says, "Do whatever you need to train Gregory by then. Bring in temps, whatever. Sell him on the job, and we'll meet with him right after, to formally make an offer."

Bird says it like it's the final decision, and Alex seems to agree because he stands and speaks in a wistful tone. "Three things I want you to know, Mia. First, you've been a huge part of the growth of *The Barker*, and we are going to miss the hell out of you. Second, once you get up and running down there, let us know. We'll write a couple stories, throw some traffic your way. Third, you have a job here whenever you want. If the website doesn't work out or whatever."

That last one stings. It triggers that little nest of doubt that's been living in my belly since Peter offered me the money. I can't tell if it's Alex's passive-aggressive way of suggesting that my site *won't* work out, but it's too late to let doubt stop me.

After a moment, Bird stands as well. "Alex, don't say *that*. It's going to work out, Mia. You're heading over the rainbow, and we're happy for you."

"Thanks, Bird. Even if things go well, one way or another the site will probably end after July. Once we have a winner, the site is over."

"But you might do it again," Alex says. "2024 or whatever."

"Maybe, but I wouldn't be shocked if I'm back here in early July asking for my job back."

"Either way," Alex says. "We're proud of you. I'm not super political or anything, but what you're trying to do is great, from what I know of it."

He steps around the desk and we hug, then Bird steps over and hugs me tight. Bird is closer to my size and age, and he's the one I'll miss most of all.

After work, I head over to Angelina's, a small wine bar on the ground floor of the office building my best friend Steph works in. I prefer cheaper, out-of-the-way places, but this is her favorite joint and I'm going to miss the chic glass tables, modern furniture, and bright lighting.

Steph and I meet here at least once a week for an after-work drink, but today she's nowhere to be found, despite the fact that she said she'd be right down when I texted.

I sit at the bar and take out a Moleskine notebook. Even though I have twenty apps on my phone that would be better for keeping lists, I still prefer real paper and a classic Bic ballpoint. My mother has given me a ten-pack every Christmas since I was eight years old.

1. Quit job

I cross that one out right away, which gives me a tingle of satisfaction.

2. Hire Steph

That's why I'm here. Steph is the human resources manager for Door Knockers, a company that manages volunteers for various political causes, and I'm planning to convince her to join me in California.

3. Negotiate end of lease

I'm not too worried about this one. I only have four months left anyway, and if I can't talk my way out of it, I'll just eat the cost. It still blows me away that 'eat the cost' is something I can do now, but I've done the math and I can.

4. Pack

My plan is to pack two large suitcases and a box or two of necessities, then put the rest of my stuff in storage. When you're a single woman living in a 600-square foot apartment, that's not much stuff. When I rent an apartment in Santa Clarissa, I can have it shipped.

5. Charge Bluebird

Other than my designer leather T-straps, Bluebird is the only cool, extravagant thing I own. It's a baby-blue 1964 Mustang with a cream-colored, convertible top. But it's not just any Mustang. Bluebird is an electric hybrid and, as far as I know, the only electric 1964 Mustang on earth.

On my thirtieth birthday, I got some unexpected money from my dad—about whom we *do not speak*—bought the car for twelve grand, then had it converted by a local electric car guru. That cost another thirty thousand, and now I can charge it at any Tesla-compatible charging station in the country. I know I could have just bought a Prius, but in a life dominated by safe choices, rational thinking, and the maintenance of efficient office systems, sometimes whimsy is required.

By six-thirty I've finished a glass of wine, and I'm worried about Steph, so I take the elevator up to her office, where something big seems to be going on. Door Knockers occupies a large, open space of about two thousand square feet, but the employees aren't on phones or at computers like normal. A few walk briskly back and forth between corner offices, and a crowd of around thirty are gathered in a corner, all craning to see a computer screen.

I stand by the elevator, looking from face to face, but I don't see Steph.

I haven't yet told her about the money. She knew I was in California for Project X, but she and I made a pact never to text about important things. We met at singles night at a bar filled with awesome ladies and far-less-awesome guys, and bonded over our shared belief in the power of face-to-face conversations in an increasingly digital world. Sure, we text to set up meeting times or just to say hi, but the big, life-changing stuff, we do in person.

Which is why I'm bummed, and worried that I don't see her. I walk to the back of the crowd, not close enough to see the screen everyone is huddled around, but close enough to over-hear some of the conversation.

"It's final?" a man asks, sounding dejected.

"Doesn't say," another replies.

"When?" a woman asks from the center of the crowd.

"Month, month and a half."

"Why?"

"Shift to digital," a voice says behind me, and it's Steph, who just walked out of one of the corner offices. "More and more political causes are shifting to digital. Facebook ads, email campaigns, even Twitter bots—though most won't admit to that. They just don't need people going house-to-house anymore."

Ten people in the group try to speak at once, but Steph raises her large hands to quiet them. "We're not going to have any more information tonight, but I've just spoken with Mr. and Mrs.

Baker, and they confirmed it. I'm sorry to say that Door Knockers is closing."

Again, people try to speak, but not as many. A few groans and sighs come from the crowd as Steph steps up onto a chair. Shoeless and standing on the ground, she's half a foot taller than me, so now she looks like a giant.

But it's not just her size that allows her to command the room. Steph has a deep, booming voice and a combination of charisma and authority that makes people listen when she speaks. Outside the office, she's a jeans and t-shirt kind of woman, but now she's wearing one of the six identical green pantsuits she wears to work, which I helped her pick out when she got the job.

"People," she says, nodding at me to acknowledge my presence. "Listen! I know this is a shock, and I will meet with you one-on-one tomorrow, starting at eight. For now, go home. We. Are. Not. Going. To. Have. More. Information. For. You. Tonight."

She surveys the crowd as a few more groans rise out of it, but the people quickly disperse and Steph hops down from the chair.

"Bad day at the office?" I ask as she leans in to hug me.

"It's complicated. A business blog reported that we're closing and I just found out it's true. Someone on the board leaked it before a single staffer heard."

"Oh no, I'm so sorry. So are you just out of a job now?"

I'm genuinely sorry, but I have to admit that the predatory part of my brain thinks that Steph needing a job is not the worst news from my perspective.

"I'm not...it's complicated..." she replies uncomfortably. "I'll tell you, but...I was in my boss's office and...well...now I really do need that glass of wine."

~

At the bar, we order wine—red for her and white for me, as always.

"Before we get into my shitstorm," Steph says, "tell me how it went in California. You won't hear the results for a week, right?"

She sips her wine and I wait for her to put it down. "Remember how I said that the winner gets a hundred fifty thousand dollars?" I ask.

"Yeah."

I smile widely, but I'm nervous to tell her about the money. Like saying it out loud will somehow wake me from the dream.

She sees my smile and matches it. "What, girl? Spill it."

"Peter Colton is donating five million dollars."

Steph sips her wine again. "To what?"

"To my site. To Ameritocracy."

"Huh?" Her phone buzzes and she reaches into her purse to silence it.

Clearly, she doesn't understand me. "Steph. Turn your phone off. Look at me." I wait as she powers down her phone. "Peter Colton is giving me five million dollars. I quit my job. Friday is my last day at *The Barker*. I'm moving to California on Saturday."

She stares, her look of confusion shifting to a skeptical smile. "You're serious?"

"I am."

"You're *serious*?"

"I'm serious, and I want to hire you."

Steph catches the eye of the waiter. "Champagne. *Veuve Clicquot Brut Rosé.*"

Her French accent is perfect and the waiter turns on a dime. I know she speaks the language fluently, but I'm consistently amazed by how confidently she moves through any situation, whether ordering champagne, telling thirty people they just lost their jobs, or covering Beyoncé at karaoke night, which she does regularly.

She smiles. "Start from the beginning."

By the time I finish telling her about my trip, we're each on our second glass of champagne. "And the timing is perfect," I conclude. "If Door Knockers is closing, you can come with me."

Steph leans away. "Oh Mia, wow. I don't know, I—"

"You're gonna be laid off anyway, right?"

She closes her eyes, and I can tell she's trying to figure out how to tell me something difficult. "Not exactly," she says, opening her eyes. "Mr. and Mrs. Baker already offered me something new. Door Knockers is closing, but they have another company, a political...thing. They offered me a promotion. More money, more staff. It's a big deal."

The air leaves my chest. Though my brain knew there was a chance she wouldn't join me, I never expected her to turn me down. I've been counting on having her with me. "That's why you said it was complicated?"

"I'm really sorry."

"What's the 'political thing'?"

She sighs and stares into her champagne flute. "A Democratic super-PAC."

"What?"

"I know, I know."

We've spent so many hours talking about the need to get big money out of politics that this is the last thing I expected. "Haven't you said that the super-PAC is the single biggest threat to democracy since Louis the Fourteenth?"

"Louis the Sixteenth, but I'm a girl on a budget, Mia. They're offering me two hundred grand a year. That's a *much* better budget. Seattle rents aren't getting any..."

She trails off, probably because she can tell I'm halfway between disappointed and disgusted. "Please tell me you're kidding. You're *not* going to work for a super-PAC. You *can't*."

"They work on issues I care about."

"Issues you care about?"

"Poverty, environment, net neutrality, campaign finance reform."

"You're gonna fight for campaign finance reform by running a super-PAC?"

"We've gotta fight fire with fire and—"

"I get it. I do." I don't usually interrupt people, especially Steph, but right now I don't want to hear her justifications. "You might be able to do some good there, buying congressmen before they can be bought by another super-PAC with competing interests. You've got the brains for it, and two hundred grand is not a small deal. All I've got to offer is that if you come with me you have the chance to do something people will be talking about in a hundred years."

It's my best argument, and I'm afraid to look up at Steph because I don't know if she's gonna buy it.

"We can't all run off and just do whatever we want," she says. "I've got my brother to think about, my mom. My kids, when I have them someday. I need to save money and—"

"That's such *bullshit*." I'm embarrassed that I'm angry, and I go quiet. Instead of calling her a sell-out, I should be congratulating her.

We sip champagne in silence, then Steph powers on her phone, and scrolls for a while. "Just out of curiosity," she says, not looking up, "what could you offer me?"

"I'm thinking forty-two grand for me and the top few people."

She scoffs. "You're gonna move to Silicon Valley on forty-two grand a year?"

"I have savings."

She scoffs again, louder this time.

"Like, eight thousand." I know how ridiculous it sounds. Silicon Valley is one of the most expensive areas of the country, and my savings will barely cover the first and last month on a decent apartment.

"Mia, take me out of the equation for a minute—and I'm saying this as a friend—are you sure about this? I mean, why not stay here, keep your job, think this through. If this five million dollars is real, why not pace yourself, build over time?"

I have a theory, a silly oversimplification of human nature that I use to help understand people. At the very least, it's a good way to understand Steph and me. The idea is that there are two types of people, categorizable by how they get into a cold swimming pool.

There are people who ease in over a few minutes, slowly exposing more and more of their bodies to the water. Others run straight for the deep end and dive in head first.

I'm a head-first diver, Steph is a slow easer. Some might think that the head-first divers are braver, but I don't see it that way. I know that if I feel how cold the water is, I'll run screaming in the other direction, but if I dive all the way in, I'm committed. No takebacks. I can block out the thought of the cold water just long enough to run and jump, and by then it's too late. Steph is more cautious, always thinking of long term effects and unintended consequences.

Both ways have their virtues, and it's why we make a good pair.

"Honestly," I say, "I can't stand another year of this. You're one of the smartest women in your field, and if you're selling out to run a super-PAC, to add more negative attack ads to the never-ending bombardment of bullshit on TV and online...well... I'm sorry, it's not your fault."

I pause, hoping she'll say something, but she's stone-faced.

"I'm sorry," I say again. "Look, the election is in sixteen months. Ameritocracy will crown a winner in under twelve. One way or another, much of the next sixteen months will be dominated by politics and political news. I know it might be stupid, and I know I might regret it, but I just can't get through another election cycle without doing my best to inject some hope into it. Some transparency. Some fairness. I just can't go through it all again without putting up a fight."

"I get it," Steph says. "I really do. And I'm going to be your biggest fan. It's just too risky for me right now. I'm sorry." Her cheeks are tight, her lips held together firmly. It's a resolute look. Right or wrong, she's made up her mind.

"It's okay," I say with as much optimism as I can muster.

Without her, this will be *a lot* harder. But what's really killing me is that, when I jump into the deep end without Steph, I usually regret it.

[7]

A week later, I pull Bluebird into Santa Clarissa and park in front of Baker's Dozen. It's about to close for the night, so I order a Cobb salad to go, then grab my bag and stumble up the stairs into the second-floor office. I can unpack the rest of the car tomorrow.

After fumbling around in the dark, I find a dimmer switch, but it only illuminates the corners of the office, giving the whole space a kind of haunted-castle vibe. The office looks the same as when I left it, except now there's a bed and a nightstand in the corner. On the nightstand is a small vase of red and yellow tulips with a card.

Mia-

My best web guy will meet you at nine tomorrow. Welcome to your new life!

Peter

I flop onto the bed, which seems to have been brought from the dorms at the campus because it's narrower than a standard twin bed. As I eat my salad, I contemplate Peter's note. There's something right about the phrase he chose.

New life.

Until now, I considered this a continuation of my old life. But sitting in the half-dark in a new city, eating a fancy salad on a crummy bed in an office that would likely cost ten grand a month on the open market, I can't argue that this isn't, in fact, a new life.

In the last week, I quit my job, gave up my apartment, and moved a thousand miles with nothing I couldn't fit in the back seat of Bluebird.

I dove into the pool head-first.

I also tried and failed multiple times to hire Steph. After our talk at the wine bar, I emailed her pictures of the offices, a link to a story about Santa Clarissa, and a few articles about Peter Colton's philanthropy. I even sent her a link to the online menu of Baker's Dozen, promising her the best biscuits west of the Mississippi.

None of it worked.

I set the salad on the floor, brush my teeth in the large employee restroom, and curl back into bed. I barely paid attention to the site over the last week because of the ten-hour days at *The Barker* and evenings spent packing, canceling my utilities, and saying goodbye to friends.

I toss and turn for nearly an hour, both because the bed is uncomfortable and because I'm teeming with excitement about tomorrow. There's so much to do that I'm tempted to get up and write a list, but I roll over onto my back and stare at the ceiling.

I can't help myself. As I fall asleep, I'm composing a to-do list in my head.

I wake to chirp after chirp, like a family of birds is having a discussion on the nightstand. My cellphone's text alert.

I wonder where I am. The first light barely peeks through

the large office windows, and I realize that it wasn't a dream. I'm in a kickass loft-like office in Santa Clarissa, a half-eaten Cobb salad on the floor next to me.

Stretching my legs, I remember the narrow width of the bed and carefully flip over into child pose. I'm not much of a yogi, but it feels good to start the day with a few stretches.

Next, I check my texts, and that's when my pleasant morning ends.

Mom: *Is something wrong with your site?*

Malcolm: *Odd candidate movement on Ameritocracy. What's going on?*

Peter: *Is everything okay?*

I climb out of bed, almost falling again because it's not only too narrow, it's also high off the floor. After looking for coffee for a few minutes, I give up and grab my laptop, then slide back under my covers and open the homepage. I know right away that something is wrong.

The number one spot is no longer occupied by Destiny O'Neill. She's all the way down at number four, and my top three candidates are all cartoon characters.

Ranked number one—the leading figure in my attempt to transform American democracy—is a green frog, apparently named Pepe. His candidate statement, which I can barely understand through the bad writing and misspellings, reads, "FEELS GOOD MAN. SUPPORT OPOSING AN END TO NEGATIVE DEPLORABLE FACISTS AND THEIR FACES. DO MORE WITH LESS AND SHEIT."

Ranked number two is a wild-haired cartoon figure named Rick Sanchez, who I vaguely recognize from T-shirts. I think he's a mad scientist on a show I've never gotten around to watching. His candidate statement promises to "Make Anime Real" and has a number of firm policy positions about video games I'm not familiar with.

My stomach is in knots, my head spinning with the realization that Ameritocracy has been hacked.

It gets worse. At number three is a crude drawing of an obese woman with glasses, her name listed as "Cupid Stunt." Her candidate statement is mostly about how she wants to be raped by various ethnic and religious minorities, but I can't even finish reading it before a dry heave surfaces.

When I'm certain I'm not actually going to throw up, my first text is to Peter.

Me: *Someone hacked the site or something. Not sure yet. Can your web guy come any sooner?*

Peter: *Don't know, but I'll tell him to get over ASAP.*

Me: *Thanks.*

I check the site again, going through the pages one by one to make sure everything else is as it should be. As far as I can tell, nothing else has changed since last night.

I check my email. Around one a.m., I received three messages, one right after the other, and I begin to understand what happened.

When I set up the site, I arranged it so new candidates do not need to be approved before their pages go live. All they need to do is fill out the information and their profile becomes visible within a few minutes. In the following week, we verify their identity, address, proof of citizenship, and age.

Judging by timestamps on the three emails, three candidates registered in rapid succession, changing only the name to get around the site's requirement that candidates not register a name that's already in use. But how did they get so many votes?

As I ponder this, a piece of paper slides under the office door. Startled, I look around feeling paranoid, then walk over and find that it's a menu from the Baker's Dozen downstairs. Stapled to the menu is a note: *We don't usually deliver, but we'd be happy to bring you food anytime between 6 a.m. and 10 p.m.*

I order coffee, French toast, and a fruit cup, deciding to wait for Peter's web guy before freaking out completely. I'm going to have to pace myself if I want to stay sane through the next year.

As I wait for the food, I arrange about a hundred sticky Post-it notes on my desk. Over the last week, I promised myself I wouldn't obsess too much about the site. Every time I had an idea, I just noted it and moved on. Now it's time to get organized. I break them into ten different categories, then rank them in order of importance.

Next, I scroll through my emails and find that another candidate registered late last night. A real candidate. Her name is Wendy Kahananui, a name that sounds familiar. Her Candidate Statement reads: "Government must serve all equally. Self-empowerment, compassion, unity of all beings."

In her profile picture, she appears to be around fifty, deeply tanned, and standing on a beach wearing flowing white robes. I click through to her Platform Page, where I learn that she's a spiritual teacher and yoga master from Hawaii.

She describes herself as half Japanese, half Caucasian, raised in four different countries, and fluent in five languages. After starting a successful yoga studio in Honolulu, she began teaching workshops on self-empowerment, which she now does all over the world.

With a few clicks, I learn that she has one of the top self-help channels on YouTube, where she teaches yoga and meditation to millions of people. That's why I know her name. I did one of her yoga videos in my apartment last year. Taken all together, she's a pretty big celebrity. She was even on *Ellen* once.

According to her page, "As President, I will bring higher values to the White House. I don't hold fast to positions or ideologies. Instead, I will respond to all problems and situations from within the moment. I will lead with empathy and compassion, but also with the sword of truth and justice, as personified by the goddess Kali."

Her page is short on specifics about policy or political involvement, but this is still great for the site. She's easily the most high-profile candidate we've had. I'm about to check her social media to find out if she's shared her Ameritocracy page when a knock at the door interrupts me.

My food and, more importantly, *my coffee.* I leap out of bed, jog to the door, swing it open and...Benjamin Singh stands before me, the only-sorta-creepy guy from the party. The one with the computer screen cowboy hat with miserable pickup lines.

He must be Peter's web guy.

"Um, hi," I say.

He looks at the floor. "Hi."

"Did Peter send you over?"

"Yes."

I step aside. "Come in, please."

He doesn't move.

"I'm Mia, and I think you're here to help me. Do you want to come in?"

He looks up briefly, then back at the floor. With his dirty jeans, plain black t-shirt, and unkempt hair nearly covering his eyes, he looks like he got the short end of an all-nighter. Then again, I'm in pajama pants and a tank top, and God alone knows what my hair is doing, so I'm in no position to judge.

Still standing in the doorway, he starts rocking back and forth from foot to foot.

"Are you okay?" I ask.

"Yes."

I step into the doorway and put a hand on his shoulder. "You're Benjamin, right? I met you at the party the other night."

"Yes."

"And you're here to help me with my site?"

"Yes."

He still doesn't come in, and I'm halfway between confused and frustrated. The door opens at the bottom of the stairwell. *Coffee.*

"Benjamin, there's a guy coming up the stairs with coffee and food. You'll need to move out of the way. In or out, buddy."

He glances down the stairwell, thinks for a moment, and steps into the office.

By the time I've paid for the food, Benjamin is already on his laptop at one of the desks. "4Chan," he says, not looking up.

"Yes! Thank you. What's going on?"

He doesn't respond, so I rinse out two Colton Industries coffee mugs and fill them from the large silver pitcher.

"Thanks," he says as I set one down next to him and peer over his shoulder at the screen.

"No problem. Are you feeling better?"

He doesn't respond to my question, but says, "Your site was the target of a botnet last night. They'd been planning it for a few days. This was probably inevitable because there's been a little more buzz about your site in tech circles the last week or so. There are posts about it all over the Chan boards. Nothing major. Just teenagers looking for attention. Can I have your passwords?"

I write my passwords on a Post-it and stick it to the corner of his screen. "How'd they do it?"

"Just registered their candidates, then sent an army of bots over to register fake user accounts and vote thousands of times."

"But you're not allowed to vote until your account is verified, which means providing proof of citizenship and identity. There's a whole process, that—"

"Yeah. They hacked that. Probably took them twenty minutes. Would've taken me five."

"Can you fix it?"

He sighs, but doesn't answer. One of the downsides of being a generalist who's trying to run a website is that I don't fully understand my own technology. He's already accessed the back end of my site, but I have no idea what he's doing. Until now, I've paid a freelancer forty bucks an hour to troubleshoot issues on my site, and I can tell immediately that Benjamin knows what he's doing.

"Benjamin, please. Can you fix it?"

"Yeah. That's the easy part."

"And?"

"And what?"

"What's the hard part?" I ask, annoyed.

He stops typing and gives me an irritated look. "Making sure this doesn't happen again. Look, I'm gonna need some time with this. I'm gonna need to bring in a few people, and we're going to need machines."

"Like, weed whackers or industrial wind turbines?"

"Computers."

"Of course. Order whatever you need. And thank you. Really."

I'm about to head to my office when he says something that surprises me. "I'd do anything for Peter."

I detect a whiff of human emotion from him, and put a hand on his shoulder. "What do you mean?"

"I owe him my life."

"Your life? Explain."

"Not my life, literally. But yeah, he hired me when I was sixteen. I'd only been in the States for six months, mom and dad mopped floors so I could go to a good high school in Palo Alto."

"How'd you meet him?"

"Interned through a summer program, then Peter hired me before my junior year. Never looked back."

"And where are your mom and dad now?"

Benjamin smiles for the first time. "Not mopping floors anymore." With that, his eyes are back on the screen.

Happy to have him around, but frustrated by my own helplessness when it comes to tech, I head to my office, the largest of the three glassed-in spaces in the otherwise loft-like office. There, I plan to get back to my notes and ease my frustrations by creating the mother of all to-do lists.

I freeze at the door when I notice movement behind the desk. My Post-it notes are scattered across the floor, some shredded. I step back and look around the office, which is empty except for Benjamin. "Hello?" I say quietly. "Hello?"

I'm about to conclude that the movement was just my imagination, and that the carefully arranged Post-its were blown onto the floor by a random gust of air.

Then I see the cat.

[8]

I see its tail first, black and waving at me from behind the desk—*my* desk—like it's the most natural thing in the world.

"Hey," I say. The tail disappears, and I walk around the desk. "Kitty, kitty, kitty."

He's sitting under my office chair, as though that's a perfectly reasonable place to sit. The rest of the cat is also black except for four large white spots, two on one side, one on the other, and one on the top of its head. He looks up at me and blinks noncommittally, a look I interpret as something between "What are *you* doing here?" and "Your Post-it notes? I wouldn't know *anything* about those."

I crouch to gather my notes, and my heart drops when I see that most of them are mangled beyond repair. When you've put your brain on paper, and that paper is destroyed, it feels as though a piece of your brain has been destroyed.

I sit on the floor next to him, trying to piece together parts of notes and wet corners of others. I see words like "challenge," "democracy," "interns," and, for some odd reason, "pineapple."

It's no use. Half my notes are lost forever, the rest are wildly disorganized, and here I sit on the floor of my new office, a mystery-cat rubbing his ribcage against my leg.

"Benjamin!" I call out into hallway. "Is this your cat?"

He doesn't respond, but I know it's not. There's no way he snuck a cat in under his shirt. The cat doesn't have a tag, so I figure he's a stray who smelled food and came in when the door was open.

Or maybe he was here all night. Maybe he just came with the office. Maybe he's the spirit of a failed startup, reincarnated as a cat until he eats enough important Post-it notes to digest their informational karma. Maybe I need some food to go with this coffee, because I'm running three cartoons for president and starting to believe in ghost cats.

My first day hasn't gotten off to the start I'd hoped for, but just when I'm about to lose it, I remember that there's a box of warm French toast out in the main office space. Things could be much worse.

By noon, I've consumed two orders of French toast, accepted a delivery of eight new computers, and welcomed three of Benjamin's assistants, on loan from Colton Industries. Somewhere in there I showered and changed out of my pajamas and into jeans, a white button-down, and a blue blazer.

The computers have been set up and networked, and Benjamin assured me multiple times that he's doing everything he can to solve the 4Chan attack.

But still I hover behind his desk, watching over his shoulder. "Are you sure there's nothing I can do?" I ask for the sixth or seventh time.

The last couple times, Benjamin ignored me, but now he

turns slowly in his chair, glaring. "I. Will. Fix. This. Don't you have a company to run?"

I retreat to my desk, where our mystery cat stalks around my ankles. It's not easy, but I settle into the fact that there's truly nothing I can do, that the fate of my site is in the hands of a dude with a computer hat full of offensive pickup lines, and three other tech people I just met.

One way or another, we'll get out of this mess, and I decide to write my list. As a pool jumper, I learned early on that I need lists. They help keep me from spinning out of control.

After a respectful pause to mourn my destroyed Post-its, I write down the big things—the must-dos.

1. Hire an Executive Director.

This is priority one because I need someone to hire personnel and manage the day-to-day operations so I can focus on the media strategy, fundraising, and other big picture tasks. Someone to hire interns, manage the staff, and handle at least a few of the crises that are sure to arise every day. Steph was my first choice, but she's in Seattle.

2. Create Media Strategy

Assuming Benjamin and his crew can get the 4Chan hack fixed, I want to launch a mainstream media blitz starting late this week. The more media we get, the more legitimate we will seem. The more legitimate we seem, the more good candidates we will attract. The more good candidates we attract, the more donations we will get and the more legitimate we'll seem. Starting with a bang in the public eye is crucial.

Wendy Kahananui shared her profile across her social media platforms, and even uploaded a video to YouTube to announce her candidacy. I need to figure out how to capitalize on that.

According to Benjamin, our number of unique visitors per hour has doubled since he arrived this morning, largely due to Kahananui's registration. Voter registrations have increased as well. Instead of getting new voters at the rate of five a day, we're getting five an hour. But we need mainstream print and TV media attention to hit the next level.

3. Build an app.

I didn't have the money to develop an app when I started Ameritocracy, but now I do. I expect that I can get Benjamin and his team to take care of this. Though the site works on phones, a dedicated app will be a crucial part of achieving the exponential growth I'm aiming for.

4. Create Fundraising Strategy

Democrats and Republicans often spend over $100 million on a general election campaign. For an eventual Ameritocracy candidate to have any chance, we need a campaign war chest of at least $10 million to start. That amount, combined with the celebrity I plan to create around our winning candidate, should be enough to compete. So, in addition to the donations that should come in with more candidates and voters, I plan to target individual donors around the country.

5. Find an apartment.

I look through my office window and across the office, my eyes landing on the bed in the corner. To my embarrassment, I didn't make it before Benjamin and his team showed up. My half-eaten Cobb salad is still browning on the floor beside it.

I'll need an apartment eventually, but I have a clean bed in a comfortable space and a restaurant that will bring me three meals a day. I've gotten by on less. Come to think of it, this is better than most of the places I've ever lived. Promising to make the bed tomorrow, I cross "Find an apartment" off my list and add "Deal with cat."

Happy to have a basic plan, though still a little irritated that the cat destroyed my notes, I stroll into the office to check on Benjamin, then stop dead in my tracks.

Steph stands near the doorway looking confused. She doesn't see me.

"Steph!"

She meets my eyes across the office and smiles. "Does a Mia Rhodes work here?"

I try to read her expression, but before I can, I read her outfit. She's wearing one of her green pantsuits, which means she's here to work. I jog across the room and jump into her arms. She hugs me hard, lifting me up like a mom with her kid.

"You came," I say.

She sets me down. "I heard this joint was hiring."

"Oh my God are you really here? Like, *here*?"

She scans the office. "Is this your staff?"

"I don't have a staff. These are computer guys and gals on loan. My first day is going..."

I trail off as the cat emerges from my office and brushes against my ankle.

"Poorly?" Steph asks.

"You could say we're experiencing growing pains, as I'm sure all Silicon Valley startups do."

"You got a cat, at least."

"Seriously," I say loudly to the room, "does anyone know whose cat this is?"

Everyone looks up from their screens, but no one speaks.

"What's his name?" Steph asks. "And when did you have time to get a cat?"

"It's a...strange story. His name is, uhhhhh...His name is Post-it."

Steph crouches down and reaches for him. "Kitty, kitty. *Heeeeeere*, kitty kitty."

Tentatively, Post-it strolls over and lets Steph pet him, but only for a moment before returning to my ankles.

"Are you really here to help me?" I ask.

"Mostly to try those biscuits you told me about, but yeah. I'm here. And, from the look of it, we've got a lot of work to do."

"Executive Director?"

"Is that an offer?"

"More of a desperate plea, but yeah."

Steph surveys the office, her eyes landing on Benjamin, who is huddled over his laptop, typing as two people talk to him at once. "What's his deal?" she asks.

"We got hacked this morning. He's helping, I think. I hope." I sigh deeply. "This first day has been a bit of a nightmare."

"He's cute," Steph says in a loud whisper.

I crouch to scratch Post-it behind the ears. "Yeah, he's cute. But, we have to call animal control or get him to the animal shelter, right?"

"I meant Benjamin, not the cat."

Standing, I say, "I guess. If you're into the disheveled-computer-genius look."

"Maybe I am, maybe I'm not," Steph says, eyes still on Benjamin.

"A couple girls I met at Peter's party last week warned me that he's mildly creepy, and he has this weird hat thing with pickup lines."

"Huh?"

"Then I saw the three of them leave the same room the next morning."

"So?"

"Just saying."

Steph is still staring, and I snap my fingers in front of her eyes. "Steph!"

She blinks a few times, then looks at me. "Executive Director?"

"That's right. We can work out the details, but I see this as a partnership. You handle the day-to-day, I focus on media and fundraising."

"So I get shit done, you tell the world about it?"

I laugh. "Basically, yeah."

She nods toward the glassed-in offices. "And one of those would be mine?"

"Yup."

She thinks, looks at Benjamin, then at Post-it.

Finally, she looks at me with a determined smile that makes me feel for the first time today like everything is going to work out. "I'm proud of you, Mia. I accept."

We decide to iron out the details of her employment over drinks that evening, and though I'm eager to talk about big picture stuff, we're in crisis mode. Back in my office, I reach someone at the local Humane Society, who takes down Post-it's description, then regrets to inform me that their shelter is full.

I roll my eyes at Steph and agree to care for the cat until its owners reclaim him. I call to arrange for cat supplies, then Steph and I draft a couple press releases related to the hack.

Both convey roughly the same thing: the site was hacked, it's not a huge deal, and our crack team of experts returned the site to normal. The main difference is that the first version of the press release is dated today, and highlights the speed with which Benjamin and his crew solved the problem. This version down-plays the significance of the prank.

The second version presents a picture of a more sophisti-cated attack and contains a blank space to insert the date, which we will fill in when we actually solve the problem. Both versions have spaces to insert technical language describing the hack and, more importantly, all the steps we're taking to ensure that this never happens again.

I don't know which version we'll need, but after another check-in with Benjamin—who shoos me away without a word—I admit there's nothing more Steph and I can do right now, so we split up.

I cross "Hire an Executive Director" off my list and watch through my office window as she introduces herself to Benjamin and the other tech people he brought in. It's clear from moment one that she's in charge, and it puts me at ease.

At my urging, Peter kept the donation quiet so I could announce it when I was ready, and now I'm ready. I begin by writing two more press releases. The first is from Ameritocracy, the official not-for-profit entity that owns and manages the website. In it, I describe the donation, lay out the expansion plan, the timetable for voting and debates, and the ultimate goal of the site.

The second press release is from the perspective of Colton Industries, highlighting that the donation grew out of a standard Project X application and that Ameritocracy will be 100% independent from all Colton Industries business interests and employees. In a sense, I'm marking my territory. In the media, you never get a second chance to make a first impression, so I want to ensure that the initial stories focus on the site, not on Colton Industries or on Peter. As happy as I am to use his celebrity to build buzz around the site, I don't want him to be the story.

I email the second press release to Peter, figuring he'll have his staff edit it, slap it on company stationery, and send it out.

After running it by Steph, who is already posting job openings all over the internet, I paste my press release onto Ameritocracy letterhead, which includes a stars and stripes flag logo. Once I'm happy, I send it to every contact I have in the news business, including Alex, Bird and the reporters and news executives I got to know over the years working at *The Barker*.

I also share the release to Ameritocracy's email list, Facebook page, and Twitter account which, at the moment, has a measly two thousand followers. Next, I record a brief video, announcing the donation and walking viewers through our new offices, leaving out my bed and the salad that I still haven't cleaned up.

By early evening, *The Barker* has already posted a short blog hit about the donation, and I've given quotes to a couple other websites that will be running features.

Through a local agency, Steph has hired three office temps who start tomorrow, and placed ads for the three full-time positions we need to fill immediately: Office Manager, a role I am *thrilled* not to be filling myself, Chief Financial Officer, someone to keep the books and track the money, and Social Media Director, someone who will monitor every mention of Ameritocracy on social media, manage our accounts, and engage with users. With Benjamin and his team on loan from Peter, we'll save hundreds of thousands on tech help.

Wiped out, Steph and I are about to head downstairs for an early dinner when Benjamin shouts like a madman. "Done! I'm done!"

I walk around two of Benjamin's assistants, each hunched over a laptop in the middle of the floor, meeting Steph behind Benjamin's office chair. "Tell us everything," I say, but his eyes are on Steph, who's looking at him like a cartoon bear staring at a turkey.

"Benjamin! Did you fix it?"

This snaps him back in. "Fixed, locked down against future attacks, and a lot of those script kiddies are going to find their passwords posted in places they won't be happy about."

He still hasn't looked directly at me, but he speaks with total confidence and a hint of badassery. Standing in the doorway earlier, he reminded me of Dustin Hoffman from *Rain Man*, but now he sounds like Arnold from *T2*. My working theory is that he only feels like himself when he's touching a computer.

"What places?" I ask.

"Places where much better hackers will open up their Steam and Netflix accounts and run up charges they'll have to explain to mom and dad. So, y'know, it ends up as a story they tell to the next little prick who tries to screw with Ameritocracy."

I'm taken aback. I hadn't asked him to do...most of that. Not that I'm complaining. "Right, yes, okay. But are our top three candidates no longer cartoon characters? Is *that* fixed?"

"Oh yeah, had that done hours ago. Deleted their candidate profiles, blocked the bots they were using to vote. Your home-page is fixed, and it doesn't look like any other candidates were affected. Your top twenty is back to normal. I spent the rest of the afternoon installing new security features so this can't happen again."

"And their passwords?"

"That was for fun. And, like I said, a deterrent." He finally faces me. "Keep in mind, what I've just installed brings your security up from a zero out of ten to maybe, like, a three. When we build out the site, we'll want to take that to a ten, or as close as we can get."

I don't know what to say. I don't love the fact that I'm relying on a somewhat creepy guy who showed up on my doorstep with Peter's recommendation, and it doesn't help that he uses the same one-to-ten scale on which he was rated a Silicon Valley creeper the first night I met him. Further confusing the matter is that Steph appears to be interested in him. But right now, Benjamin is who I've got.

His eyes drift back to the screen, and I lean in and hug him from behind. His back is rigid, his shoulders stiff, and I think he could use it.

"Thanks," I say. "We've got to send the press releases and do a couple other things first, but do you want to come to dinner with us?"

"Yeah," Steph says. "Come eat."

"Nah. I gotta get some new security stuff going here. We need to start verifying the information users enter by using confirmatory data. IP addresses, browser versions, image searches on avatar pictures, and so on. I'm gonna stick around here and do that."

"But you have to eat, too," Steph says.

He turns and gives her a look I can't read. "Bring me something."

"We will," Steph says.

[9]

We collapse into a booth in Baker's Dozen and order two glasses of wine—red for her, white for me—and I sigh with the satisfaction that only comes after a hard day at work doing something you love. "We're really doing it."

Steph undoes the top button on her shirt. "We are."

After Benjamin explained his fixes, we updated and sent out the first version of the press release, then made a half dozen calls each to contacts in the media, encouraging them to focus on the Colton donation and downplaying the significance of the hack.

Now, I can finally ask Steph the question that nagged at me all day. "What made you change your mind?"

"Biscuits. This is the place, right?"

"I think they only serve them at breakfast. Seriously, though."

"You really want to know?" Steph's face is ponderous, and I can tell she's about to tell me more than I expected to hear when I asked the question.

"I do."

"I went to one meeting at the super-PAC last week, Americans for Justice, they're called. It was just a get-to-know-you kind of thing. Everyone was all, 'Glad you're joining us!' and 'Can't wait for you to get started!' And—"

"That sounds good."

"Lemme finish. The place was downtown, two whole floors in the White Crown Building. Probably fifty employees, and I'm the *only* black person in the room, the only black person at an organization trying to support politicians who'll fight poverty. All that is...it is what it is...it's not the point. The point is the offices, where we're supposed to work on *poverty* issues, were like Roman-emperor-level expensive. I'm about to make two hundred grand a year—and I'm only middle management—and everyone is sitting in eight-hundred-dollar chairs around this glass conference table that must have cost...I don't even know. They even had a goddamn vintage espresso machine in the center of the main office space. One of those gold metal ones from Italy."

"Oooohhhh, I *love* those." After just three sips of wine, I'm tipsy and full of joy. For a moment at least, everything is great and the world is a wonderful place. "All the copper knobs and silver buttons and—"

"Mia!" Steph gives me a look and takes a long swig of wine. "Look, I'm all for espresso, and I'm all for making money, but just standing in that room, I couldn't shake the thought: What the hell am I doing here? What are any of us doing here? I passed six homeless people on my walk through downtown Seattle. Sitting up in that high-rise, I couldn't help but think, how far removed from doing any *actual good* can I get? I'm gonna miss the salary, and I'll be a little pissed if this decision means my future-maybe-children have to eat peanut butter and jelly in public school cafeterias, but—"

"You know you're a bit of an elitist snob, right?"

"Hey! I wear the 'elite coastal liberal' badge with pride."

I wait to see if she's going to say anything more, but she doesn't. Politically, Steph leans pretty far left, whereas I'm closer to the center. Even when we disagree, though, I admire the way she fights for what she believes in, and now I admire her decision to put her money where her mouth is, especially given the money-to-mouth ratio in this case.

"I'm sleeping in the office for now," I say when I'm sure she's done. "Where are you gonna stay?"

"Negotiated a weekly rate on a place fifteen minutes away. We're going to be working sixteen hour days, side by side, for the next..." She pauses to do the calculation in her head. "...Eleven months and thirteen days. Last thing I need in the remaining eight hours is to listen to you snore."

"You really think we'll make it to the debate on July Fourth? I mean, we set up all these deadlines and schedules and plans but...something in me still expects this all to fall apart before then. I—"

"Mia," she interrupts, "I think you may be suffering from imposter syndrome, so let me tell you something, as someone who's been in the political world—or at least the fringes of it—since I volunteered for the DNC back in my junior year at Georgetown. You belong in this world."

She waits for me to look up, and when I do her brown eyes have a familiar look in them, like she's going to look at me as hard as she can until I agree with her. She usually reserves that look for when she's trying to convince me of something about the world, but now she's trying to convince me of something about myself.

"You *belong* in this world," she repeats. "We have the money and soon we'll have the staff. This *is* happening. I don't know if we'll get a candidate who can win in 2020, but by July Fourth—eleven months and thirteen days from now—we will have built Ameritocracy into something *everyone* in America is following."

The look in her eyes almost has me believing her, and I'm close to tears when my phone chirps with a text. "It's Bird."

"Begging you to come back already?"

"No it's...oh no."

"What?"

I don't respond because I'm too busy reading the first article openly mocking Ameritocracy.

"Mia, what?"

I scan the article, barely noticing when our food arrives, then read the headline to Steph. "It's a blog piece from *The Washington Insider*. The title reads *Anybody for President?*"

"*The Washington Insider* is tiny. They're nothing."

"But still, listen to this."

"Come around."

I slide into Steph's side of the booth and hand her the phone, reading over her shoulder and scoffing at the more insulting phrases.

Anybody for President?

In the zaniest development yet of an already-absurd 2020 election cycle, a Seattle office manager with no political experience wants to make it possible for anyone to run for president.

And she means ANYONE.

Her online political competition, Ameritocracy2020.org, allows users to run for president, and promises to donate a large sum of money to the eventual winners' campaign after the final debate, scheduled for July Fourth. Those of us at The Washington Insider doubt she'll make it that far.

So far, her website has attracted about as much attention as any other stoned-college-freshman-level fringe political site. But this sideshow got a boost recently from eccentric tech mogul Peter Colton, who is ready to double down on the "eccentric" label. According to a press release emailed by Ms. Rhodes herself, the five million dollar donation will be used to "expand the platform, hire new staff, develop an app, and produce live events for the leading candidates."

Rather than laugh at "develop an app" as a serious press-release phrase, since she brought up the "leading candidates," let's discuss them. Though screenshots circulating online indicate that, earlier today, the site was hacked so its leading candidates were obscene cartoon characters, the real leaderboard isn't much better.

Made up of nutjobs from the fringes of American politics and others who appear to be using the platform to boost their own online presence, the top ten candidates make us here at The Washington Insider long for the days of party bosses in smoke-filled back rooms choosing the president.

Don't believe us? Here's a sample:

Coming in at number 10: Wendy Kahananui, a patchouli-scented guru with no political experience who joined the site twelve hours ago.

At number 9: Asher Gull, a leftist activist so far out there he was disavowed by the Democratic Socialists as "too radical."

And who's currently leading this debacle? Destiny O'Neill, a self-described "Second Amendment MILF," whose candidate videos could be used to audition for the leading role in an adult film.

Candidates 2 through 8 aren't any better.

Though we certainly respect Ms. Rhodes' passion for democracy, the verdict of The Washington Insiders: leave presidential politics to the grown-ups.

By the time Steph finishes reading, I'm fuming. But to my surprise, she's not hurt at all.

In fact, she's laughing. "You have to admit, 'patchouli-scented' is a pretty good phrase."

I whack her arm, then return to my side of the booth. "That's not the type of emotional support I was looking for."

"Eat your dinner. There will be a lot of these. We're going to have to grow thick skins. Did you see what FiveThirtyEight wrote?"

I cringe. FiveThirtyEight.com is one of the most-respected polling analysis sites in the business since their founder predicted fifty out of fifty states correctly in the 2012 election. "At least they wrote an article about us," I say weakly. "That's good news, right?"

"Not an article," Steph says. "But they sent a Tweet. Well, actually a reply to someone else's Tweet. They said that Ameritocracy isn't even worth polling about."

For a few minutes, I dig into my Cobb salad, always a favorite but one I usually can't afford. Baker's Dozen makes the best I've ever tasted, but even my comfort food is no comfort. The emotions well up and I know that Steph can handle them.

She's halfway through a ribeye steak when I say, "The hack, the article, the move. That damn cat...well the cat is cute but destructive to my Post-it-note system. Anyway, I just can't."

I haven't cried, but I'm in the emotional place just before tears.

"Mia, calm down. We've had a rough first day. And, okay, it's gonna get worse, but—"

"Worse?"

"Sure, but do you know *why* it's gonna get worse?"

"Hold on, let me chug this wine before you tell me."

I'm only half-joking. I take a long sip of my wine as Steph gives me a quizzical look that I take to mean "How concerned should I be?"

I hold back the tears, reassured by the authority Steph brings to every situation. "I'm okay," I say. "I'm better. Now, tell me why it's going to get worse."

"Because you're going to be famous."

"Famous?"

"Mo' money, mo' problems."

"I'm gonna be just as broke at the end of this thing as I was at the beginning."

"Yeah, but everyone will be talking about Ameritocracy. *Everyone*. And, like it or not, you're going to be the face of it. That comes with a lot of crap from all directions."

Steph's words don't help. "I barely know what I'm doing. We got hacked on *day one*."

"You'll need to find some sanity, Mia. There will be problems. Little ones *and* big ones. You're going to have to learn to delegate and trust the people around you. If Benjamin is the best Peter has, that means he's one of the best on earth. He'll make sure this doesn't happen again and, in a few weeks, this will be a tiny bump on the track of the runaway train that is Ameritocracy and Mia Rhodes."

I raise an eyebrow. "You come up with that line yourself?"

"It's true. Mia, look at me."

My eyes trace the wood grain on the table before I look up.

"You need to get your shit together, Mia. We just went from pee-wee football to the NFL playoffs overnight. We're headed for the Super Bowl."

"What's with all the analogies?"

"I just quit a job that paid two hundred grand a year to work for an idealistic startup. Poetry is all I've got."

"Okay, but trains *and* football? Better to stick to one metaphor at a time."

"You're gonna write the press releases, okay?"

"Okay."

"Plus..." She trails off and digs back into her steak.

"Plus what?"

"Wouldn't hurt you to...find a man."

"I don't need a man to—"

"I'm not saying you need a man. You're an amazing woman, kicking ass and taking names."

"A hobo cat brought me to tears today. I'm not feeling like much of a superhero."

"You're gonna have to fake it 'til you make it. But my point is, of course you don't *need* a man, but don't you want one? Someone to get away from the office with? Someone to...you know."

She raises her eyebrows and rubs her hands together in a gesture I assume I'm supposed to associate with sex.

"I don't have time for that."

"Okay," she says, "but it might help keep you sane."

We eat in silence as I ponder her suggestion. The more I think about it, the more I suspect that it's less a suggestion and more a warning of something she's going to do.

I'm about to ask her, but I think better of it. Steph has always had an ease with men that I don't. She gets them, and gets what she wants from them. Whether it's a one-night-stand, a cocktail party full of doctors and lawyers, or a lust-at-first-site interaction with my tech guy, she knows what she's doing with men.

Me...not so much.

And, even if she's right, I have other things to think about. As we finish our meal, my mind races forward to the first big Ameritocracy rally.

Since the moment I started the site, I envisioned a rally at which I'd introduce the candidates to America. TV stations from around the country would be there, along with frumpy print reporters scribbling in the front row.

Until recently, it seemed an absurd fantasy. Now it takes on the air of real possibility, and I quell my anxiety like I always do —by making plans.

When Steph excuses herself to the restroom, I open the Notes app on my phone and start a new note, smiling inside at the fact that Post-it has no chance to destroy this one.

I start typing:

Ameritocracy: The Rally
Introduce the idea.

Introduce the candidates.

November, 2019

Los Angeles, CA

Typing it makes it feel real, and I stare at the screen for a good three minutes, letting Steph's confidence in the success of Ameritocracy wash over me.

I must be in some kind of trance, because Steph is sitting across from me again before I know it.

"Mia?"

I look up slowly.

"Mia, why do you look far away? Are you fantasizing about the rally again?"

She's the only person I've shared my vision of the rally with. "I am," I say. "But don't worry. It's not a fantasy anymore. We're doing this."

"What's next?"

"We finish our wine, and start bright and early tomorrow. It's time to get to work."

[PART 2]

[10]

Two months later, Steph and I stand side by side, grinning like fools at the large flatscreen TV Benjamin recently installed in my office. The TV displays the Ameritocracy leaderboard, mirrored from our homepage, and shows that Destiny O'Neill has just dropped to number three, down from number two.

She lost the number one spot to Wendy Kahananui a few days ago, and now she's been bumped down another notch by the recently-joined radio host Tanner Futch. I'm not rooting for Futch or anyone else, but I haven't trusted Destiny O'Neill from the beginning.

"She's still top five, though," I say.

"It's not like Futch is much better," Steph counters. "Worse, if you ask me."

"At least he actually *wants* to be president."

"I guess, but would *you* want him as president?"

"I'm committed to neutrality. I'm Switzerland."

Steph just rolls her eyes.

Futch took the site by storm when he launched his campaign a few days after the press release. The son of West Virginia coal miners, Futch is a jowly, smooth-talking radio host in L.A. who represents the views of alt-right conspiracy theorist types. His key beliefs are that the government needs to be taken back from the oligarchs who own both parties, that 9/11 was an inside job, and that most mass shootings are false flags aimed at curtailing the second amendment. His Candidate Statement reads: *America is being destroyed by its political ruling class. States' Rights. America First. Don't defend; attack!*

He's not a candidate I could support, but he represents the views—or *shapes* the views—of many Americans, and his entry caused quite a stir.

Steph walks around my desk, sits in my chair, and puts her feet up. "We did it."

I sit across from her and match her smile, though I don't know what she's talking about.

"We made it over the first hurdle," she says.

"What do you mean?"

Post-it jumps onto Steph's lap and presses his body into her. Steph pets him slowly. "When I got here, I had a few benchmarks in my head, things that needed to happen over the first couple months. Benchmark one was staffing."

She gestures into the main space through the window of my private office. Across a dozen scattered desks and tables, Benjamin works with his team, joined by five new full-time staff members. Two interns, an office manager, a social media manager, and a secretary. "We succeeded at that."

"*You* succeeded at that."

"True enough," she laughs. "I handled all that. But you handled benchmark number two: get some good press."

"We got more bad press than good."

Over the last month, Ameritocracy was the subject of quite a few articles and even a newscast or two. All but two had a mocking tone similar to the piece published by *The Washington Insider*. Most of them mentioned Destiny O'Neill, because if you want to mock our seriousness, she's tailor-made.

"True," Steph says, "but we got good coverage from *The Barker* and, what was that one site?"

"Buster's Political Scoops dot US. Not quite the same caliber as *The Washington Post*."

"Still, a rave review."

"I guess. What was your third benchmark?"

"That we stay friends."

I look up, and she's still smiling. I feel crummy about my inability to generate more positive coverage for the site, but as always, Steph's reassurance makes me feel better. "So far, so good."

"Seriously, though. Running a company with friends destroys the friendship a lot of the time, and we made it through a rough period. We may not be in love with our candidates yet, but if we keep doing what we're doing, amazing human beings are going to start walking through the door."

"Or maybe just registering online?"

"It was a *metaphor*," she says.

"I know what a metaphor is. I majored in English for two semesters and...Steph?"

She's stopped listening. I follow her wide eyes to the corner of the office, where Benjamin and his crew have set up four tables and covered them with twenty grand worth of computers. But I don't see Benjamin.

I see Destiny O'Neill.

Steph stands suddenly. "What the what?"

"You took the words right out of my mouth," I say, also standing.

Destiny is hanging out near the bank of computers, chatting with Benjamin's assistants in blue jeans so tight I think they must be sprayed on. She laughs and pats one of them on the shoulder, then leans over a chair and points at one of the screens, her huge breasts almost spilling out of her ribbed white tank top.

"See her hat?" Steph says.

I hadn't noticed Destiny's trucker hat until now. It reads: MILFS FOR THE SECOND AMENDMENT.

"Oh no." I offer Steph a panicked look. "What's she doing here?"

"I don't know, but candidate relations is your department. Plus, I've got the CFO candidate interviews to prep for."

"So what you're saying is that this is my problem, right?"

Steph smiles and nods.

"In that case," I say, "benchmark three is still up in the air."

Steph pets Post-it slowly, then laughs like an evil genius from a cartoon. "You better get her away from Benjamin's guys before they lose their virginity without taking off their pants."

I scowl, but in a loving way, then turn on my heels and stride into the main office space like I run the place. I do run the place, but right now Destiny O'Neill is acting like she's in charge.

As I make my way around desks, I trip over a recycling container, catch myself, then continue my stride as though I hadn't. I hear Destiny's voice—flirty and sweet as high-fructose corn syrup—"Can't you just tweak the algorithm a teensy-weensy bit, for me?"

She's talking to one of Benjamin's assistants, whose name I knew last week but have since forgotten. "Well, possibly," he says. "It's actually easy, we'd just—"

"Oh, can't you do it for me?" she says, her voice a little twangy, like a northerner doing a bad southern accent.

"Ahem!" I say, standing up as straight as I can, hands on my hips.

Destiny sees me and turns. "If it isn't Mia Rhodes herself! I was just telling these sexy young men how unfair the algorithm is to your *longest-running* top candidate. I was saying that—"

"What are you doing here?" I ask, as firmly as possible.

Destiny takes off her trucker hat, puts it backward onto the head of the assistant she'd been speaking with, leans down, and pecks him on the cheek. "I'll be back for *you* later." Then, to me, "Walk and talk? Show me the office?"

Before I can respond, she's leading me around the office, touching the desks and windows, even running her hands over the leaves of the potted plants like it's foreplay for some weird fetish I've never heard of. I watch her and watch the rest of the staff, who are trying their best not to be caught staring.

"Destiny," I say when we're alone in the far corner of the office, "what are you doing here?"

"You heard me before. I came to talk about the algorithm."

"The...really?"

"Truly. I was in California to protest against the ridiculous anti-gun measures they're trying to get on the ballot in 2020, and to sign panties at a car show. Thought I'd stop by."

"Please tell me you weren't really signing panties at a car show?"

"They weren't, like, used panties. That expense was all on the car show. Paid for my flight, a $2,000 appearance fee, and a crate of my favorite white thong panties. I'm kinda known for them."

"That I did know," I say, still trying to wrap my brain around the fact that this conversation is actually happening. And worse, that I actually *did* know that.

I glance through the glass into my office, where Steph is still sitting behind my desk, petting Post-it. The smirk on her face says she's been watching the whole scene.

"Anyway," Destiny continues. "Is there somewhere we can talk?"

It's almost noon, and I figure the only way I'll get through a full conversation with Destiny O'Neill is if food is involved.

I nod toward the door. "I know a place."

~

Steph and I have eaten at Baker's Dozen at least once a day since she arrived. Walt, the waiter who brought me the French toast and coffee on my first day, knows me well.

As Destiny and I take a seat, he says, "Welcome back, Mia. Cobb Salad and iced tea?"

"Yes, please." I offer him a weak smile. "But she'll need a menu."

Destiny looks at Walt with what must be her default look: seduction. "Are you on the menu?"

Walt, entirely uninterested in her charms, hands her a menu. "No, honey, but we *are* known for our biscuits."

Destiny laughs, scanning the menu. "Carbs? At lunch? I'll have the steak sandwich, hold the bread."

"Fries?"

"Raw carrots. For my skin."

Walt looks confused, but scribbles a note on his pad. "And to drink?"

"Watermelon juice with ginseng. For the libido."

Walt glances at me, eyebrows raised in his best *is-she-serious?* look, then frowns at Destiny. "We don't have that."

Destiny looks around like she might storm out of the place. "Iced tea will be fine. No sugar."

Walt leaves, and before Destiny can say anything, I try to take control of the conversation. "Do your followers know that you're so picky about your food and drink? Isn't it kinda off-brand to sub out raw carrots for good old-fashioned freedom fries?"

Destiny stares at me, but with none of the charm she heaps on every man in her presence. "My followers love me for who I am."

"Do you believe anything you say, though?"

She shrugs. "A lot of it. Look, for most of my fans, Government and Society are the same thing as Mom. Always telling them to stop smoking weed, stop being so disrespectful, don't use that kind of language, all those video games can't be good for you, eat healthier, I know what's best and I'm only trying to look out for you, so do what I tell you. And they *hate* that. So I give them a replacement. Instead of Killjoy Mommy, I'm Sexy Mommy who agrees with them about everything. And I've managed to make that a full-time job because I'm very good at it."

I'm simultaneously stunned at the depth of her cynicism and a little impressed at how well she understands her audience and her business model. "Wow, okay. And my site is a part of your, what, marketing plan?"

She smirks. "Lemme turn it back on you, Mia. Do *you* believe any of the stuff you say?"

"Of course I believe in Ameritocracy!" I say.

I'm about to continue when she cuts me off.

"I believe you can say the word 'Ameritocracy' with a straight face, which must have taken practice, but c'mon, Mia. It's just us girls here. You don't seriously think the next president is going to be anyone from your site, least of all me. And that's okay. Neither do I. But whoever your site picks is going to have several months to build *your* brand, to make *you* more famous. And when it comes to that, Red, I'm your best option. If you think I look good on YouTube, give them an excuse to point TV cameras at me. I'll get more coverage than dried-up old Wendy Whatserface or that creepy toad Futch, because I'll be better for everyone's ratings. That's millions in free advertising for *your* site. Your price on the speaking-fee circuit will be mid-six-figures before you know it. So let's talk about your algorithm. Just us girls."

Internally, I amend my earlier opinion of her cynicism, the depths of which I had wildly underestimated. My opinion of her business savvy remains, though. She's right that news programs would rather air footage of a well-endowed woman in a low-cut top than a jowly man in a suit. It's one of the exact things I started Ameritocracy to combat.

Swallowing my first several responses, I arrive at, "You think our ranking algorithm should be changed in your favor?"

"Yes. It's wildly unfair."

"We haven't even announced how it works."

"You must know people are trying to reverse-engineer it based on how it responds."

I do know that, though I'm surprised at how fluently Destiny talks about algorithms. She's not the person she presents to men, and I'm not sure I can hold my own in this conversation.

"What exactly are your issues with our algorithm?" I ask.

"Mia!"

When I hear my name from the front of the restaurant, I turn to see Peter, who strides in wearing a black suit and skinny red tie, like he's ready for the red carpet.

When he reaches our table, he says, "Steph said you were down here. I dropped in to see if you'd like to have lunch. And here you are, having lunch." He turns to Destiny. "And you must be Destiny O'Neill. I've seen you on the site. Your campaign has been truly...inspirational."

I think he's making fun of her, but Destiny doesn't notice, because she's switching modes. The scarily insightful woman is gone, and I'm back at a table with Libertarian Jessica Rabbit.

Sliding over, she says, "Have a seat, Peter. Join us. We've only just ordered. But I should warn you, they don't serve watermelon juice with ginseng."

Her accent is different, I notice. Gone is the slight twang she adds in her videos. In its place she's installed a more refined tone. Less Scarlett O'Hara, more Katharine Hepburn.

She leans toward Peter, and his eyes dart briefly to her chest, which strains at her shirt so hard I'm worried I might get hit with boob shrapnel.

"You know what?" He stands. "I'm just gonna..." He sits next to me. "Is this alright, Mia? I think, yeah. I'll just sit here."

"Fine," I say.

Peter catches Walter's eye and nods, his sign that, as usual, he'll have the eggs Benedict and a champagne flute of Red Bull. Then he turns to Destiny. "So, what are you doing in town?"

"She came to complain about the algorithm," I say.

"It's unfair," Destiny pouts.

"Why's that?" Peter asks

"Well, I know that you haven't officially announced how it works, but we know that you're using ranked candidate voting and that somehow you're taking social media mentions and shares into account."

"Right," I say. "That's nothing we haven't talked about publicly. Hell, that's on our website."

"But," Destiny says, "it's clear you're missing a key metric: longevity."

"How do you mean?" Peter asks.

Destiny leans across the table toward Peter, again exposing her cleavage. "I'm so glad you asked, Peter." She practically breathes his name, and I get a sense of the person she's become for Peter. Tech-savvy, but submissive. Smart, but never smarter than the man she's talking to. "What I mean is that it's clear from the algorithm, and from the way that prissy ass guru Wendy

Kakablani or whatever rose in the standings, that there's a recency bias in your algorithm."

"It's not my algorithm," Peter says. "Complaints like that are Mia's department."

"What I mean—"

"I know what you mean," I interrupt.

Walter arrives with the food, and I'm glad to have a moment to collect myself. The recency bias Destiny is referring to has to do with how we choose to weight the value of social media shares and mentions over time. And, though we could debate whether we were right or wrong to set it up the way we did, to my astonishment, Destiny is right about the basic facts.

Social media mentions are worth a fraction of a point in the algorithm, but it's not cumulative. So, let's say that someone gets ten thousand Twitter mentions on a Monday, that's worth about six hundred points in our algorithm. Combine those points with actual votes, and you get their total score, and their rank is based on that.

But they don't keep those points forever. We assign a half-life to social media mentions, whereby every week they lose half their value. So, the next Monday, the mentions from last Monday only add three hundred points to the total. The next Monday, one hundred fifty points, and so on. All the while, of course, new mentions from that week count for full points.

Destiny stabs at bits of her steak-hold-the-sandwich, making almost imperceptible growling noises while staring hungrily at Peter. For a woman like Destiny, landing a man like Peter, even for just an hour, is social media gold. If she managed to get a photo of his butt sticking out of some unkempt sheets in a hotel room, it would make the mainstream tabloids.

And hell, there's always the chance of a quickie marriage to a multibillionaire—and everything that comes with that—especially if she can talk him out of a prenup. She's laying it on embarrassingly thick, but I've come to understand her thinking. Peter's a lottery ticket. Odds aren't great that she'll win, but the payout is huge, so she's making the most of what might be her only shot.

Peter isn't biting. In fact, unless I'm crazy, he's been giving me little looks, the kind that tell me he might be interested in more than my algorithm. Come to think of it, he *did* show up out of nowhere to have lunch with me.

"So," Destiny says loudly between bites of a carrot. "I don't see how you can justify dropping the weight of all the social media I've gotten over the last six months—which, by the way, has driven a ton of traffic to Ameritocracy. You let some Gandhi-come-lately stroll in and use her YouTube fame to bump herself up in the standing overnight. And—"

"First of all," I say, "you don't know the algorithm as well as you think you do. Most of Wendy Kahananui's rise was due to votes—actual votes. All her YouTube fans are real fans, and she has a lot more of them than you. Secondly, Tanner Futch isn't big on social media, and he overtook you this morning, so you really don't know what you're talking about."

"But I'm right about the way you weight social media over time?"

"It's not something we've talked about publicly, but we were going to release a statement about it anyway, in response to inquiries we've gotten. All I'll say is that, yes, we weight social over time. It's not just one big accumulation of points. Why do we do it that way? Because it more closely reflects practical election dynamics. Think about it. No, don't interrupt."

Destiny tries to get a word in, but I hold my hand up to stop her. Peter watches the whole thing, wearing that bemused smile I've come to expect from him.

"Seriously, think about it," I continue. "In a regular election, a candidate can build up all sorts of goodwill for months, but then a scandal breaks and she loses half of her voters overnight. All the great stuff she did or said four months ago is no longer relevant."

"But that's exactly it," Destiny says. "If you're tracking social media mentions, and you have no way of knowing whether they are positive or negative mentions, a scandal might actually *help* someone. Someone could just do terrible things and get people talking, and—"

"Maybe that explains why you've been number one for so long," Peter interjects.

I suppress a laugh by popping a black olive in my mouth. Destiny either doesn't get Peter's joke, or is just happy he's speaking about her. "I *have* been number one for a long time," she says. "And Mia, we need each other. That's my point." She shoots me a glance that says, *Remember what I said about media coverage before the hot guy came in.*

We eat in silence for a few minutes, but a couple times I catch Peter staring at me. Destiny's bosom takes up half of my peripheral vision and, though I hate to admit it, I'm surprised and flattered that Peter seems to have zero interest in her obvious advances.

Finally I say, "None of this matters. As we've said publicly on multiple occasions, we use social media points in our algorithm at the beginning, partially to reflect the pulse of what people are saying, but partially to generate discussion of our site. And as you know, Destiny, actual votes are weighted much more heavily. So, it's not like if Kanye West enters the race he'd suddenly be number one because of all the talk about him on Twitter. He'd need actual votes."

"And he'd probably get them," Peter says in between sips of Red Bull.

"You *can't* let celebrities enter," Destiny says, clearly terrified at the idea of trying to out-YouTube Kanye.

"Aren't *you* a celebrity?" I ask.

This time, she can tell I'm poking fun, and she gives Peter a wounded puppy dog look. "Are you gonna let Mia talk to me that way?"

"I'm just here because they have the best hollandaise sauce in the valley. And the smartest political mind."

I open my mouth to say something clever, but swallow hard as the compliment sinks in.

Destiny notices my hesitation, and Peter's flirtation. "Don't tell me you two..."

She looks genuinely hurt, and I'm genuinely uncomfortable.

Regaining my composure, I say, "The bottom line is that we're not changing the algorithm. Plus, and this is big, the social media points go out the window at the end anyway. At the end it will all come down to the vote."

"But how you get to the final ten people *will* be determined by the social media points," Destiny insists.

I've stopped listening.

As we finish our food over the next twenty minutes, Destiny tries a bunch of arguments and proposes a few ideas for ways to promote the site, all of which involve promoting her.

I eat quickly, eager to get back to work and distracted by Peter's sideways glances.

Not long after the unexpected visit from Destiny O'Neill, I'm in my office working on the plan for the rally, our first large Ameritocracy public event. It's only a month away, and will be held at a nice Los Angeles hotel called The Q. I chose Los Angeles because it's got more media than any other west coast city, and I chose November 3rd because it's exactly a year before the next election.

The rally is our coming-out party, the moment we introduce Ameritocracy to the nation. If it goes as planned, everyone in America will be talking about the site and our candidates by the end.

Exactly one week before the rally, we'll temporarily lock our voting system and invite the top ten candidates. I've already told all the candidates in the top fifty to hold the date open.

The question is, what should the public events look like?

My first thought is to present the candidates one at a time as the crowd and the press watch, but that feels wrong somehow. The more I think about it, the more I want all the candidates together on a stage, both to communicate the weight of the contest, and to give viewers a reason to check out the site. I don't know who the top ten will be at that time, but everyone watching will like at least one or two of them. I don't want anyone tuning out because the first five people are losers, and missing out on the two candidates at the end they'd have loved.

I consider making the event a debate, but it's too soon for that. Just getting all these people in a room together will be a herculean task. Trying to moderate a debate would be something else entirely.

Plus, I've already announced a series of debates for the spring and early summer, and I doubt many of my candidates would come out of a ten-person debate looking especially good right now. Debating is a skill, and the more time they have to prepare, the better.

What about a roundtable discussion? I put that in the maybe column, but even that could get weird. Someone like Tanner Futch, who talks for a living, would have a distinct advantage over someone like Beverly Johnson, a self-described housewife from the Pacific Northwest, who has been rising in the polls lately with a blend of fiscal conservatism, strident advocacy for children, and videos of herself demonstrating recipes from her Scandinavian heritage.

No, I think the way to go is a presentation by either Steph or me, maybe both of us, followed by a chance for the ten candidates to introduce themselves one by one and take questions from the audience and the moderator. That way, viewers will see the top ten candidates on stage together, each of them at their best.

After the presentation, we'll do a smaller event where candidates can meet members of the press and superfans of the site in a more intimate setting. And, of course, Steph and I will be meeting with them all before the public events to thank them for participating and talk them through the rules and the schedule for the rest of the year.

I'm about to start typing up a formal plan to send to Steph for feedback when shouting erupts outside my office door. Looking up, I see a handsome, broad-shouldered black man standing next to Steph. And he's got a GoPro video camera strapped to his chest.

"You can't film here!" Steph says, but he's not listening.

Instead, the man walks a lap around the perimeter of the office, a huge smile across his face, shaking hands with our staff members one by one. He's wearing a tan suit and shiny black shoes. I'm pretty sure I recognize him, though I don't remember from where.

He introduces himself to a pasty-faced social media intern, who looks terrified. "Marlon Dixon," he says, shaking the kid's hand vigorously before moving on.

"Marlon Dixon," he says to one of Benjamin's assistants.

When he makes it to Benjamin, he again says, "Marlon Dixon," but adds, "I hear you're the man in charge of the site, and you *know* I've got some questions."

Benjamin shakes his hand awkwardly, and sits, flummoxed, on the armrest of his chair before losing his balance and falling to the floor.

I've seen enough.

Scurrying across the office, I shout, "What's going on?"

The man helps Benjamin up, apologizing profusely, and I step between them. "Who *are* you?"

"The Reverend Marlon Dixon," he says, extending a hand and shaking mine so hard it nearly breaks. The man is only a few inches taller than me, but barrel-shaped and muscular. His face is clean-shaven and, the more I stare at him, the more I think I've seen his face go by on a meme on Twitter or Facebook.

"Are you? Wait, are you?" I'm trying to place him, but the little red camera light blinking on his chest throws me off.

"Marlon Dixon," he says again. His voice is full of passion and a slight accent I think of as southern, but can't place.

"I got that," I say, "but who? Why?"

"He's Marlon Dixon," Steph says, walking up next to me, reading from her phone. "Southern Baptist minister from Abilene, Texas."

Recognition hits me. "Aren't you the minister who got arrested for—"

"For serving food to the homeless? Yes I did, and I'm proud of it! I've been smeared in the papers for bailing out prostitutes and preaching to junkies in the park in the wee hours of the morning. Yes I have, and I'm proud of it! I've been arrested for sheltering undocumented immigrants in the basement of my Church, and I'm proud of it! I even got hauled in for gathering with my congregation on the steps of the Supreme Court of these United States to read from the Gospel of Matthew. And you know what? I'm *proud* of it! Yes, ma'am, I've been arrested. Twelve times altogether—once for each of Jesus's apostles."

"Given that speech before?" Steph says.

"Once or twice," Dixon admits with a disarming *aw-ya-got-me* smile. "It's a question I've gotten before, and sister, any preacher who says he's never reused a sermon is lying."

I recall a profile of Dixon after his first arrest about five years ago. For two decades, he'd worked on hunger issues in Texas, but when Galveston passed an ordinance against feeding the homeless, Dixon kicked into action. Wearing his GoPro body cam, he gathered thirty members of his church on a Saturday, filled a van with food, and spent the day handing it out in a park while dressed in his white and gold preaching robes.

When the police dragged him away, Bible in one hand, wooden spoon covered in gravy in the other, he was reading from John, 3:17. "But if anyone has the world's goods and sees his brother in need, yet closes his heart against him, how does God's love abide in him? Little children, let us not love in word or talk but in deed and in truth."

The video went viral within hours of his release on bail. Dixon received a small fine, plus three months of probation and community service hours, but the episode thrust him into the national spotlight and sparked an intense online debate about Christian activism.

Since the arrest, Dixon had been wearing a GoPro most of the day, uploading thousands of hours of video on his church website, as well as to YouTube and other video sites.

He's much shorter in person, but his voice is the same—impassioned and loud enough to echo off the walls of the office. That raises a question: what is he doing in my office?

"Mr. Dixon," I say. "Welcome to Ameritocracy headquarters. First, I need to ask you to stop filming." I give him my firmest look, and, before he can object, I add, "Now."

"Happy to oblige," he says, pressing a button on the side of the camera.

"I'd like to hear why you're here, but my staff is hard at work. Will you come to my office?"

"Happy to oblige."

He follows me, Steph right on his heels. The three of us sit, me behind my desk, Steph in the chair next to me, and Dixon across from us. "Can we get you a water or a coffee or anything?" I ask.

"Thank you. A water, please."

His "please" comes with a dazzling smile that, to my surprise, doesn't look affected or fake. Steph hands him a water from the mini-fridge in the corner, and he drinks half of it, then wipes the glistening sweat from his bald head.

"So," I say, "how can I help you?"

He downs the water in three large chugs, then places the empty bottle on the desk. "I do apologize if the filming made you uncomfortable. It's just my habit. I believe in holding people accountable for their misdeeds, so I make it easy to hold me accountable for mine. More than that, if I can share with the world how beautiful and rewarding the Lord's work is, maybe a few more people decide to take part in that work. But my mission isn't yours, and I'm sorry if I filmed anything I shouldn't have."

"It's okay," I say. "But why are you here?"

"Well, Ms. Rhodes, I'd like to interview you and your staff, if you'll allow it. I'm thinking about running for President of these United States, and I came to see whether your site is the place to do it."

Half an hour later, Dixon has explained that he flew in from Texas that morning to make a surprise visit to the office. His plan was to interview the Ameritocracy staff to find out if we were "for real," and to let his tens of thousands of viewers around the world determine whether he should use our platform to run for president.

He also explained his politics, some of which I could have guessed, but pieces of which surprised me.

Dixon aligns with the left on taxes ("Let the usurers pay their fair share"), racial justice ("End the legacy of slavery that is the U.S. prison system"), healthcare ("Is anyone among you sick? Let him call for the elders of the church, and let them pray over him, anointing him with oil in the name of the Lord"—quoting James, 5:13-15) and the environment ("For the land is Mine; for you are but aliens and sojourners with Me"—Leviticus 25:23).

On abortion, he aligns with the Christian right, opposing it for the same reason he opposes the death penalty. "Life is absolute."

He explains how, in his early forties, the Texas Democratic Party tried to draft him to run for Congress, but he turned them down when they pressed him on softening his abortion stance. Unlike most politicians, he wasn't willing to cave on an issue that, to him, was a moral absolute. Plus, his openness in the form of his videos shows a radical transparency that makes me certain that he is who is says he is.

He speaks with a passion simultaneously practiced and unfaked, and though I disagree with about half of what he says, I like him more and more as he speaks. Above anything, what drives me nuts about politics is hypocrisy, and Marlon Dixon is one of the most genuine people I've ever shared a room with.

My respect for his sincerity is why I agreed to his request to interview the staff. That and the fact that I knew it would bring new people to our site.

So Dixon spent the last hour chatting with members of our team, asking them about the platform, asking why they support Ameritocracy, and how they see the competition playing out. The staff responded to his intensity and infectious enthusiasm, perking up and looking more alive after only a few minutes with him. Like he was drawing the best out of each of them as they spoke.

He even got Benjamin Singh excited when he asked whether it would be possible to stream live video from his GoPro straight onto his candidate page on the Ameritocracy website. That's a technology that, while possible, Steph and I decided not to pursue because of the potential legal implications of showing unfiltered live video.

During the interviews, Post-it followed Dixon from desk to desk, interview to interview, rubbing up against his ankles and slapping him with his tail lovingly. The cat's affection only affirmed my trust in the folksy preacher.

And now in my office, it's my turn in front of the camera.

Sitting across from me, Dixon removes the GoPro from his chest and sets it up on the corner of my desk. "So, Ms. Rhodes—"

"Call me Mia, please."

"Alright then, Mia. Why'd you start Ameritocracy?"

Nervous, I fall back on clichés, offering the same answer I used during the presentation. "I wanted to make democracy more transparent, level the playing field, to get around entrenched interests and corrupt campaigns. American politics had turned into a reality show, and I figured that it ought to at least be a reality show without commercials."

I've said these words a dozen times to a dozen reporters over the last few weeks, but, in Dixon's presence, they ring hollow. It's not that they aren't true, but they're not what he's looking for, and I know it. He lives in a world of passion and emotion, of true belief. He wants me to join him there.

But instead of calling me on my canned answer, Dixon levels his dark eyes at me and reaches out a hand which, to my surprise, I take.

His hand is cool and strong, and he squeezes mine with just the right amount of pressure. "I want to know your heart," he says.

He holds my gaze another second, and my eyes well up. Before I know it, tears roll down my cheeks. Eyes unfocused, I gaze at my desk, its hard corners and glossy surfaces becoming merely a soft arrangement of earth tones.

Then I say something I never would have expected. "I love the world so much. I love this country so much." I wipe my eyes on my hand, then wipe my hand on my pants. "I honestly couldn't stand to live through another election and watch this country devolve." Gaining inner strength as I speak, I wipe my eyes again and there are no more tears. "I don't agree with all our candidates, and I don't agree with you, either. But that's not the point. The point is to have real discussion, hear from real people. I feel like America is about to split apart at the seams. Radical times call for radical new ideas. I don't know if this idea will work. I don't know if we'll make it to November, or even to the July Fourth debate. And even if we do, I don't know if we'll have a candidate with a shot of winning. I just needed to do... something. I love everything too much not to."

Dixon's eyes are soft as he hands me a handkerchief from the inside pocket of his suit jacket. It's soft white linen and smells like some sort of fabric softener that tickles my nose.

"Thank you," he says. "I hoped you'd say something like that. You'll be seeing these videos online by tomorrow, and you'll see my candidate page on the Ameritocracy page before that."

[12]

I'm on the third floor, in a small room in the corner next to the bathroom. One of Malcolm's YouTube mixes plays through my phone into a Bluetooth speaker I've just finished mounting on the wall of the room, which I've started calling "my apartment."

Soon after arriving in Santa Clarissa, I spent a day driving Bluebird around looking for a real apartment. Though I saw some nice places, they were all smaller than I expected and, for $3,000 per month, I decided I could live at the office a while longer. Plus, our staff isn't yet large enough to have spread to the third floor.

I stare at the basket of unfolded laundry, then lie on the bed and close my eyes, listening to Malcolm's dubstep remix of Ray Charles's famous version of "America the Beautiful."

With the bump from Marlon Dixon's videos, we saw an influx of new candidates over the week since he stormed our office. And his seriousness as a candidate brought a lot of new interest from certain segments of the left, who are describing him as "Jimmy Carter's heart and soul in Terry Crews' body."

Though we declined his request to stream on our site live, he posted over a hundred videos that show him to be a gifted, fiery speaker. Dixon feeding the homeless, Dixon meeting with community leaders, Dixon attending the summer football games of his high school alma mater, where he played halfback and still holds the record for rushing yards in a season. Though I often find myself disagreeing with him, he never comes across as phony, which puts him ahead of most politicians in my book.

By early this morning, Dixon had climbed all the way to number fifteen, and is already the highest-ranked candidate who represents the political views of the left. Many of them, at least.

Feeling good, I set Sunday aside to do laundry and finish unpacking. Instead, I spent most of the morning listening to music, staring at the ceiling, and coming to terms with how quickly my life has changed.

My phone chirps with a text notification.

Peter: *What are you up to today? Thought maybe we could grab brunch.*

I haven't seen Peter since the day Destiny O'Neill came to town, though we text almost daily. I'm no expert at reading men, but as far as I can tell, he's been flirting consistently. Just little things, like pointing out good PR we're getting, or commenting that he saw a great picture of me attached to some blog post he read.

But I told myself today was for unpacking, for getting my life in order.

Me: *Can't. Unpacking.*

Peter: *Awesome! You found a place?*

Me: *Kinda. Decided to stay in the office.*

Peter: *That's cool. But seriously, an old college friend of mine is in town. Wants to meet you. Can we stop by in a bit? Won't take long and we can help unpack.*

I think about his offer for a moment. It's odd that a friend of

Peter's would want to meet me, but I need help moving an old recliner up from the office's storage area to my new "bedroom."

Me: *Sure, come by anytime.*

As I put my phone down, it chirps again, and I expect another text from Peter, but this one is from Steph.

Steph: *BOOM! This just posted online. Will run in print edition Monday morning.*

Underneath the text, she's included a link to a *New York Times* article. After almost dropping the phone, I scan the article so fast that I don't retain a single word of what I've read.

I look away, take three deep breaths, and read again more slowly.

Peter Colton Funds Ambitious Political Startup

Colton Industries founder and renowned philanthropist Peter Colton has donated five million dollars to a small nonprofit website, Ameritocracy2020.org, which is hosting an online competition to support an independent presidential bid in 2020. According to founder Mia Rhodes, "We're looking for the most innovative, compelling voices in American politics. But we're also looking for voices that have been ignored by the political process."

To that end, the competition rules stipulate that elected politicians from the Republican and Democratic parties are not permitted to enter, though independents who currently hold elected office are.

The current leaders are mostly fringe candidates, but since the announcement of Colton's donation, an influx of new candidates has raised the credibility of the site. For example, the Reverend Marlon Dixon—known for his criticism of income inequality and racial injustice—has been climbing the leaderboard lately.

But skeptics see flaws in the premise. "Is the two-party system perfect? Of course not," says DNC chairman Martin Romano. "But pulling candidates from the ranks of amateurs is not the solution."

Colton defends the project. "The political system is broken, and technology is the best option we have to fix it. For decades, Americans have complained about a system where money rules, where entrenched power rules, and where innovators like Mia Rhodes are ignored, or outright fought. That ends now."

Time will tell whether the idea will grow fast enough to have any impact on the 2020 election, but with the backing of forward-thinking Colton, political operatives on both sides of the aisle are sitting up and taking note.

So are the few government officials who managed to get elected by third parties or as independents. "I think it's great," said Dwight Lerner, a Green Party congressman from Vermont. "I'd join myself if I had any ambition to run for president."

I wiggle with delight in my bed before finishing the article. It's listed as "Business," which probably means that it will run on page B23 of the print edition, but it's already cracked the list of the site's "top twenty most-shared articles." It's our first coverage in *The Times*, our first coverage by any of the big, national newspapers.

Though I would have preferred if they'd written more about the site and our contestants, using Peter's fame as a hook is understandable. Of course, I'd love a front page story written by the *Times'* lead political writers, but, baby steps.

I tap back over to my exchange with Steph.

Me: *We rock!*

Steph: *We really do.*

Me: *We absolutely do.*

Steph: *We rock, and occasionally roll.*

I begin typing another cheesy response, but look up when Peter arrives in my doorway, flanked by the best-looking man I've ever seen in person.

It's not just any handsome man. It's David Benson, star of the blockbuster series of *Atlantis* films, and *People Magazine's* sexiest man alive from a couple years ago.

Leaping from the bed, I avert my eyes from David Benson

and throw a *why-didn't-you-tell-me* look at Peter. "*This* is your college friend?"

"Mia, meet DB, as we used to call him back in the dorm."

David Benson winks at me and smiles, and I'm more than happy to call him DB.

He grasps my hand with the well-practiced confidence of lead actors everywhere. "Pleased to meet you, Mia. I'm a big admirer of yours."

He plays a badass ex-CIA agent with a New York accent in the *Atlantis* movies, but in real life he's got a wisp of a Midwest drawl, his vowels just a touch longer than they need to be.

"Wait," I say, "you're an admirer of *mine*? You're, like, David Benson. I mean DB." I cast glances around my half-unpacked room, wishing I'd folded the basket of laundry occupying the office chair I've been using as a bedside table. I suppress the urge to remind him of scenes from his movies that have been racing through my mind.

"I get that a lot," DB says. "I'm a big Ameritocracy fan. Check your site. I registered to vote over three months ago."

Doubtful, I glance at Peter, who says, "Seriously. DB texted me the minute he heard I donated money."

Don't get me wrong, I was never the girl who had posters of Hollywood hunks on her wall, but this makes me swoon. DB is known for political activism. To hear he's a fan of the site means a lot. Plus, he's just as charismatic in person as he is on screen, and I want his approval. I'm smart enough to notice that, but not smart enough to make it not true.

"I saw the piece in *The Times* this morning," DB says.

"*The New York Times*?" Peter asks.

"No, the *Santa Clarissa Times*," DB says. "If I'm not mistaken, that's the first coverage of Ameritocracy in *The Times*."

"It is," I say, still reeling.

"Congrats," Peter says.

"That's gotta feel good," DB adds.

I want to say it feels incredible, and follow up with something suave like, "Not as incredible as welcoming you to my bedroom." But it's not my bedroom, and that's way more forward than I'm comfortable with. He probably hears similar lines from women like Destiny O'Neill twenty times a day, and I don't want to end up in the same universe as Destiny O'Neill in DB's mind.

Instead I say, "It's nice. It'll help grow the site." I gesture to the bed. "Please, have a seat."

"No way," Peter says. "We're here to help unpack."

"Yeah, give us orders."

I barely resist the urge to blurt a double-entendre as I look around the room. A bra sticks out from a drawer, which only intensifies my impulse to get them out of here so I can clean up. "Well, there is a chair that needs moving. The blue recliner in the storage room."

"One flight down," Peter says to DB. "We're on it."

They disappear, and, after cramming the rogue bra back in the drawer, making my bed and stashing my laundry under it, I text Steph.

Me: *Peter and David Benson—yes THAT David Benson—are in my room.*

Steph: *What the what? Seriously?*

Me: *Seriously.*

Steph: *Why?*

Me: *Because I no longer live in a reality I recognize.*

Steph: *Tell me everything.*

The sounds of their grunts and footfalls travel up the stairs as Peter and David approach with the chair.

Me: *Gotta go.*

Steph: *Text me later and TELL ME EVERYTHING.*

Peter and DB are in my doorway with the chair. "Where do you want this?" DB asks.

"In the corner." I watch DB's tight grey t-shirt bulge as he squats with the chair.

Unsure what to do next, I rearrange books on the shelf. "So, how'd you first hear about the site? And please, have a seat."

Peter flops on the bed. DB takes the new chair.

"I'm active in L.A. politics," DB says. "Been a strong Democrat since college. After failing for my first five years in Hollywood, I thought about going back home and running for mayor in my hometown. Then I got the first *Atlantis* movie and, well..."

I stop shelving books and sit next to Peter on the bed. "And you became the hottest movie star on the planet."

"He's too modest to say that," Peter says.

"Who's your favorite candidate?" I ask.

"Can't you track that on the backend of your site?"

"We can see who individual voters are voting for, but we have too many users for me to track anyone individually. Even if I knew you were on the site, which I didn't."

"Justine Hall," he says.

"Really? You struck me as a Marlon Dixon kind of guy."

"I would be," DB says. "But I can't get over his stance on abortion. I get that he thinks of it as a moral absolute. But I figure that men have been forcing their moral absolutes on women long enough."

Peter laughs. "Are you sure you don't prefer Justine Hall because she's smokin' hot?"

"Everyone I meet all day is smokin' hot, and half of them are assholes," DB says, waving a hand dismissively. "Myself included. I really think Hall would be good for the country. Political experience, which is more than Dixon has. And I like her 'whatever works' approach. I feel like I've had enough ideology, y'know?"

Justine Hall is Steph's favorite candidate, too.

She joined the competition just over a month ago and immediately became the candidate with the highest elected position.

As a left-leaning independent, four years ago she was elected mayor of Denver in a ridiculously close three-way race, a race she never wanted to enter.

For the first fifteen years of her working life, she was a Unitarian pastor, working in the poorest communities of Denver. After that she became a successful community organizer, working with city officials to create drug programs and homeless shelters, but she had no ambitions to run for office herself.

She was widely respected and viewed as above partisan politics, so members of her church banded together with her husband and practically forced her to run. They gathered the signatures to get her on the ballot, and she got the hang of politics quickly.

She won the mayoral race with only 36% of the vote, but gained popularity quickly after proving to be a strong executive. In her first month, she negotiated better healthcare for all city employees, and she united business and environmental groups by creating the best incentives in the country for clean energy job creation. She leans further left than I do, but she's one of the most serious candidates in the field.

Peter's right, though. She is smokin' hot in a *too-busy-to-care-about-my-looks* kinda way.

"I won't deny she's beautiful," I say, suppressing a twinge of jealousy. "And she has a shot. Not sure how serious she is about Ameritocracy, though. She doesn't post much, doesn't make many statements."

"She's busy running the city of Denver," DB says. "You watch. I bet she hits the top ten before your rally. I plan to come, by the way."

"That would be great," I say. "That'll probably double the number of reporters who show up."

He laughs. "It'll certainly bring out reporters, but maybe not the kind you want. I don't think TMZ and *The National Enquirer* are your target news outlets."

I laugh. "All press is good press."

DB's phone rings. He looks at it, winces, and steps out into the hall.

I cross my legs on the bed and face Peter. "Can't believe David friggin' Benson is your old dorm buddy."

"I hope it's okay that I brought him. He really is a big fan."

"I know. I can tell from his...from what he said."

"Then why do you look so skeptical?"

"It's just odd to have Peter Colton and David Benson sitting around, helping me unpack, you know? I can't believe this is my life."

"You belong in this world."

I hold his gaze as his smile intensifies. It's his *I-know-some-thing-you-don't-know* smile, and it's working. I fall into his eyes, and have to steady myself on the bed. I don't know exactly what he means by "this world," but it's one that includes David Benson and him in it.

That's hard to ignore.

"Sorry to interrupt," DB says from the doorway. "That was my agent. I've gotta run to the airport. Emergency voiceovers for the fourth *Atlantis* movie."

Peter stands. "Need a ride? I'll call my car back."

"Nah." DB waves Peter away. "Got an Uber on the way." Turning to me, he says, "Great to meet you. Keep up the good work, and good luck unpacking."

With that, he's gone, and I'm alone in my so-called bedroom with Peter.

After an awkward half hour—during which I folded my laundry

and sent Peter down to Bluebird for the lamp I bought at Pier One yesterday—I offer to drive him home. As expected, he tells me he can have his driver come, but I'm genuinely curious about where he lives.

Unless I'm crazy, he's been flirting with me ever since that day Destiny O'Neill arrived, and it makes me nervous. I always gain confidence when I'm behind the wheel of my beloved Bluebird, so that's where we end up.

Peter runs a hand over the cream-colored leather seat. "Ah, the famous Bluebird."

"This is her. The one thing I own that I actually care about."

"Wouldn't have pegged you for a muscle car woman, but now that I see you in her, it works."

It's seventy degrees out, so I retract the top and tie my hair into a ponytail.

"You spent thirty grand on the electric conversion?" he asks.

"Yup."

"That's a lot. With the work my company is doing in solar, that's gonna be ten grand in a few years."

"Wasn't really my money," I say, pulling onto the main road of Santa Clarissa.

"What do you mean?"

"Got it from my father."

"We don't talk about your father." Peter's face is guarded, as though he's worried he's crossed a line.

We pass Baker's Dozen and Mama Mia, where Malcolm bought me the dress on my first day in Santa Clarissa. I throw on my sunglasses as the bright sun flashes across the car. "No, we don't."

My hair is wild, my face windburnt but cool from the night air. The black sky is full of stars.

"Here." Peter gestures down a long stone driveway that leads to the largest house I've ever seen.

For the last four hours, he's given me a guided tour of the area. We saw Stanford University, the Google campus, and the house where Steve Jobs and Steve Wozniak built the first Apple computer. We stopped for snacks at a gas station where we could charge Bluebird, and neither he nor I looked at our phones the entire time.

At a security booth, Peter waves at a bored-looking man before the wrought-iron gate swings open. I ease Bluebird into a circular driveway and turn off the engine.

The house is stone, with a large central section and two distinct wings to the north and south, each with a turret. Vines climb up the sides toward windows too numerous to count.

Turning to him, I say, "So, you hired an architect and just said 'Hogwarts'?"

"I like the old styles," he replies, but he doesn't sound even slightly interested in his house. His eyes are fixed on me and he's wearing that megawatt smile.

I'm uncomfortable, so I say, "You smile like you know something no one else does."

"I do." He inches toward me.

I lean away, but not because I'm threatened. I just like my space. "What's your secret?"

"I want to kiss you."

"Why?"

He looks puzzled, and I blush. Steph tells me that I'm terrible at picking up on signals, and she's right. It's odd, really. I *knew* he'd been flirting with me, but my mind didn't connect it to physical reality. I couldn't believe it was anything more than banter. Even as he scooched towards me, I figured he was just...I don't know what I figured.

The exterior lights from his mansion shine down in what I can only describe as "romance movie lighting." His hair blows in the warm evening air, and well...there's the whole Antonio Banderas thing.

I want him to kiss me. But I'm conflicted, and not sure why. "We work together," I say.

"We don't."

"Maybe it's that...I don't...I don't want to be described as 'Peter Colton's girlfriend' in the caption of some magazine photo three weeks from now."

He leans away. "*That's* what you're worried about?"

"One of the things."

"Mia, please. Did you see the way DB looked at you? You're a powerful, beautiful woman. A magazine is just as likely to call me 'Mia Rhodes' boyfriend.'"

That's a lie. It's sweet, but it's a lie.

Even with all the press Ameritocracy received lately, I'm nowhere near as famous as Peter, who is approaching household-name status in the way Bill Gates did in the nineties and Mark Zuckerberg did in the last decade. But the fact that he said it thaws me and, for the first time, I see myself through his eyes. Through DB's eyes.

The reality of the day, of the last two months, hits me all at once. This is happening.

I lean forward—or maybe it's more of a lunge—and kiss him. He pulls me in as I press him against the passenger side door.

His hands move down my back, around my waist. He gives a slight tug and I'm halfway onto his lap. As he squeezes my ass, I bite his lip, one of my go-to moves. He's a skillful kisser. Just the right balance of tenderness and control.

A man's voice tears us apart before I can invite myself inside. "Mr. Colton, you have a call."

He shoots a look towards the house, where a man in a white suit stands on the stone steps.

"Who is it?"

"Mrs. Zhang. It's eleven a.m. in Beijing."

"Damn," Peter says.

I scoot off him and slide behind the wheel.

"I have to take this. Would you like to come in and wait? Should only be fifteen or twenty minutes."

Part of me wants to say yes, but another part wants to get back to the office and obsess about the article in *The Times*, about our leaderboard, and about the site in general.

The second part speaks loudest. "I should get back."

He looks back at the man on the steps, leans in to peck me on the cheek, and hops out. When he reaches the steps, he turns and calls, "I'll text you later."

"Okay," I say, though not loud enough to reach him as he disappears into the house.

[13]

I'm driving to The Colton Industries campus for the regular Friday night party, eager to hear Malcolm DJ for the first time since the night of my presentation. Mostly, I'm eager to see Peter for the first time since the kiss.

As it turned out, his Beijing call led to a trip, which took him out of town for nearly a week. And when he returned, I came up with excuses not to see him. I'm not sure why. It has something to do with the nagging feeling that the first time a paparazzo catches us together, I'll appear next to him with the dreaded caption: *Peter Colton's Latest Girlfriend*.

I wonder whether I'll kiss him again. I wonder whether I want his staff to know about our...I don't know what to call it. "Attraction" is the best I can come up with.

But I'm distracted by something else—some movement on the site that, while not alarming, has bugged me since going over our leaderboard a few hours ago. I park in front of Building 7 as a partygoer passes my car wearing a sexy librarian costume that looks like it was designed on a war-torn planet in deep space.

The party is just starting so I decide to satisfy my curiosity.

First I check our top ten list. To be honest, I'm obsessive about the list. As things progressed from real to realer over the fall, as we got more press, more money, and more candidates, I began checking it ten or twenty times a day. Okay, maybe it's more like fifty or sixty.

You know that feeling when you log onto Facebook and see that little red number of notifications? Or when you get a new text but your phone is across the room and you have a few seconds of anticipation, wondering who messaged you?

I have that feeling a hundred times a day now. Every time I refresh our homepage. Even when, like tonight, the leaderboard is right where I left it earlier in the day.

1. Marlon Dixon

Since he joined, the Reverend Marlon Dixon has been the rockstar of Ameritocracy. Charismatic, engaged, and constantly self-promoting, he's held onto the number one spot for the last two weeks, with no sign of slowing.

2. Tom Morton

Morton entered in mid-September and, for the first few weeks, didn't make much of a splash. A former Ambassador to Ukraine and a Washington insider with a decade of high-level consulting for oil and gas interests, he has a decent résumé. But he's not a great fit for the site. He's as deep in the Washington swamp as you can get and still be breathing.

In his late fifties, he cuts a severe profile, with graying blonde hair, a sharp nose and an apparent inability to show emotion. In his two or three dozen videos, he speaks in a smooth, almost mechanical cadence, saying nice, patriotic things without any real feeling behind them. And his candidate statement reads: *Believe in America. Restore Faith in Our Most Cherished Dreams.*

It's the kind of thing a politician would say in a bad Hallmark movie. The kind of thing that sounds good at first, but doesn't *say* anything. Given that the whole point of Ameritocracy is to eliminate meaningless political speech, his style stands out for its blandness.

Between his hundreds of Facebook posts, position papers, and videos, he doesn't get much more specific. Though we made a sacred pact to be neutral about the outcome of the election— our algorithms were designed around this idea—it doesn't mean that Steph and I don't form opinions about candidates. As far as we can tell, Tom Morton is in favor of puppies, ice cream, America, freedom, and a few other buzzwords, but he's a soggy slice of generic white bread.

Much to our chagrin, Morton has slowly moved up the leaderboard. For the life of us, Steph and I can't figure out what he's for and what he's against, and we can't tell which political party he'd be a member of under ordinary circumstances. Our best guess as to why people vote for him is that he's good-looking for a man in his late fifties. Tall, good build, a solid jaw.

In an antiquated, stereotypical way, he looks *presidential*.

3. Orin Gottlieb

An aging libertarian author with white hair and ten best-sellers to his name, Gottlieb is one of two academics in our top ten. A prominent voice among political conservatives, he single-handedly made libertarian politics cool again, bringing a philosophical underpinning to the arguments that others lacked. He comes off as full of himself, but a lot of folks buy his books, and a lot of them joined Ameritocracy.

4. Cecilia Mason

A seventy-year-old real estate billionaire from New York, Mason entered just after Orin Gottlieb, and has been getting by on celebrity and hugely active social media accounts. She owns two professional sports teams, a private island near Jamaica, and a world-class collection of music memorabilia from the sixties and seventies, including John Lennon's piano and the private jet Led Zeppelin used on their first U.S. tour.

Her political positions are pro-business, anti-gun, anti-pornography, anti-drugs, and anti-video games. Though she's popular with older women, she's been dubbed "Nanny State Mason" on the forums, and has been unable to crack the top three. But she's smart and willing to spend her own money to get her name out there, and it's working.

5. Tanner Futch

The right-wing shock jock has done well for himself landing appearances on Howard Stern's show and a couple of the top podcasts on the far right. Even a few mainstream Republicans have praised him lately, though they did so without mentioning the conspiracy theories that are his stock in trade.

6. Wendy Kahananui

Our friend from Hawaii dropped off after a couple embarrassingly vague interviews, but she's in the top ten due to her massive online audience of devoted fans. As more experienced candidates join the field, I doubt her brand of crunchy New Age granola will convince new voters to support her.

7. Beverly Johnson

Best known for her YouTube channel, *Pacific Northwest Home*, Johnson is a self-proclaimed "proud housewife." She's a short, round, good-natured lady with red hair a few shades lighter than mine.

In addition to sharing recipes on her YouTube channel, she's active in the community. She's pro-choice, but spends much of her time counseling women to choose adoption over abortion, which makes her sympathetic to some of the less fervent pro-lifers. And she's adopted six children, so no one can accuse her of failing to practice what she preaches.

Politically, she's hard to align with either party. Socially liberal, but fiscally conservative, she favors a balanced budget amendment—"If families have to balance their budget, so should government." She's also made education a major part of her platform, favoring more money for schools, higher teacher pay, and a longer school year.

Of all the candidates, Beverly Johnson seems most like a real person, which explains her popularity. She fights food cravings, has trouble getting her videos to upload, and is happy to talk about it all.

8. Avery Axum

I'm not supposed to play favorites, and I don't, but Avery Axum is my favorite.

The second academic in our top ten, he joined the site about a month ago and rose steadily up the rankings. Before accepting a professorship at the George Washington Law School in D.C., Axum worked in the legal offices of three presidents—two Republican, one Democrat. He also wrote six books, including the definitive history of the legal aspects of the Civil War and an alternate-history novel in which the Supreme Court decided the other way in the 1803 *Marbury vs. Madison* case.

I keep telling myself I'll find time to read it. If what I've heard about its sales is true, I might be the first person to do so.

Axum is in favor of radically overhauling the prison system and ending the war on drugs, positions embraced by the left, but he also favors states' rights and a strong military, positions usually associated with the right. All in all, he's a brilliant, right-leaning centrist with the academic background and graying good looks to bring dignity and integrity to the political process. Unfortunately, being his fan feels like loving an obscure cult movie: you find yourself repeatedly explaining how it's not *that* boring if you give it a chance. In contrast to Gottlieb, who has a gift for the sound bite, Axum seems unable to deliver an argument in under ten minutes.

9. Destiny O'Neill

To my delight, Destiny has fallen in the rankings over the last month. Don't get me wrong, if she climbs the leaderboard again and wins Ameritocracy, she *will* get the money. I'm one hundred percent committed keeping the playing field level. But she makes me feel like we still have a cartoon character in the top ten, given how much of her is a performance.

10. Justine Hall

David Benson tweeted about Justine Hall constantly over the last week, and she needed the help because she wasn't doing much to support her own candidacy. Her position papers and the few videos she added to our site were all solid, and a couple of them were among our most-shared pieces, but she doesn't directly engage the voters much.

In fact, seeing this makes me wonder about our entire project. When a talented, intelligent mayor of a major city trails a YouTube con artist due to lack of social media hustle, there might be a flaw in the system.

I tell myself it's nothing I can fix tonight as I roll down the window, hoping to catch a note or two of the music Malcolm is creating inside. The cool evening air feels good, and part of me wants to head straight into the party, but instead I open Twitter, promising myself I will only work for five minutes.

I run a quick search for Tom Morton. His official account is full of bland position statements, probably tweeted out by an intern in his office, and a search for mentions of his Twitter handle brings up just a few hundred tweets.

Some are making fun of him, some are praising him, but most are just retweets of his bland posts with one or two words added. For example, an account called @UtahMom7691 quoted one of his tweets that read, "America must once again become the indispensable nation," adding only, "Strongly agree!"

Another account, @RockstarSkaterJohn, retweeted one of his tweets that read "Families make up the backbone of this great nation, and must be supported," adding only "Hell yeah."

I run the same search for Orin Gottlieb, which is a whole

different experience. Morton has only a few hundred tweets using his name over the last day. Gottlieb has thousands. People tweet about him constantly, both positively and negatively. Memes are everywhere, some making fun of his libertarian politics, others touting him as something close to a Messiah. People have strong opinions about Gottlieb, and share them online.

Something about the discrepancy in their mentions doesn't sit right with me. Yes, Gottlieb is a bestselling author with a strong personality. Yes, he provokes controversy, and Morton doesn't. But that night-and-day difference when searching for them feels...inorganic somehow.

I cast a look at the front door of Building 7, where a man and a woman, both wearing tuxedos, walk hand in hand through the door. As much as I want to hear Malcolm DJ again, dance with Peter, drink ridiculous cocktails, and be around actual people, my worry over unusual Twitter activity is stronger than that.

Sighing deeply, I open a new text to Peter.

Me: *Something is up. Gotta go back to the office.*

Before he can respond, I write to Steph.

Me: *You still in the office?*

Steph: *I'm here.*

Me: *Wait there. Coming back. Benjamin still there?*

Steph: *He's here.*

Me: *Wait, why's he there? Thought he was coming to the party.*

Steph:...

Me: *Let's dish about what ... means tomorrow. Something's up tho. Have him pull up the stats on social media mentions for our top ten.*

I start the car, but before I can put my phone on driving mode, a new text arrives.

Peter: *What is it? Can I help?*

I read the text twice, start typing a reply, then delete it and pull Bluebird out through the security gate.

~

When I arrive at the office, Steph is hunched over her laptop, a half glass of wine on the desk next to her.

"What's going on?" she says, not looking up.

"You might want to get yourself another glass of wine first. Never mind. I'll get you one while I get one for myself."

A minute later, I'm back from the kitchenette, a glass of Sauvignon Blanc in my hand and the open bottle of zin for Steph.

To my surprise, Benjamin Singh now sits where Steph sat, having returned from the bathroom. A look passes between them, but I'm too worked up to give it much thought.

"I pulled up social media stats," Benjamin says. "What are you trying to figure out?"

"Morton's slow and steady climb has seemed odd, right? The vanilla ice cream candidate flourishing on a site otherwise dominated by folks on the further extremes."

"Right," Benjamin says. "That I knew."

"And I've been feeling like I just don't see people talking about him much online. He doesn't have a large platform on YouTube or Facebook or anything. When I pulled up his Twitter mentions, it was crickets."

"And yet," Steph says, "he's getting votes."

"Exactly."

"So," Benjamin says, "you're wondering whether you're imagining things. Wondering where his votes are coming from?"

"Right. Can you do something like a graph that compares his social media mentions with other candidates?"

Benjamin turns to his computer. "I can do better than that."

Benjamin pulls up a graph of blue and red lines that reminds me of something from calculus class in high school. "Haven't had much time with this, but I've been working on a new thing." He points at a fairly stable red line, moving from left to right across the screen. There are a few dips and spikes, but it's close to horizontal. "That line charts the average ratio of votes each candidate has to the amount of organic discussion of that candidate on our Forum."

One of the major innovations of the last two months was the Ameritocracy Forum. Tens of thousands of users spend time there each day, discussing candidates, debating issues, explaining their votes, and sometimes even interacting with candidates who run Ask Me Anything hours and answer questions posed by users. A team of six moderators work remotely in eight-hour shifts, reading comments, banning abusive users, and working like mad to keep things civil.

"I don't get it," I say.

Steph takes a big sip of her wine. "Remember when I told you that we were trying to figure out how to make sure no one is gaming the system? This is one of the ways Ben came up with. The red line shows how much discussion a candidate generates relative to their vote totals."

Steph puts her hand on Ben's shoulder. The "..." text and the fact that Benjamin is using her computer makes sense. They're sleeping together.

"Tell her about the D Score," Steph continues as my mind adjusts to this new reality.

Benjamin speaks with an excitement that's rare for him. "At any given time, we can see a candidate's D Score. An average score is ten. Less than ten, they're getting fewer votes than we'd expect, given the amount of discussion of them on our forums. More than ten means they're getting more votes than we'd expect."

He clicks his mouse and a dark green line appears on the screen.

"This is Destiny O'Neill's line for the last two months. You can see that it's consistently a little bit above the red line. Her average D Score is fourteen. That's high, but still in the range of normal. It means that she's getting forty percent more votes than we'd expect her to get, based on the number of mentions she gets on the Forum."

"But it makes sense," Steph interjects, "because we know she has a huge following on Reddit and YouTube, so many of her voters just aren't migrating to our Forum."

"They're discussing her on YouTube and Reddit instead?" I ask.

"Exactly," Benjamin says.

"Please don't tell Destiny what we're calling this metric," Steph pleads, squeezing his shoulder. "If she starts recording videos about how she's scoring more D than the other candidates, I may literally go insane."

Benjamin nods, still absorbed in his graphs. He clicks two more times, causing a bright blue line and a black line to appear.

"The black line is Orin Gottlieb."

The line runs a little below the original red line, and his D Score is nine. I ask, "So that means he's getting ten percent fewer votes that you'd expect, given the level of discussion of him on the forums?"

"Right," Steph says. "And the blue line is Marlon Dixon, who's at a twelve."

"Okay, I think I get it. What about Tom Morton?"

Benjamin clicks his mouse again, and a purple line pops up. It starts well below the red line, trends upward for a few weeks, then crosses the red line before spiking.

Benjamin taps the screen at the spike. "One week ago, he achieved the highest D Score we've seen in the system—a sixteen—meaning he got sixty percent more votes than we'd expect, given the number of mentions he's getting. Now, he's at a nineteen, almost twice as many as we'd expect."

"That goes with the sense I got looking at his Twitter mentions," I say, "but that could just be because there's not much to say about him. Still wigs me out, though."

"It should," Steph says, "because at least it means that something odd is happening, and it *could* be something nefarious."

I look at Steph nervously. "Why do you think it's nefarious?"

"Because *no one* likes the guy. Even his mentions on the Forum are mostly people making fun of him. People call him Marshmallow Morton."

"Is there a way to quantify positive and negative mentions?" I ask Benjamin.

"Not yet," he says. "If we could track positive mentions and determine likely voting behavior based on it...well...that would be a game changer."

"The point," Steph says, before swigging the rest of her wine, "is that it looks odd and we need to figure out what's going on."

Steph and I have often discussed the fact that the biggest danger to Ameritocracy is if users don't see the voting as fair. The whole point of the site is that we are providing the most neutral platform ever created on which one can make a political decision. We cut out the political parties, the DNC and the RNC, the TV stations, and the debate committees. We created something to reach straight to real people, and anything that erodes the credibility of the platform will doom the project.

As the last hope that I'll make it back to the party fades, I ask, "What do we do next?"

Steph steps around to the other side of the desk and opens a laptop. "I'm gonna read through Morton's social media posts for the last week to check whether his level of engagement has spiked, whether he's rolled out any interesting policies or theories that he hasn't added to our site yet."

"And I'm going to dig into our numbers," Benjamin says. "Who's voting for him? Ages, locations, which candidates they're moving votes from when they switch to him, that kind of thing."

"What should I do?" I ask, overwhelmed by the thought that someone or something could be manipulating the site, but impressed by how quickly they're kicking into gear.

"You should take the wider view," Steph says. "Read through his stuff again, along with the others in the top ten. Think about the demographics. The key question is: Assuming I'm wrong, and that everything is on the up and up, *why the hell* are people voting for this guy?"

"Got it," I say, walking into my office.

Before I can open my laptop, I see that Peter has texted me back.

Peter: *Missing you at the party. Malcolm is killing it. Just did a trap version of Willie Nelson's "Crazy." Let me know if I can do anything to help with whatever's going on. And if I can see you later.*

I start to respond to his text, but can't figure out what to say. So, as I always do when I can't figure out what to do about a man, I focus on my work.

I read through every public statement I can find about Morton, finding more of the same: milquetoast positions and a good public résumé, but nothing interesting or noteworthy.

The more I think about the candidates, the more I can't understand the votes Tom Morton is receiving. When I started Ameritocracy, one of my driving ambitions was to bring real candidates into the political system. Candidates who wouldn't have to pretend to be something they're not, candidates who would be transparent about their pasts, their positions, and their plans if elected. Morton is the opposite of this, and not only does it bother me, it confuses me.

"Oh no! No, no, no!" It's Benjamin's voice from the other room, sounding panicked.

I'm at his side a moment later. "What?"

Steph runs in from the kitchen area, holding the bottle of red wine. "What?" she asks, leaning over his other shoulder.

Benjamin looks at me over his shoulder. "This guy might be a fake candidate."

"What do you mean a 'fake candidate'?" I ask.

"I found a bunch of things," Benjamin says, turning back to his screen. "First, look here."

He taps on his screen and I see a list of some of our top candidates, with numbers of Twitter followers next to each name:

Tom Morton: 3,452,980
Orin Gottlieb: 800,832
Justine Hall: 286,733
Cecilia Mason: 1,982,234
Tanner Futch: 4,455,211

Benjamin clicks another button and a red number pops up to the right of each number. "The new numbers are the number of fake followers each candidate has."

I see that Morton has almost three million fake followers, roughly eighty percent of his total following, while the other candidates have far fewer. "What's a fake follower?" I ask.

"A Twitterbot."

"Define 'Twitterbot'."

"It's a type of software that controls a Twitter account via the Twitter API. The bot can autonomously perform actions such as tweeting, retweeting, liking, following, unfollowing, or direct messaging other accounts."

"So there's not a real person there?" I ask.

"There *are* real people there," Benjamin says, "but there's often one person behind thousands or even tens of thousands of accounts."

Steph says, "That's bad, but what else did you find?"

"It's beyond bad," Benjamin says. "Look at the other candidates. None of them have more than twenty percent bots as followers. Someone is trying to prop up Thomas Morton."

"Not necessarily," Steph says. "He may have had all those followers before Ameritocracy. Maybe he was just vain and bought Twitter followers to pump up his consulting brand. A lot of people do that."

Benjamin clicks on Morton's name on the screen, which leads to a detail page of his Twitter followers. "Nope."

I can see that, from 2015 to 2019, Morton's follower growth was steady, but a series of huge spikes occurred recently.

"What the hell?" Steph says. "He gained over three million followers since joining the site. That's gotta be more than anyone else."

"Way more," Benjamin says. "Most candidates see steady growth in their Twitter followings after joining the site, but Tom Morton is buying followers, or someone is buying them for him. Grab a seat and I'll show you how a Twitterbot works."

This is going to get complicated, so I pull up chairs for me and Steph, then grab the bottle of Sauvignon Blanc from the kitchen.

"This is gonna be a three-glass kinda night," Steph says.

"Or four," I say, filling my glass to the top.

[14]

The next morning, I wake up bleary-eyed and a little hungover. Post-it is draped across my neck, purring like a warm, vibrating choker. Steph, Benjamin and I worked until two in the morning, but gave up without any clarity about Morton.

I lift Post-it off my neck and take the stairs from my makeshift bedroom down to the main office space, where Benjamin is asleep on his keyboard. A document is open in front of him, displaying an endless stream of the letter "L," the letter his cheek happened to fall on whenever he passed out. Steph is stretched out on the couch in the corner of the office, her long legs dangling off the side.

I'm far from a morning person, but lately I've been getting up earlier and earlier. Possibly because I have more to do than ever before, but I think the real reason is that my days are so full that I've come to cherish the quiet moments before the office goes nuts.

I stagger to the kitchen to fill a quart-sized Mason jar with cold brew. Today is going to be nuts. One way or another, we have to figure out what's going on with Thomas Morton.

Though it's possible it's nothing nefarious, I doubt it, and I'm worried that we'll discover something that sinks Ameritocracy.

I gulp down my first twelve ounces of coffee in four sips while leaning on the fridge, then head into my office and sit at the computer, trying to reboot my brain where it left off the previous evening.

Scrolling through my phone, I see a new text from Peter from four in the morning, just an hour ago.

Peter: *Robert Mast? Are you serious?*

I'm not sure what he's talking about, but I know that he only texts me for two reasons. The first is to flirt, the second is to chat about the site. So unless I'm dating a guy named "Mast" and Peter was late-night drunk texting out of jealousy, he's talking about a new candidate. Plus, the name rings a bell.

I'm about to pull up the website when my phone rings. It's Peter.

"Morning, Peter, how'd you know you wouldn't be waking me up?"

"I saw the text I sent go from 'delivered' to 'read' so I knew you were on your phone."

I can't tell if that's cute, a little stalkery, or just a coincidence. "Waiting by the phone?" I ask.

"Nah, I was on my phone doing other stuff. But I *am* excited. You didn't tell me Bobby Mast was a candidate!"

I struggle to place the name. "Is that the general who's always talking about military preparedness?"

"Former general, and yes."

"He's *not* a candidate."

"Where have you been for the last twelve hours?"

"Dealing with a...with a thing."

I try to pull up our homepage, but my laptop is acting wonky, loading and loading without displaying anything.

Peter is clearly pumped. "You mean to tell me you don't even know about the new candidates on your own site?"

He's messing with me, but I get defensive anyway. "No, I've been too busy *running* that site."

One thing I've learned after months surrounded by tech geniuses is that restarting a computer will fix three-quarters of problems, so I hold down the button until the screen goes dark, then lights back up.

"When did he...I mean, are you on the site? My computer is being weird. Read me his profile."

Peter clears his throat and shifts to an official-sounding voice. "Robert Mast, age sixty-two. Candidate statement reads: 'America can once again be a Shining City on a Hill.'"

"Okay, not sure exactly what that means. Go to his platform page."

Reading from the page, Peter says, "'Robert Mast believes in American leadership around the world, in terms of values *and* in terms of military strength. Democrats and Republicans have allowed the U.S. military to fall behind technologically, and, as President, I will change that.' Then it goes into his bio, but you know that already, right?"

I do. Mast is a retired three-star general and author of the bestseller, *A Flag of Promise*. He's also a regular guest on all the cable news channels, where he argues for increased military spending and American leadership. Every election cycle for the last twelve years, his name has popped up as a potential Republican candidate, but he's never run for anything, or even publicly confirmed that he's a Republican. He's handsome in a silver-haired kind of way, well-spoken and known for being tough as leather.

"I know a bit," I say, "but read me what he wrote."

"'Mast joined the army on his eighteenth birthday, served in Vietnam, commanded troops in both Iraq wars, and achieved the rank of three-star general before retiring in 2011. He believes in traditional Christian values, and in restoring America's leadership around the world.' Then there's a long quote from him from a recent interview. 'Throughout history, America's actions haven't been perfect. But our *ideals* have been, and still are. We hold doors open for our women, they stone them. We integrate our society, they segregate it. We help our poor, they leave them to die. There's a reason that Christian values spread around the world in the last century. It's because they're more inclusive, more progressive. Our foes will respect us when we win. If need be, we'll bomb them into freedom.' After that, he's got a detailed history of his military service."

I was pacing the office as Peter read, but the last line stops me in my tracks. "Bomb them into freedom? Gah! Does his profile really say that?"

"It does."

I sit at my computer, which has completed its relaunch. Our homepage opens, and I click through to confirm that Peter isn't messing with me.

In his profile picture, Mast wears a dark green uniform, the breast adorned with medals and the shoulder affixed with three silver stars. His hair is silver, streaked with white, and short, like he was issued a haircut by the United States Army and never considered changing it. His eyes are light blue, and full of a gentleness I didn't anticipate, given his bombing-based rhetoric.

"Mia, are you there?"

"Sorry," I say, "I was reading his profile. I'm just—"

"Stunned."

I'm beyond stunned, but I don't want to admit it. Peter is just excited for me, but I don't like anyone to know about developments on my site before I do. "I don't know what I am."

"But you know this is *huge*, right? Major Republican donors have been courting Mast for eight years."

151

"Twelve," I say. "I remember the *will-he-or-won't-he* chatter about whether he'd jump into the 2008 Republican primaries."

"He's the candidate you need."

"For what?"

"To blow up the site. I mean, for the site to blow up. To take off. You know what I mean."

He's right. Thanks to the launch of our app, Ameritocracy had about forty thousand new voters register over the last week, and just under three hundred new candidates, but Mast is the most credible, by far.

Mast is already leading our "Hot New Candidates" page, though he doesn't rank anywhere near the top hundred overall. It's only a matter of time, though. He's a decorated veteran and, though I'll need to study his positions more thoroughly, he espouses a view of America that's shared by much of the country. He's the first candidate to join who's already a household name, at least among cable news viewers.

"You're right," I say. "This will shift our coverage from mostly online to all over the news channels."

"Then why do you sound upset?"

"The coffee hasn't kicked in yet."

"Mia, c'mon. I can tell from your voice that you're upset."

"'*Bomb* them into freedom'?"

"I thought you promised to remain neutral about your candidates."

"I am neutral, but..."

"You've gotta lighten up, Mia. Take it easy on yourself. Enjoy this. He probably won't win anyway, and if you can't enjoy the roller coaster ride you're about to go on, well, what's the point? You're about to get more exposure than you've had in the last two years."

I know he's right, but something about Mast's candidacy doesn't sit well with me.

"I'm sorry," he continues. "I don't mean to be the mansplainer-in-chief, but after I sold my first company, it took me a year to realize I could slow down. That I was a billionaire and could do pretty much anything I wanted."

"I've never liked roller-coasters, and I'm no billionaire."

"What I mean is...you have no idea who will win. But, like you said, Republicans have been trying to get Mast to run for twelve years. He's seen as adhering to many Republican values while being above politics. This is going to be *massive* for Ameritocracy. News outlets you were begging for coverage are gonna bust down your door."

For the last five minutes, the landline at our front desk has been ringing constantly, and it dawns on me that Peter's right. We *are* entering a new phase. "I gotta let you go," I say. "Need to get my office people in here."

"Good idea," Peter says, "you may be a household name by the end of the day."

I take a swig of coffee, pondering whether that's a good thing. "I'll talk to you later."

"Wait, Mia, before you hang up. Tomorrow I'm going to the Future Now Transformational Festival out in the redwoods. Would you come as my guest?"

"The what?"

"Future Now Transformational Festival. It's like Burning Man, but for rich people."

"I thought Burning Man was already for rich people."

"Rich-*er* people."

One thing I like about Peter is that he jokes about his money in a way that puts me at ease. Though he lives a ridiculously lavish lifestyle, he does so with just enough self-deprecation to keep him from entering Scrooge-McDuck-level self-parody.

"Would this be...um...a date?" I ask.

"Let's just call it a transformational experience. Fabulous

food, yoga, music. You know you want to see me get my krump on again."

"Is Malcolm playing?"

"Malcolm, are you serious? *Absolution* is playing."

"Who's that?"

"Hottest DJ on earth?"

"Oh, I like Malcolm's music."

"Me, too, but Absolution is...Mia, you're stalling."

I am.

My eyes are on Mast's profile picture, the phone at the front desk is still ringing, and my attention is tugged in a hundred directions at once. I'm in no position to decide anything about anything other than Ameritocracy.

Then, as if it knows I need a way out of this conversation, my laptop dings with a new email. Scanning it, I know my day is about to get even weirder. "Peter, I have to go. CNN wants me live in-studio for Anderson Cooper 360 tonight."

Half an hour later, Steph and I are at Baker's Dozen, spreading jam on warm biscuits and talking through the ramifications of Mast joining the race.

"He'll be top ten within weeks," Steph says.

"Too late for him to make the top ten for the rally, though. That list locks tonight."

"How nervous are you?" Steph asks between bites of biscuit.

"Nervous, why?"

"Duh! The CNN thing. Anderson Cooper grilling you as millions of viewers watch."

"I haven't even written back yet."

I didn't reply to the email, thinking I should run it by Steph first. But we both know I'll accept. "Honestly, I've never been more nervous. This is happening way faster than I thought possible."

"Mast will be a game changer."

I push a half-eaten strawberry around my plate. "Can we talk about something else?"

"What else is there? Today will be the craziest day in the history of the site. Bummer that we drank too much wine and only got a few hours of sleep, but you're acting like a teenager who just rolled out of bed hungover with a bad attitude."

I ignore her, searching for a way to change the subject. Coming up empty, I just change it. "Are you sleeping with Benjamin?"

Steph leans back, sipping her orange juice with a wry smile. "Maybe."

"Maybe since when?"

"Maybe for about a month."

"He's...you know I told you about the pick-up lines he was using at the party my first day here. He's—"

"He's cute, and he used one on me. 'My servers never go down, but I do.'"

"Gross," I whisper, hoping the couple at the adjacent table didn't hear Steph. "How can that have worked on you?"

"Mia, please. You think that line worked on me? Of course it didn't. It was just a damn joke, anyway. He's shy, not real polished when it comes to flirting. Plus, you know, all humor has a kernel of truth."

"Don't tell me more. I *don't* want the details. But you guys are good at hiding it, I'll give you that."

"You know me. I dated my boss for six months once, and was practically engaged to Damien, remember? I was his direct supervisor, and we made it work. The key is keeping work separate."

She studies my face, trying to read me. "Why'd you bring that up? I figured you knew he was gonna make my booty list. But why now?" She tilts her head sideways. She's on to me. "Ooooh... You've got something to hide."

I say nothing.

"Mia?"

"I kissed Peter."

"What the what? I'm not you—I *want* details."

I tell her the short version of the visit to my room, the drive, and the kiss, but my heart's not in it.

"Okay," Steph says when I finish. "Unless you regret not pouncing on David damn Benson when he was *in your bedroom*, which I understand, why do you look miserable that you made out with a hot billionaire?"

It's a good question. Between the stone driveway, the lighting, and Peter's looks and intense charisma, it should have been the kiss beyond all kisses. The world should have fallen away, a moment frozen in time, and I should still be tingling with aftershocks. Instead it was just...nice. Not thrilling, but nice.

It's not just that he funded my project. I *have* worried about that, but Steph's ability to keep things separate with Benjamin gives me confidence that I can navigate it.

And it's not because I have any interest in playing hard to get, or playing any other games for that matter. I'm a grown woman and I'll do what I damn well please. It's something about Peter I can't put my finger on.

"I don't know. He invited me to some festival. Burning Man for the super-rich, or something."

"Future Now?"

"That's it."

"You're going. That's an invitation-only thing for, like, CEOs and their mistresses."

I give her a look.

"Or their *wives*," Steph says. "And there are plenty of women

CEOs who bring their boy-toys, too. It's a big deal, though, and it'll be fun."

"I'm not going."

"You really are."

"I'm *really* not."

"If not because of Peter, go for our site. You'll probably meet potential donors there."

She's right, but I'm distracted by the subtle panic that's been rising in me ever since that email from the CNN producer.

Plus, during breakfast I've been watching through the window as our staff filtered up to the office, and I know I need to get up there and lead them. We need to develop a press strategy for the Mast story and begin to get back to the dozens of journalists calling for comment.

"What are you gonna do about Peter?" Steph asks.

"I don't know yet, but let's go. We've got work to do, and I need to figure out what to wear on CNN tonight."

15

After the busiest day in Ameritocracy history, I drove Bluebird thirty miles north for my interview with Anderson Cooper. Now I sit in front of a green screen in a padded closet, microphone clipped to my chest. The air is stale and a bit too warm, and I try to remain calm as I stare into a large TV camera.

I take a few breaths, recalling the cool breeze that blow through my hair on the ride from Santa Clarissa to the CNN studio in South San Francisco. An earpiece relays the voice of a manic producer along with the deep, comforting voice of Anderson, who opens his show and goes over the big national news of the day.

Like I've said, I'm a bit of a Monica, so I arrived half an hour early, and now I have nothing to do until we go live.

"Seventeen minutes before you're live." The producer's voice is in my ear, intense and focused, like if a triple espresso could talk.

Pulling out my phone, I check my email one last time. My daily media summary has come in, and I scan the list of news articles that mention Ameritocracy, our candidates, or me personally.

One link takes me to a video from a local newscast, KGTV out of Reno, Nevada, where a makeup-caked news anchor speaks dryly and with a forced sense of humor. "On the lighter side tonight, it's Uber for the presidency, as a startup website tries to take the political primary process by storm."

The video changes to a still shot of the Ameritocracy homepage, where Destiny O'Neill still holds the number one spot. It's a screenshot from a couple weeks ago, which pisses me off slightly because she's barely clinging to the top ten. But, as Steph loves to point out, all coverage is good coverage.

The anchor continues, "Like many of you, secretary Mia Rhodes was fed up with politics. But unlike most, *she* did something about it, starting a website called Ameritocracy just after the 2016 election. For the first couple years, she attracted only a few followers.

"After a five million dollar donation from billionaire Peter Colton, she's turning that around. The site allows anyone to run for president as an independent, and promises the fame and money to compete with the Republican and Democratic nominees in the summer and fall of 2020."

The video shifts to a montage of Destiny O'Neill from her Platform page. She wasn't wrong about TV wanting to put her on screen. "If the current leaderboard is any indication, the site is attracting only fringe candidates. Candidates like Destiny O'Neill, a scantily clad YouTube star with controversial views, and Thomas Morton, a former ambassador to the Ukraine with no experience in elected government.

"But a major PR push is underway, and only time will tell whether Ameritocracy will give an independent candidate the first real chance since Ross Perot, or whether it will flounder like Peter Colton's ill-fated private-plane-sharing app."

Three different articles posted today all say a version of the same point: Mast's entry signals a turning point for Ameritocracy. One right-leaning blog worries that Mast will siphon votes from their favorite candidate, Tanner Futch. A left-leaning blog argues that Mast's entry signals the end for Ameritocracy, not a new beginning, because he's "the military-industrial complex in a human skinsuit."

Another piece quotes a Republican strategist bemoaning the fact that, if Mast wins Ameritocracy, he could pull votes from the Republican candidate in the 2020 general election, given that most of his views align with the party platform. All in all, the coverage is positive, and it's clear to me that the CNN interview isn't a fluke. Ameritocracy is spreading into the public consciousness and may be reaching a tipping point.

I haven't yet seen stats on new registrations, but Mast climbed all the way to number 211 in our rankings in twenty-four hours, the fastest one-day rise in site history.

The producer is in my ear again. "Ten minutes, Mia. Do you have everything you need?"

"I'm all set," I say, still staring at my phone.

"Anderson wanted you to know that we expanded the panel."

I sit up and speak into the camera, feeling ridiculous because I'm unsure whether the producer can see me. "I thought this was just a one-on-one."

"We needed some alternative perspectives, so we brought in one of your candidates." She pauses for a moment as I run over our top ten in my head, wondering who it could be. "Tanner Futch," she continues. "Plus an independent congresswoman. Maria Ortiz Morales."

"I've heard of her," I say, trying to fill time as I adjust to this new reality.

"First Latina member of Congress from Ohio. First independent to win a congressional election in ten years. She'll have a great perspective on your site. Expect questions about Mast, about Ameritocracy in general. You've done this a million times. You'll be fine."

"Right," I lie. "A million times."

"Seven minutes. You'll hear Anderson in your earpiece when we're back from break."

It's too late to think through what it means that I'll be live with Tanner Futch and Maria Ortiz Morales, so I glance at my phone, planning to power it down and take deep breaths until showtime.

Then, in the very last line of the email, I see my name in a headline: *1988 Spoiler Mia Rhodes is Getting Back into Politics*

"No, no, *no*," I whisper.

"What is it?" the producer asks.

"Nothing. Sorry. I didn't mean to say that out loud."

"Are you sure you're okay?"

"Fine," I manage, but I'm anything but fine.

Someone wrote about me and my father. Against my better judgement, I click the link to an article on PoliticalMuck-raker.com.

1988 Spoiler Mia Rhodes is Getting Back into Politics

With the expansion of her political reality-show competition, Ameritocracy, and its recent funding by eccentric billionaire Peter Colton, Seattle resident Mia Rhodes is looking to shake up the democratic process.

For the second time.

According to previous media accounts and hospital records obtained by Political Muckraker, *Mia Rhodes is the daughter of former Connecticut Senator Payton Rhodes.*

Mr. Rhodes, who served as Connecticut's Senator from 1970 to 1988, was the frontrunner for the presidential nomination in the 1988 Democratic primaries until scandal rocked his campaign.

The scandal was Mia herself, who was born to waitress

Alexandra Dimakos on the night of the Iowa caucus, February 8, 1988.

At the time of the affair with Ms. Dimakos, Mr. Rhodes was married to prominent health insurance executive Cecilia Rhodes. The couple had two young children—son Elliot Rhodes and daughter Patricia Ann Rhodes.

In the early months of the 1988 Democratic primary campaign, Mr. Rhodes was seen as the Democrats' best chance to challenge the Republicans after eight years of Ronald Reagan, largely because of his centrist positions, strong ties to the financial and insurance sectors, and stable family life. Early polling showed him favored by over ten points against any of the Republican candidates in the field.

Word of Rhodes' affair with Ms. Dimakos, however, began leaking in January of 1988 and, by Super Tuesday, Mia Rhodes was national news, forcing her father to drop out of the race, paving the way for Michael Dukakis, who eventually lost to George Bush in the 1988 general election.

Political reporters quickly moved on, but for a brief period, Mia Rhodes was known as the child who decided the 1988 election.

Though he and Mrs. Rhodes remained married, Mr. Rhodes left politics and went on to become a successful executive in the health insurance industry in Connecticut.

It's unclear whether Mia Rhodes and her father have a relationship, and whether her recent efforts to upend the democratic process are an attempt to vindicate her father.

The phone drops out of my hand and lands on the padded floor with a dull thud. My cheeks are hot, and I know they're taking on a shade of red that usually means I've had a couple glasses of wine.

But I'm not fighting back tears.

I'm fighting back rage.

"Thirty seconds back, Mia." It's the caffeinated woman's

voice. "By the way. Expect fireworks. Futch and Morales *hate* each other."

I should have seen this coming, but I didn't.

The smooth voice of Anderson Cooper fills in my ears. "In political news tonight..."

My head pounds, my ears ring, and I hear only fractured words and phrases as he introduces the site, and me.

"...Ameritocracy...Bold concept..."

I always expected the story about my father to come out, but hoped it wouldn't. It sounds crazy, but somehow I convinced myself that if I didn't address it, it might just go away.

"...Upending the two-party system...Recent addition of Robert Mast..."

I look around the sound booth, wishing for something, someone to distract me. It's like I'm in a dream. I press my feet onto the floor, and, for some odd reason, I feel myself back in the car with Malcolm, the night he took me shopping before the party with Peter.

"You should be hyped," he told me then, and as Anderson Cooper says my name, I push the memories of my father away long enough to get hyped for the interview. Or at least to get through it.

The producer is back. "Video live in five, four, three, two, one."

"Mia Rhodes, welcome to AC360," Anderson says.

I throw a smile on my face. "Great to be with you, Anderson."

I fake my way through the first five minutes, during which I explain the origin of Ameritocracy, laugh when Anderson jokes that we're like '*The Voice* meets *Mr. Smith Goes to Washington*,' and say a silent prayer that he doesn't ask me about my father.

By this point, I've repeated the responses so many times that many come automatically, and the knowledge I'm being watched by millions fades as I get going.

Anderson's next question is to Maria Ortiz Morales. "Ms. Morales, I'd like to get your perspective on this. You lost a leg in the war in Afghanistan at the age of thirty-three, were honorably discharged from the Navy, and served ten years as an intelligence analyst for the CIA. When your husband passed away, you returned home to Cincinnati and ran for Congress. A decorated war hero, how would you feel about taking orders from a commander-in-chief elected by an Internet poll?"

I want to object, but the question wasn't to me. "First of all," Morales says, her voice steady and quiet, "as a member of Congress, I don't take orders from anyone except the voters in my district. But I have to say that the concept troubles me greatly. I—"

"You like the system as it is because it benefits the politically correct status quo." It's Tanner Futch, loud and bombastic, interrupting Morales.

"Please let her finish," Anderson interjects.

"Thank you," Morales says. "As a service member, I learned to set aside my personal partisan beliefs to serve the mission. I served under commanders-in-chief from both parties, and though I chose to run for Congress as an independent, I respect both parties."

Futch grabs the first opening he can. "You respect special interests. You're the token independent in Congress. You're like the one black dude in an all-white fraternity. They let you in so they can say they have an independent member. Ohhh, *looooook. Anyone* can run for Congress in America."

I'm speechless, but like the producer instructed, I gaze straight into the camera, motionless, a pleasant look glued to my face.

"Are you saying Ms. Morales isn't independent?" Anderson asks.

"I'm saying that no one *can be* independent in the current system," Futch says. "That's what makes Ameritocracy so important. For the first time, we're going to hear the voice of the people. Not the special interests. Not the deep state. Not the bankers in Europe and Asia who want to destroy America by taking away our guns and opening our borders. The voice of the people! I disagree with Maria Ortiz Morales about everything. I despise her gay-rights, pro-Latino, pro-immigration, so-called progressivism. But I'd welcome her to join Ameritocracy. Let's find out where the *people* stand on these issues. Not the bankers and media elite who fall all over themselves just because she's Latino and happened to get hit by an RPG on a hill outside Kabul. What do you say, Maria? Do you want to join the most transparent, most democratic political experiment of all time?"

Futch's rant is the most passionate case for Ameritocracy that has been made on national TV, and though I don't love the fact that it came from him, I have to admire his ability to articulate the vision.

"I don't know where to start with that," Anderson says. "I have a question for Ms. Rhodes, but you should have a chance to respond, Ms. Morales."

"Usually with Tanner Futch, when you filter out all the xenophobia, conspiracies, and insults, all you have left is a few prepositions. In this case, though, it's prepositions and one thing I agree with, which is a nice first. We *do* need better representation of people's real concerns. So thanks, Tanner. I'll give your suggestion serious consideration. Just not the rest of your boilerplate bluster."

"You will?" Anderson asks.

"I will," Morales replies. "Now if only Mr. Futch would cut out his racist—"

"Ra-racist? Racist. *Racist?*" Futch is stammering like a madman, but that's part of his act. Over the last couple months, I've watched his videos and tuned into his podcast from time to time, and I get the sense he may not believe half of what he says. He comes across like an old musician, playing the hits for his fans.

Interrupt a woman, check. Blame the deep state, check. Blame European bankers, check. Close the borders, check. Interrupt a woman again, check and check.

This time, though, Morales talks right over him. "We *all* know what you mean by 'European bankers.' I've read your site."

"Didn't know you were a fan," Futch laughs.

"Ms. Rhodes, what do you make of this?" Anderson says loudly, cutting off the cross talk. "Here you have one of your leading candidates espousing what we can at least say are controversial ideas. Yet, as the leader of the project, you've promised to remain neutral."

"For me, it's about the platform," I say. "Though I can't condone everything Mr. Futch says, and I don't officially endorse any candidate or position, I believe in his right to say it. And I believe that, with Ameritocracy, we're providing the most transparent, most democratic platform in the history of elections. I know that TV hosts—no offense, Anderson—like to compare Ameritocracy to reality television, but our aim is earnest."

"And if I can interrupt," Anderson says, "would you say the announcement by Robert Mast is evidence that you're being taken more seriously?"

I open my mouth to speak, but Futch's voice is in my ear. "It's evidence that establishment thinkers are trying to co-opt the revolution."

"That was a question for Ms. Rhodes," Anderson scolds. "So, what do you think, Mia?"

"I think..." I trail off, head spinning, anger rising in my chest.

"They call it the deep state for a reason," Futch barks. "You know, this goes all the way back to—"

"No!" I say, and everyone goes quiet.

The emotion I stuffed down after reading the article about my dad is back. The sadness, frustration, and rage I squashed for decades hits me all at once, intensified by months of long days and short nights.

I have no more fucks left to give. "I think that men like Tanner Futch have been talking over me for too long. Talking over women for far, far too long."

Futch tries to interject in my earpiece. "No!" I say again, gaining confidence. "You're not going to talk over me. If you win Ameritocracy, I'll be the first to congratulate you, but you're not going to talk over me."

I pause just long enough to ensure I've shut him up. "Three things, Anderson. There are three things I want your viewers to know, and thanks for giving me this platform. First of all, to answer your question, Robert Mast is an excellent addition to our pool of candidates. His military service should be respected, and his ideas should be listened to.

"But no more so than our other candidates. Candidates like Beverly Johnson, a housewife from Washington state, or Justine Hall, the mayor of Denver, Colorado, or Avery Axum, who your viewers may not have heard of but who's served under *three* different presidents—Democrat and Republican. While your network was stoking the partisan fires for ratings, he served.

"Or Cecilia Mason, who started six different companies and brought billions of dollars into the New York economy. Or Destiny O'Neill, who...well...I hope you'll invite all of them on your show. Not just the candidates your viewers have already heard of, like Robert Mast. Or the ones who will say something controversial, like our friend Mr. Futch.

"If you care about democracy at all, and not just keeping the stock price of your parent company high, you'll spend a couple time slots you've set aside between ads for Buicks and pharmaceuticals to introduce our candidates to the world."

Anderson tries to say something conciliatory, but I'm on a roll. "Second, over half of Ameritocracy's top hundred candidates are women, whereas only twenty percent of nationally elected officials are women. I hope that's something you cover as well. One thing Mr. Futch and I agree on is that Ms. Morales would be a welcome addition to Ameritocracy.

"Third, and I can't stress this enough. As the leader of Ameritocracy, I *will* remain neutral. We've done everything we can to create a fair, neutral platform that allows the American people to decide. Only half of eligible voters voted in the 2016 election. Less than forty percent in the midterms. So I want to say this directly to your audience. The moms and dads on their couches at home, the business traveler standing in an airport, the teenager illegally streaming this online, go register at Ameritocracy2020.org." I pause for effect. "Do it. Right now. If you like Tanner Futch, vote for him. But take the time to get to know our other candidates. No matter who you vote for: vote. Don't let someone else make the decision for you."

There's something about saying what needs saying that frees a person. Something about not pretending to be small that makes me bigger than I could ever have imagined.

Now I walk on air as I leave the studio and cross the parking lot. I slide into the familiar leather seat of Bluebird and power on my phone, tempted to re-read the story about my dad. Instead, I open a series of texts from Peter.

The first text is a photo of a silver helicopter, the words "Colton Industries" painted on the side in black.

The second text is another photo, a little blurry, taken from high in the air, looking down on a sea of tall trees as a golden sun sets over them.

The third text is a note.

Peter: *Nice job on TV. Handled Futch perfectly. Registrations will go nuts. On my way to Future Now. Chopper could grab you late tonight or tomorrow morning. Join me?*

I wait to see if he sends anything else, then tap out a reply.

Me: *Maybe tomorrow. Send pics when you arrive and I'll decide.*

Before I press send, a new text arrives.

Steph: *Oh my God you killed it on TV! Right now Anderson is like, "What the hell just happened? I thought this was AC360, not the Mia Rhodes hour of power." That article about your dad, tho...You okay?*

I delete the text to Peter.

My performance in the interview made me feel better, but the truth is that I am anything but okay. I don't like talking about my father, but having other people talk about him is even worse.

I should have known that our history would come out, but I wall off my feelings about my past to figure out whether the revelation can damage Ameritocracy.

First, I decide to respond publicly, which I do via a one-paragraph statement I text to an intern with instructions to slap it on Ameritocracy letterhead and post to our Twitter account. The statement acknowledges that my father is my father, that he has nothing to do with Ameritocracy, and thanks the press in advance for respecting our family privacy.

If my father doesn't go on TV or give quotes to reporters, the story will go away in a couple days, most likely. Though he's well known around Connecticut, his name has long since fallen out of the national political conversation. If he lays low, our past will still come up from time to time, I decide, but won't do any damage to Ameritocracy.

But as I pull out of the parking lot and begin driving south, I know it's damaged me.

I've never spoken to my father. Not once in my thirty-one and a half years on earth. The total sum of our contact has been three birthday cards, each delivered through my mother, who kept my father at a distance since he broke off the affair when it became public.

The first card arrived the day I turned ten. It was a picture of a red and yellow clown holding a bunch of blue balloons. On the inside of the card, my father wrote:

Happy Birthday!

-Payton Rhodes

He included $500 cash, which I offered to my mom because she was struggling to pay the rent at that time. But she refused. We would not rely on his money for day-to-day expenses—not now, not ever.

She insisted I buy anything I wanted. I picked out a brand new scooter and a PlayStation, but lost interest in both quickly.

When I was twenty, he sent me $5,000. This time the check arrived inside a card with a picture of a bird on the front. It wasn't even a bird wearing a birthday hat or making a joke, like "Happy *Bird* Day." It was just a cheesy hotel-art bird with brown feathers. Probably the same design his secretary sent to Washington lobbyists on his behalf to thank them for helping him rig the health insurance markets.

Again, he wrote:

Happy Birthday!

-Payton Rhodes

At the time, I was broke and going into debt, so I considered using the money to pay for a portion of my junior year tuition at The University of Washington. Then I remembered my mom's admonition, so I used it on a three-month backpacking trip through Europe between my junior and senior years.

Ten years later I heard from him again, and by this point I'd studied political history and largely come to terms with my accidental role in it. A couple weeks after I turned thirty, my mom forwarded me a check for $50,000. Through a Google search for salaries of top insurance company executives, I determined that this was roughly one percent of his earnings that year. This time there was no card, just a handwritten note on a plain white piece of paper.

Dear Mia,

I hear you graduated from University of Washington with a degree in political philosophy. This makes me very happy. I hope you use this money to pay off school loans or otherwise advance your life.

Love,

Your father, Payton Rhodes

Thinking of it now brings waves of sadness.

Your father.

He never admitted to the affair in public, never acknowledged I was his daughter. Not to the press, not even in the cards he sent. He just slithered away from the '88 campaign and issued a vague statement about 'mistakes,' 'deep regrets,' and 'repairing the damage done to his family.' He meant his *real* family— Cecilia, Elliot, and Patricia. Not my mother, the striking Greek waitress he slept with for a year. And not me.

Worried for his political career, he'd pressured her to have an abortion, even threatened her with public shame and financial ruin. From his twisted perspective back in 1988, it made sense. He had a good shot of becoming president if I *wasn't* born. A rumored affair is one thing. A child out of wedlock who shares your last name is an entirely different level of scandal. One from which—in 1988 at least—politicians didn't recover.

Once I was born, he *did* offer to send money regularly, though not through the court system, but my mom refused. As

171

she put it to me over and over, "If he didn't want you to be born, I don't want his money anywhere near our family."

The birthday cards were the only exception.

He probably had a team of political consultants sitting around him as he wrote the first two birthday cards, advising him against admitting parentage in case he ever wanted to get back into politics. It took him thirty years to write "Your Father," and it shatters me to think about it. Thirty years of deliberately obscuring the truth, a truth finally admitted in the most mundane way possible.

I sometimes wish I'd taken his advice to pay off my student loans, but my mother's admonition had landed deep within me. So I took his $50,000 and did the most magnificently self-indulgent thing I could think of at the time.

I bought Bluebird.

Or, more accurately, I had Bluebird built for me. The baby blue 1964 Mustang cost me $14,000, and I found an electric car pioneer named Rich to do the rest. For $36,000, he converted the car to electric, installing dozens of lithium ion batteries in the trunk and adding a Tesla charging kit.

As I pull into my usual spot in front of Baker's Dozen, I contemplate my decision to buy Bluebird. My most-beloved possession was purchased with guilt money from a father I know only through press clippings, grainy YouTube videos, and occasional denigrations muttered by my mother.

As much as I've tried to convince myself that I have no interest in a relationship with him, I wonder whether it's an accident that I spent his money on a car that constantly reminds me of his existence.

16

My mini-rant on AC360 went viral overnight. Tens of thousands of new voters registered, and over five hundred new candidates signed up, at least a few of whom are serious. The most serious is Maria Ortiz Morales, who sent in her official registration at 3 a.m. local time.

The press release about my father went out during my drive back from the studio, and this morning there are a few dozen messages requesting interviews and further comment. But I don't have time to bask in the afterglow of my CNN appearance. It's two weeks to the rally, and I've got work to do.

First, I email a schedule to Gwen Winters, the KPBS anchor I've lined up to host the main event, where our candidates will be introduced to the world. Next, I spend an hour with a team of interns, setting up a contest whereby representatives from each of our forums are selected to attend a special cocktail reception the night of the rally.

Finally, it's time to call the top ten candidates, the ones invited to the rally.

1. Thomas Morton—the I-Guess-He'll-Do candidate.

2. Marlon Dixon—on a mission from God to feed the hungry and house the needy.

3. Tanner Futch—the bombastic voice of the alt-right.

4. Cecilia Mason—genteel old money come to life, with a strong business background.

5. Justine Hall—the only top-ten candidate with executive-level political experience, but she's too busy to talk about it.

6. Orin Gottlieb—the rockstar representative of small-government libertarians.

7. Charles Blass—a modern-day Trotsky, with millions of millennial followers.

8. Wendy Kahananui—who believes that all political problems are spiritual problems.

9. Beverly Johnson—the queen of suburban moms, and a hell of a cook.

10. Destiny O'Neill—the cartoon in a 13-year-old boy's math notebook come to life.

After dropping out late in the summer, Blass re-entered the competition a week ago and rose quickly, propelled up our rankings by an army of young, idealistic voters, mostly from California. They'd created a Facebook group called The Blass Meme Repository, and memes featuring Blass are spreading like wildfire, announcing his presence as a sort of political Santa Claus, promising equality for all.

I spent the morning calling the candidates in reverse order, and besides the awkwardness when Destiny O'Neill asked me whether I was sleeping with Peter yet, things went as expected.

On our call, Blass assured me that his heart condition was under control and that he was in Ameritocracy to win it. Futch called me "little lady" three times and praised Destiny O'Neill as a "true patriot." Wendy Kahananui tried to convince me that she'd be more informed on the issues at the rally.

I saved Thomas Morton for last, and I dread the call.

Steph and Benjamin are still working on figuring out what's going on with his voting, but we decided that, for now, we have to keep up the appearance of normalcy.

Sitting behind my desk, Post-it curled up on my closed laptop like it's some kind of throne, I dial Morton's D.C. cellphone.

He picks up after just one ring. "This is Tom Morton."

"Mr. Morton. Mia Rhodes from Ameritocracy."

"Yes, my assistant said you'd be calling."

"Yes, yes. Good. Are you aware of the public rally we're planning in Los Angeles?"

"Yes."

"And are you aware that you're currently the top-ranked candidate on our site?"

"Yes."

"And are you planning to attend?"

"I am."

Under normal circumstances, his short answers wouldn't seem especially odd, but I feel like a woman who's just found out that her husband is cheating so she reads way too much into every little word and gesture.

I'm sure he's hiding something, so I try to draw him out. "We'll give each candidate a couple minutes to introduce themselves to our audience and, most importantly, to the dozens of TV cameras we hope will be there."

"Yes."

"Any idea of what you'd say? I'm trying to get a sense of each candidate's public speaking ability for the...for the cameras."

"I'd probably say something like, 'I believe in America's most cherished dreams. I believe in the America that once was, and the America that will be once again. A vote for Thomas Morton is a vote for freedom, equality, and justice. A vote for Thomas Morton is a vote for America itself."

I give Post-it a look, hoping maybe he can decipher some of the gibberish Morton just spouted.

"Excellent, Mr. Morton. I should tell you that there will be a moderator, Gwen Winters from KPBS."

"Yes."

"What I mean is, she may ask follow-ups. She may ask for a little more specificity."

"Alright."

"Here, let me try." I adjust my voice a little to sound like a news anchor, an annoying habit I picked up from my old boss, Alex. "Mr. Morton, recent Pakistani incursions into northwestern India have raised tensions in the region. As president, what would your policy be on India-Pakistan relations?"

After a short pause, he answers, his voice smooth and robotic. "The conflict between India and Pakistan goes back hundreds of years and stems from deeply rooted religious and cultural differences. I believe America must be a leader in India-Pakistan relations. The security in that region affects us all. But, at the same time, we must focus on Americans first and not lose sight of America by placing our attentions halfway around the world. As president, I'll ensure the safety of all."

His voice is empty, as though he's reading off a cue card he doesn't fully understand. The words are all correct, but carry no meaning.

Post-it can probably sense my unease because he gets up off my laptop and starts prowling back and forth along the edge of my desk. "How about a domestic question?" I ask. "Healthcare costs have risen by over thirty percent in the last five years, and show no sign of slowing. As president, what would you do to stabilize the market?"

"That's a great question, and the American people deserve a straight answer. Healthcare costs are out of control, and I believe that every American can and should receive the affordable care he or she deserves."

Like I told you, I loathe hypocrisy. But almost as much as hypocrisy, I can't stand mealy-mouthed politicians. Folks who take five minutes to say nothing at all. "But what would you *do*?" I ask.

"A Thomas Morton administration would lower costs and raise the quality of care for all Americans."

"*How*?"

"By working closely with both insurers and the states to ensure that we achieve lower costs and a higher quality of care for *all* Americans."

I'm squeezing the phone so hard my hand is red, so I switch the call to speakerphone. One of the nice things about Ameri-tocracy is that even when I think the candidates are nuts, at least they're *specifically* nuts. At least I know what they actually think. Morton is a computer that's been programmed not to offend anyone.

And I'm out of patience. "What's your favorite kind of ice cream, Mr. Morton?"

"Why do you need to know that?"

"Uhh, dinner. We're arranging catering." It's a lie, but I'm on a mission to get him to give me a straight answer.

"I'm fine with anything."

"Chocolate or vanilla, Mr. Morton?"

"I really don't see how that—"

I lean into the phone and almost shout. "*Chocolate* or *vanilla*?"

There's a long pause, and I picture Morton, surrounded by a team of advisers, flipping through binders as they try to deter-mine which flavor of ice cream tests better with moderate voters between the ages of 28 and 62.

Finally, he says, "Is Neapolitan an option?"

After hanging up, I storm out of my office, ready to rant about Morton to anyone who will listen. Steph is at Benjamin's desk, one hand on his shoulder, watching him type.

She looks genuinely happy, so I pause halfway across the office, unsure whether I want to interrupt their moment. But she looks up before I decide, and meets me in the middle of the office.

I'm about to launch into my diatribe about Morton when she says, "Did you see it?"

"See what?"

"Your dad's press release. I forwarded it to you an hour ago."

"I've been on candidate calls all morning."

"Are they all coming?"

"They are, though I think Morton may actually be a robot sent from space to bore us all to death so aliens can take over the planet."

"It was *that* bad?"

"Worse than that. It was..." I trail off, the phrase "press release" floating through the back of my mind.

"Mia, what's wrong?"

As usual, Steph can read me. "You said there was a press release? About...about me?"

To my surprise, Steph smiles. "You're going to want to read it."

I head back to my office, shoo Post-it out of my chair, and open my email.

There I find the statement, released by my father, or someone in his office. It's on the official letterhead of Rhodes Insurance Consulting, LLC.

To whom it may concern:

In response to inquiries regarding the website Ameritocra-cy2020.org, and a recent article suggesting that the founder is the daughter of former Senator Rhodes, Mr. Rhodes issues the following statement:

"A little less than thirty-two years ago, my daughter Mia Rhodes was born. At the time, I worked to conceal her existence, as I was married and viewed the affair with Mia's mother as a shameful mistake and a political catastrophe.

Media accounts at the time made my deception impossible and forced me to resign from public office. Though I regret no longer being able to serve the people of Connecticut in a public role, I do not regret that I helped bring Mia into the world. And though she and I do not have a relationship, an arrangement I agreed to with her mother, I am as proud of her as I am of any of my children.

No child is a mistake. Ever. My greatest regret in life is that I ever viewed Mia as one.

As Mia enters the public sphere, I ask that you respect her privacy. I will have no further comment on her project, or our personal relationship, beyond this: In over twenty years serving in public office, both in the House and the Senate, I witnessed gridlock, partisan bickering, needless obstruction, and shameful political witch hunts.

There's nothing about Washington that won't be made better with some fresh ideas and fresh candidates inserted into the process.

Sincerely,

Payton Rhodes

I'm flooded with a mix of emotions that, until I was halfway through his statement, I didn't know could co-exist.

First, anger that he even mentioned my name in public. Though he is a powerful insurance industry consultant, he never appears on political shows and has largely fallen out of the public consciousness. Other than quotes in a couple books that chronicled the '88 campaign, in which he used the vague language of "regrets" and "mistakes," he hasn't spoken about me publicly since the announcement that he was dropping out of the race.

The second emotion is an odd mix of sorrow and gratitude. Sorrow at the fact that I'd lived nearly thirty-two years without knowing him, and gratitude at his kind words. Words I never knew I wanted to hear but, now that I have, feel like words I've needed my whole life. *I am as proud of her as I am of any of my children.*

Tears roll down my cheeks. I wipe them with a tissue, then close the blinds and pace around my office, crying softly.

Five minutes pass, then ten. Waves and waves of grief rise and pass through me, mixed with exquisite joy that feels as though it's caused by the grief.

No child is a mistake.

The words echo in my mind and leave me simultaneously bitter and hopeful.

The door opens a crack, startling me. "Hello?"

"It's me," Steph says from behind the door.

I'm more fragile than Steph, and she knows it. She gave me just the right amount of time on my own with the news, and now she's here to check on me.

"I'm okay," I call through the door. "Come in."

She walks in and leans on the desk. "You sure?"

"I'm fine," I say, just to say something. "Could people hear me crying out there?"

"Nah, Benjamin and his team are in the middle of a heated argument about video games. Something about franchise continuity."

I laugh. I've heard that argument two or three times since Benjamin and his crew started working in our office. "As long as they're addressing the crucial topics of the day."

Steph chuckles, walks around the desk, and opens her arms. "Get in here."

I stand before collapsing into her arms.

She bear-hugs me, and I cry for another minute before she gently eases me away. "Sorry," I say, "I'm getting your pantsuit all wet."

"I don't mind." She wipes her cheek. "But you're making me cry, too. Only one of us can fall apart at a time."

"New company policy?"

"Makes sense, right?"

"Yeah."

I check myself in the mirror I keep in my desk, and though my cheeks are almost as red as my hair, and my eyes a bit puffy, I don't care.

Steph looks at me, concerned. "Are you sure you're okay?"

"I think so. Maybe."

"Take your time," Steph says. "I read the press release, too, and I know it doesn't make up for...well, anything. It doesn't make up for *anything*. But it's better than nothing."

"It is," I say. "There's something else I've been thinking about. Do you think you can handle the shop for the rest of the day? Maybe till tomorrow?"

A big smile breaks out across Steph's face. "You're going?"

"Thinking about it."

"You're *going*."

"I don't know. Maybe it's too late, and by now Peter is probably off the grid, doing peyote with James Franco and a couple Google executives."

Steph grabs my phone and shoves it in my face.

"If he invited you, he'll keep his phone around to see if you change your mind. I'm not leaving until you text him."

She watches over my shoulder as I tap out a text.

181

Me: *Steph says my CNN performance earns me a day off. Invitation still open?*

To my surprise, by the time I've dried the tears from my face, my phone chirps.

Peter: *Drive to the heliport on the campus. Chopper will pick you up in an hour.*

[17]

The helicopter passes over mile after mile of redwoods. I see the layout of the festival from the window. It's smaller than I imagined when Peter compared it to Burning Man, and clearly more decadent.

There are no tents, no vehicles, and no dusty plains. It's a long field dotted with boulders, surrounded by a winding helix pattern of about a hundred geodesic domes. At one end of the field there's a large stage. At the other end is a sculpture of a three-dimensional heart made of barbed wire that stands at least fifty feet high.

There are also inspirational messages, spelled out on the edges of the field with white rocks.

"Epiphanies Made Here."

"Diverge!"

"Make the Future!"

"Disrupt!"

"Transform Yourself. Transform the World."

When we land, I grab my overnight bag and climb out, hair swirling in the wind. As I approach, Peter smiles from between two women who are either festival staff or high-end prostitutes from outer space.

Peter is barefoot and wears a loose-fitting white shirt, tight black pants, and a black leather necklace with a white bear claw hanging from it. He's handsome as ever, but as the helicopter flies over us and we wait for the noise to fade, I try not to laugh at the self-parodying extravagance of this place.

He leans in and hugs me, the bear claw pressing against my chest. "I'm glad you came. You've been avoiding me."

"I haven't."

"You have."

I wasn't *trying* to avoid him—at least not consciously—but I haven't seen him since the kiss.

The moment is awkward, partially because I don't know what to say, but partially because I'm distracted by the women on either side of Peter, both about six feet tall and both wearing silver leather pants, low-cut white t-shirts made of shiny fabric, and black top hats.

He sees me looking at them. "This is Melissa and Dalia. They are our Transformation Assistants."

I laugh, but it turns out he's not kidding.

"Anything we can get you," Melissa says, "just let us know. Green juice in the morning, aura cleansing in the afternoon, an old fashioned cocktail in the evening."

"Cocktails?" I ask, surprised.

"Retro cocktails are making a comeback," Peter says as either Melissa or Dalia—I've already forgotten which is which—hands me a circular black buzzer, about an inch in diameter.

"Just press the button and one of us will appear."

"Thanks," I say as Peter takes my hand and leads me along a path of blue stone that has been laid into the grass. Passing the performance stage, now empty, we enter a large white tent set up as a dining room.

"Absolution plays in an hour," Peter says. "I figured we'd eat dinner first."

I take a seat next to him. "What's an Absolution?"

"Remember? The best DJ on earth?"

"Oh right. As you've seen, I'm not much of a dancer."

"Look, I know you're here to get away from work, but I have to ask if you saw Nate Silver's piece on Ameritocracy?"

"Nate Silver did an article on us?" Nate Silver's site, FiveThirtyEight, has the best reputation on earth for reading polls accurately and predicting election trends. If he's writing about us, that's good news. "Did he say we're making a dent in the polls, or what?"

"No, it was just an analysis of how statistical modeling works differently with a ranked voting system. That's Nate for you. But it was very positive. He said that Ameritocracy will be an interesting test case of how ranked voting functions within American political dynamics."

I nod, pleased. From the statistics nerds at FiveThirtyEight, that's a ringing endorsement.

A male waiter appears, then another, and they almost look like twins. Pale skin, red hair, silver leather pants and white tank tops exposing large muscles and perfectly creamy skin. "Hello," one says. "I'm Jason. This is Brian. We'll be your dining coordinators today."

I stifle a laugh at the phrase "dining coordinators," but before I can launch my sarcasm program, Jason starts describing the meal, which grabs my attention.

"After the juice course, we'll serve a trio of raw vegetable salads, followed by a duo of sashimis, then either rack of lamb or grass-fed organic Wagyu ribeye. Most of the menu is pre-set, and designed to enhance the transformational experience of the festival. We will accommodate *any* special dietary need."

He stops talking, and Peter turns to me. "Lamb or ribeye?"

"Lamb."

"I'll have the ribeye," Peter says.

"Drinks?" Brian asks.

"Water for me," Peter says. "And a Red Bull."

"Just water," I add.

Jason and Brian nod in unison and as they walk away, I try to think of a way to make fun of this place without offending Peter. Before I can say something snarky, Peter stands abruptly and extends his hand to a woman walking towards us. "Margaret, so nice to see you."

She's a large woman, tall and stocky, and around my age. As she and Peter shake hands, a small, mousey man steps up alongside her. He's dressed in tight, 1980s-style shorts and blue cape with no shirt. He's wild-eyed and dripping with sweat.

"This is Dawson," Margaret says. "Dawson Gadschmidt. He's on my team at FMH. This is his first time."

"A Future Now virgin?" Peter asks.

Dawson steps forward and shakes his hand rapidly. "It's awesome!" he says, much louder than needed in the quiet tent.

Because I feel awkward just sitting there watching the hand-shakes, I stand.

"And this is Mia Rhodes," Peter says as I slide up next to him.

I shake Dawson's hand, which is cold and clammy, then Margaret's.

"FMH?" I ask her.

"Family Media Holdings," she says.

"Margaret is the youngest senior exec at FMH," Peter says. "And Dawson is..."

"Special Projects Assistant to Dewey Gunstott, the CEO," Margaret says.

"This is the most amazing party *ever*," Dawson says, walking a circle around the table before shaking my hand.

"Mia started Ameritocracy," Peter says.

Dawson steps closer than he should. He's sweating profusely, and his eyes don't seem to be able to land on anything for more than a couple seconds. "That's you? Very cool idea."

"What is?" Margaret asks.

"Mia's trying to save America," Peter says.

Margaret raises an eyebrow in my direction.

"Well, it's a sort of online reality competition to find an independent presidential candidate for 2020, and fund their campaign."

"Oh, that. I heard about that," Margaret says.

"It's awesome!" Dawson says. "Screw the two-party system." He walks another quick lap around the table, and I try to decide whether he's on ecstasy or peyote. "And with Mast's ad buy on CBS, that's gonna be some great pub."

"What?" I ask, thoroughly confused.

"Bobby Mast. His ad buy."

I'm still wondering what he means when Brian, our *dining coordinator*, returns and sets down the drinks. Dawson lunges forward, chugs my glass of water, then Peter's Red Bull.

"Thirsty much?" Peter looks at Dawson with concern, then at Margaret.

"He's had a...busy day," Margaret offers with a smile.

"Pace yourself," Peter says. "Absolution plays 'til dawn."

Dawson seems dazed now, staring at the ground. Margaret takes his arm. "Let's head back to the dome for a nap."

But before he leaves, I catch his eye and say, "What were you talking about? Mast? An ad buy? He just got in the competition."

As Margaret pulls him out of the dining tent, Dawson calls back over his shoulder, "Three hundred grand for spots during *The Bachelor*."

"That was odd," I say as Peter and I sit.

"Sometimes people go a little nuts at these things. I don't do any drugs, but I'm guessing he had his *Transformational Assistant* working overtime to find whatever he's on."

"That *was* weird, but I was talking about the Robert Mast ad buy thing."

"Any idea what he's talking about?" Peter asks, waving his empty Red Bull glass at Jason.

"No, but if Mast made a huge TV ad buy, I would have heard about it. And, if he did, what is he doing? Running for President in 1996?"

Peter laughs, but doesn't reply, and I let it go. After all, I'm here to get away from Ameritocracy, not to find new ways to obsess about it.

We're quiet for a moment, and I ponder the phrase "Transformational Assistant."

"What do you think of this place?" I ask. "I mean, *really*."

He looks at me long and hard, then breaks into a wry smile. "Well, it's totally *absurd*, of course."

"*Thank you*," I say, relieved. "It's like, if the poorer people of the world knew that things like this existed, they'd storm this camp and it'd be guillotine o'clock."

"Ha!" Peter says as the first courses arrive, "and we'd probably deserve it."

The juice course is actually a trio of juices—because one juice would *surely* not suffice—served in small, thin glasses, arranged from lightest to darkest from left to right across a white platter. Cucumber aloe juice. Carrot passionfruit juice. Beet kale juice.

I shoot the first one, which is ice-cold and undeniably delicious. "It's just that, for someone who grew up using ketchup instead of tomatoes on her BLTs, this level of wealth is...jarring."

Peter shoots all three of his juices in rapid succession. "We do a lot of good amidst all the opulence, too. Alvin Chang and I came up with Project X after a three-hour hot yoga class a few years back. Now I'm funding you and you're saving democracy."

"So, you *could* say that the Future Now Festival saved democracy." It's a joke, of course, but at the same time I'm trying to convince myself to be okay with the level of luxury around me.

"I know you're making fun of it, and me. Relax a little and maybe you too will *transform*."

He says the last word sarcastically, but probably because he knows that's what I want to hear.

"Maybe," I say, downing my next juice, which is even better than the first.

Maybe I *could* get used to this.

"It's not just me," Peter says. "Most of the leading innovators and investors in solar and hybrid technologies have come through here. The team that perfected the batteries that run your precious Bluebird met at an ironic kickball game here back in 2008. And the lady who coined the term 'Universal Basic Income' teaches an advanced hula hooping class on the east field. Tell *that* to your proletariat mob with torches and pitchforks."

Brian sets down our next course—three distinct salads arranged in small clumps on a giant platter. It's clear he's waiting for us to stop talking so he can explain them.

I look at Peter. "So you're saying that I can enjoy myself guilt-free for an entire evening?"

"Exactly."

After dinner, I step into what I guess is a porta-potty, because technically there's no running water at Future Now. But it's not like any porta-potty I've ever been in. Spacious, it smells of eucalyptus, and is cleaner than my bathroom has ever been. But I'm not there to use the bathroom. Despite my decision not to think about it, my father's response has been in the back of my mind since I arrived, and I want to see how it's playing online.

I open Twitter, then search for my father's name. He's not trending, but there are quite a few mentions of him. The article about us has revived old debates about the 1988 election, causing one blog to write a snarky like-father-like-daughter story. Their argument is that even though an independent candidate has no chance in 2020, one *could* get enough votes to tip the election in one direction or another.

For example, if a far-right candidate wins Ameritocracy—Tanner Futch or Orin Gottlieb—he might pull enough votes from the Republican nominee to tip the election to the Democrats.

If a left-leaning candidate wins—Marlon Dixon or Justine Hall, for example—and the Democrats pick a centrist candidate, that could tip the election to the Republicans by siphoning left-leaning Democrats.

If a centrist wins, things get weird in other, less predictable ways. Thomas Morton might pull from Republicans and Democrats alike, presumably by dominating the bland-gray-robot vote. Beverly Johnson, fiscally conservative but socially liberal, could throw the whole race into flux.

Like my father blew 1988 for the Democrats, I could blow the 2020 election for *either* party. It's pure speculation, of course, and nothing any major sites will pick up over the next few days.

I find what I'm looking for on my father's official Twitter account, which I've never checked and didn't know he had until now. The pinned Tweet links to his statement, which I re-read, savoring the key phrases.

I am as proud of her as I am of any of my children.
Then again.
No child is a mistake.

And again.

I am as proud of her as I am of any of my children.

No child is a mistake.

Tears flow, just as when I first read it in my office. This time they're quieter, and come from a deeper place. A childhood place. Like my body is slowly releasing the tears I'd held back year after year, learned to hold back when my father's name came up and my mother got tight-faced and quiet. It feels like there might be an awful lot stored up in there. I've just never checked.

Tap tap tap.

Someone's at the door, though I can't imagine that all the bathrooms are occupied. "Hello?"

"It's Peter. The music is starting."

I hear a faint beat coming from far away as I wipe my face and blow my nose, but I don't reply.

"Just wanted to make sure you're okay."

"I'm fine." I splash cool water on my face from a spigot attached to a large stainless steel tank affixed to the wall.

"Well, I'm three Red Bulls in and about to wreck the dance floor. I didn't think you'd want to miss it."

I check myself in the mirror. My cheeks are almost as red as my hair, and my eyes puffy. But I don't care.

The redwood-scented breeze cools my face when I step out. Torches have been lit all around the stage, and a melody constructed from old computer sounds fill the air, backed by an electro-trance beat.

Peter looks concerned. "Are you sure you're okay?"

"I am," I say, and I mean it.

An hour later, I stop dancing.

My heart races at the front of the small but energetic crowd. The night has cooled and the air tickles my sweaty skin. I gaze at the sky, almost white with stars. I've never felt more alive. For a moment, I wonder whether I ate or drank anything dosed with whatever Dawson Whatshisname was on, but that's just my brain trying to make excuses for my happiness.

"Mia," Peter says.

He's breathing hard, his dark hair wild, and before I know what I'm doing, I'm on my tiptoes, kissing him.

He kisses me back, pulls away for a moment to look into my eyes, then takes the back of my head and pulls me in with a perfect mix of strength and gentleness. I don't know how long we kiss, but it's long enough to forget where I am. He's not tall, but he's half a foot taller than me. Only when my calves start to burn do I pull away.

Looking around, I remember I'm standing in a field, surrounded by the most powerful CEOs in the country, many dressed in costumes, all indulging in a cartoonish level of luxury. As torn as I am about the festival, I *do* feel transformed. The thoughts of my father are still present, but they don't carry the same negative weight they did earlier. I am less encumbered.

Peter puts a hand on my lower back and we walk from our spot in front of the stage to the back of the crowd. The music fades and a voice comes through the sound system.

"Y'all ready for another set?"

It's Absolution again, back from break. The crowd erupts and a slow and strange synth melody begins. Peter turns toward the stage, and it seems he's happy to keep watching the show.

I'm not. I press my tingling fingers gently into his palm before tugging his hand. "Let's go."

He doesn't turn from the stage. "You ready to get some sleep?"

"Not in the least." It's the first time in my life I'm certain I've nailed a sexy seduction line. I pull Peter toward the geodesic domes. "Which is yours?"

Peter's face changes as he realizes that, yes, I'm trying to take him back to his place for the night. "It's, uhh, the big one at the very back." He points at a path of circular white stones that leads through the transient village. "Just follow the...um...path."

I lead the way, my whole body surging with a new, unfamiliar feeling. Two feelings actually.

On the one hand, I can't believe this is happening. I can't believe what my life has become. Four months ago I worked ten-hour days for Alex Vane at *The Barker*, now I'm surrounded by the most powerful men and women on earth, leading one of them back to what I'm sure will be a very comfortable bed. Everything is surreal, like I'm living someone else's life.

At the same time, I feel like I'm exactly where I'm supposed to be. I don't believe in destiny, but if I did I'd be certain that running Ameritocracy and being here at this festival—under the stars, as odd music thumps across the night, taking Peter to bed —is mine.

We reach his dome and Peter steps in first. "Just give me a sec. I want to put away all my work stuff."

Stopping at the doorway, I peer at the stars and do a slow twirl that reminds me of the night I met Peter, the night when I spun like a drunken fool on the dance floor and felt possibility I'd never felt before.

I'm about to tell Peter this when my phone vibrates in my purse. Reaching in to silence it—because nothing kills the mood like a phone call—I see the name "Benjamin Singh" on the caller ID.

Benjamin has never called me. Not once. He's texted me a couple times, but we speak at the office. He knows I'm out of town, and he's close enough to Steph that I assume he'd have run anything urgent by her.

If he's calling me now...

"Benjamin?" I step away from the dome. "What is it?"

"I'm...I'm sorry Mia. Sorry to bother you. I'm here with Steph and we weren't going to call, but it's urgent."

"What is it?"

There's a long pause. I want and don't want him to tell me what's going on.

"It's Thomas Morton," Benjamin says. "I figured out exactly what's going on."

"And?"

"It's much, much worse than we thought."

[18]

I never made it into Peter's geodesic dome. Instead, I offered a two-sentence excuse about "something going on with the site," and hitched a ride back to the Colton Industries campus in his helicopter.

As it lands on the helipad, my phone lights up with a series of rapid text tones.

Steph: *Don't come back to the office, you need your day off.*

Steph: *I mean come back if you want to, but you don't have to.*

Steph: *Hello? At least let me know what you're doing.*

Steph: *Are you even getting these?*

Steph: *Oh crap, you're in a damn helicopter, aren't you?*

It's midnight when I get back to the office, where Benjamin and Steph are huddled over a laptop, glaring at it like it's the bearer of bad news.

Steph turns when the office door creaks. "I was gonna get on the phone and tell you not to come back," she says, "but Ben told me you hung up."

"I just got all your texts, but I have to be here. Tell me everything."

"Hold on." Steph heads for the kitchen and emerges a minute later holding two glasses of wine. "You're gonna need this."

Benjamin is on the backend of our site, clicking through voting records. "It's complicated," he says. "And I should warn you that it's not an easy fix."

"Explain," I say.

He taps a graphic on the screen. "It's a chart detailing the age, gender, and location of the voters who have ranked Thomas Morton in their top three. Average age of his voters is about what we'd expect. Gender is split fifty-fifty. And—"

"Wait," I say. "The gender is split fifty-fifty?"

"Exactly fifty-fifty," Benjamin says. "Why?"

"Nobody splits *exactly* fifty-fifty," Steph says, half a second before I can.

"Orin Gottlieb is skewed about sixty-forty, men to women," Benjamin says. "Marlon Dixon and Beverly Johnson are about sixty-forty women to men, and Tanner Futch is nearly sixty-five percent male voters. So, the fifty-fifty split is unlikely, but not as unlikely as this."

He clicks the "location" section of the graph, which opens a detailed map of the United States, covered in thousands of tiny red dots. "Each dot represents a thousand voters who've put Morton in their top three."

There are dots all around the country, but a few distinct clusters as well. "Are those dense areas in big cities?"

Steph lets out a long sigh. "Some of them, which is what we'd expect, but some are weird. Look, this New York cluster is way upstate, nowhere near New York City or Albany. And the Nevada clusters aren't near Las Vegas or Reno."

Benjamin zooms to show a closeup of Nevada. "The weird clusters are around Indian reservations."

"Not near," Steph says. "On top of."

The three Nevada clusters *are* right on top of three reservations. In the west, the Fallon Paiute Shoshone Reservation, in the northwest, the Fort McDermitt Reservation, and to the north, the Duck Valley reservation, which covers a large swath of land on both sides of the Nevada-Idaho border.

"How is that possible?" I ask. "They can't have populations big enough to garner that many votes."

"Exactly," Benjamin says. "The voters *can't* be there."

I sigh because Benjamin sometimes goes into a mode of obfuscating computer issues as a way to lord his superior knowledge over us. "Damnit, Ben. Just get to the point!"

"Sorry. It's just that when you spend years doing boring coding, it's kinda cool to play detective for a few hours. Anyway, the reason all those dots show up in those places is that the dots represent IP addresses, *not* physical addresses. As you know, each voter must register with a physical address. And when I run the same check based on physical addresses, the map is dispersed much more evenly. More votes in big cities, spread evenly throughout the country, and so on."

"So this means what?"

"I don't know yet," Benjamin says, clicking on a browser tab. "But look at this. These are Tom Morton's hundred most-active users."

The page is a series of profile pictures, the type every voter must upload to the site, under which is the date the voter registered with the site. "So?" I ask.

He taps the screen. "See this face?" He scrolls down and taps on another. "And this one?"

"Same person," Steph says.

"But one is listed as Brian King and one as Dimitri Kronos," Benjamin says. "And here." He taps a woman's picture at the top of the screen, then scrolls down and taps another, identical picture. "They're not the same person with different pictures, they're *identical* pictures, just resized or filtered."

"And probably not the real person at all," Steph adds, angrily.

"Definitely not," Benjamin says. "I could show you a hundred more, but this is the least of our problems."

I'm growing frustrated, and a little scared. Part of me wants to curl up on the floor, but instead I take a small sip of wine. "Can we kick them out? I mean, I thought we had systems for this?"

Benjamin turns his chair slowly and talks to me like I'm five years old. "We *do* have systems, but not for what these guys are trying. This isn't a couple of 4Chan losers in mom's basement. This isn't even a hack in the conventional sense."

"Then what is it?"

He doesn't reply, but clicks back to the images of the maps with red dot clusters. "These vote clusters on Indian reservations, I have a theory."

He clicks on the western New York cluster. "This is the Seneca Nation. Population around eight thousand." He clicks again and a data box pops up. "See that? Morton got eleven thousand first place votes from within the land owned by the Seneca Nation. Plus about six thousand second- and third-place votes."

"How's that possible?" I ask.

"It's not, which is how I know something's up."

"I thought we verified people's addresses."

"We do," Steph says, "but he's saying that, regardless of where voters say they're living, those actual votes are coming from within that area."

"Exactly," Benjamin says. "And it's the same for all the other clusters. Thousands more votes than there are people."

"But how?"

"It's too early to tell for sure," Benjamin says. "My current theory is that someone, or some group with very good technical skills and a lot of money, is trying to rig Ameritocracy for Thomas Morton. They're setting up fake profiles, somehow linking them to real addresses, then voting via botnet all over the country, with command-and-control servers on Indian reservations."

"Why can't we just kick out those users?" I ask.

"We can," Steph says, "but if I'm right, Benjamin is gonna say they haven't broken any of our terms or conditions."

"Well, they *have*," Benjamin says. "We just can't prove it yet."

"Damnit." I walk a little circle around the desk. "And we can't kick out thousands of users without casting the whole project in a bad light. We can't do it without more information. More evidence."

Steph nods, and I know we're on the same page.

I'm freaking out inside, but, technically, I'm in charge, so I play it cool and make a decision. "Benjamin, I know you're exhausted, but if you can spend the rest of the night on this, I'd appreciate it. We need to know who is behind this, how many voters and votes are involved, and whether anything else like this is going on with other candidates."

"I'll need help."

"Bring in as many people as you need," Steph says. "We can afford it for a couple days."

"Right," I say. "This is priority one. If the credibility of our voting drops, the site is finished."

Benjamin nods and picks up the phone. "It'll take me the rest of the night to figure this out if I'm lucky—probably longer. I know some people who can help. White-hat hackers who may have a better idea of what's going on than I do."

"Can you trust them?" I ask. "We *cannot* afford for this to get out. We need to figure it out and stay ahead of the story."

"I won't tell them enough for them to leak anything," Benjamin says. "But you guys have to do one important thing.

Assuming I figure out exactly what's going on here, you need to figure out how to handle it in the press."

I gesture for Steph to join me in my office to plan for the fall-out, but another thought strikes me. "One last question. Assuming you're right that this is being run by servers on Indian reservations, why? I mean, why reservations?"

Benjamin glances up from his phone. "I have no idea."

The next morning, I stumble out of my office—where I slept on the floor—and scan the main office space. Steph went home to grab a couple hours of sleep, and now stands over Benjamin, who is either passed out at his keyboard or actually dead.

Last night, as Benjamin worked on figuring out the details of the hijacking, Steph and I talked about a media strategy, deciding to remain silent until we know exactly what happened and, more importantly, what to do about it.

"Steph." I shake off my grogginess. "What's going on?"

"Just got here. Ben was like this when I showed up."

"When was that?"

"Five minutes ago."

"You've been standing over him talking for five minutes and he hasn't woken up?"

Steph nods, and I glance at the Red Bull cans, candy wrappers, and half-full coffee mugs on his desk. I tap him on the shoulder. "Benjamin."

Nothing.

"Benjamin!"

He shifts on the keyboard, causing a string of gibberish letters and numbers to appear in an open document.

"Benjamin!"

"Wha?" He sits up suddenly, wipes the drool from his cheek,

and looks around. "I had a nightmare that I worked at Uber." He shakes his head as if to clear something out. "It was *horrible*."

"What did you find?" I ask.

He taps at his keyboard and pulls up browser windows, taking long swigs of his coffee every few seconds. He's opened a dozen different documents before he leans forward, presses his face into his palms, shakes his head violently, and yells, "Wake up, Ben! Wake up!"

Steph and I are used to this. Benjamin is not a morning person, and this is his psych-up routine.

After a long, dramatic pause, he says, "The votes aren't coming from Indian reservations. They're coming from the Ukraine."

I'm speechless. All I can do is offer Steph a blank stare.

"Ukraine," he repeats, as though this is explanation enough.

"Start at the beginning," I say as calmly as I can.

"You know how I said last night that the botnet votes seem to be controlled from reservations? That's where the servers are located that are actually running the attack. But those servers are controlled by users in the Ukraine."

"Russia?" Steph asks.

"So far, just the Ukraine, but we're still checking. Brianna. Hey Brianna. Brianna!"

For the first time, I notice a small woman with long black hair sitting on the floor in the corner where my bed used to be. She looks up and pulls off her headphones reluctantly. "What is it?" she yells.

"How many unique servers have you detected?"

"Eleven. Ten in Ukraine, and a new one in Cyprus."

"Where the hell is Cyprus?" Benjamin asks.

"Island off Greece," I say.

"Okay, keep looking," Benjamin calls. Brianna puts her headphones back on and buries her face in her laptop.

"Why Indian reservations?" I ask.

"Brianna and I think it's because Indian reservations are sovereign tribal land. Whoever did this knew they'd need U.S. IP addresses to vote on our site, and it's harder for the FBI or other law enforcement guys to seize servers on Indian reservations."

"So, wait," Steph says, "computers in Ukraine and Cyprus are controlling computers on Indian reservations, which are creating fake users but using real addresses, then voting for Thomas Morton?"

Benjamin looks strangely calm. "That's right."

I am anything but calm. For Benjamin, this is just a technical mystery, one he believes he's solved. To me, this is an existential threat to Ameritocracy.

"My office," I say. "Both of you."

In my office, Steph leans on the corner of my desk as I sit behind it and Benjamin takes a chair across from us. I feel better on my own turf.

"This is serious," I say. "What can you do?"

"Already on it," he says. "First, we block the IPs and ban the users with fake accounts."

"But that won't stop them from creating new accounts from different IPs," Steph says. "The nightmare scenario is that they do this right on the eve of the final vote."

"That's what has me freaking out," I say.

"We can work on that," Benjamin says. "I promise you we can figure out a way to make it more secure. Might take some money, but—"

"Spend it," I say.

After Peter's donation, we set aside a million dollars as seed money for the winning candidate, and we've gone through one of the remaining four-million over the last months. But we still have enough money on hand to pay staff through our final vote in July, plus a quarter million in emergency money.

"Run your expenses by Steph, but spend whatever it takes."

"Okay," he says, "but there's another problem."

"The other problem is *why*," I say.

"Right," Steph says.

"That ball is in *your* court," Benjamin says. "This is the kind of hack major national governments usually have to worry about. Brianna is one of the top white-hat hackers in the Valley. First thing she did when I told her about it was compare the list of IP addresses to a couple known botnets from black-hat hacker markets on the Dark Web. She even knows which they're using. Internet-capable devices all over the country have been co-opted to move data packets that function as votes on our site. She told me...hey, Brianna? Brianna!"

He has to scream to get her attention, and we wait until she appears in the doorway. "*What?*" she demands.

"Who did you say the number one Morton supporter in California was?"

"The ATM at a gas station in Fresno."

"Thanks." Benjamin turns back to us as Brianna vanishes. "She makes ten grand a day to do a job like this, and what she dug up, *I* can barely understand. Would have taken me a week to figure out where the machines controlling the servers on the reservations were. So you two need to figure out why, and what to do about Tom Morton."

I don't like where he's going with this. "Whether he was in on it, you mean?"

He nods slowly, and my panic is back. When I said Morton was probably drawing votes from gray robots, I hadn't meant literal gray robots.

Steph says, "Assuming you're right, someone wants this empty suit elected president. If that's the case, the question is whether he knows."

"If so," I say, "we need to kick our leading candidate out of the competition."

As I say it, I flash forward to the PR nightmare this will create. I can see the headlines now.

Ameritocracy Throws Morton Out, Towel In.

"Democracy Reborn" Suffers Credibility Crib Death.

Ameritocracy: That Was Cute, Girls, But Back To Business.

Mia Rhodes Slated To Die Alone, "Total Failure" Cited As Reason.

Post-it jumps in my lap and purrs softly, but it's no comfort.

As if reading my mind, Steph says, "If he's in on it...Oh God... That will be a disaster. Even if he's not..."

I finish her thought. "It's a disaster either way."

[PART 3]

[19]

THE Q HOTEL, LOS ANGELES, CALIFORNIA

I stare into the hotel closet, wondering whether I brought an outfit that will quell the anxiety I feel. Despite the fact that I'm in Los Angeles for just three days, I brought five outfits, but I still feel like I've got nothing to wear.

Objectively, I've got plenty to wear. What I mean when I say I've got nothing to wear—what most women mean when they say that—is that I don't know if I have the outfit I need to be the woman the world needs me to be today.

And the world needs a lot from me today.

I reject a white pantsuit that Steph made me bring, then a formal skirt-and-jacket thing that is somehow too eighties. All it's missing are shoulder pads.

Finally, I land on the best I'm going to do for the day I have ahead of me. It's a navy-blue Versace pantsuit, cut sleek and

207

modern, with two columns of silver buttons down the front of the jacket, giving it a Union Army vibe. I bought the suit at an outlet mall over a year ago and haven't worn it once.

I'm usually not one to buy a dress that's a size small to encourage herself to lose weight, and I don't hoard clothes. When I bought it, I thought it looked like something a badass heroine would wear while commanding a starship in an inter-planetary war. Though I never had reason to wear it at *The Barker*, I think I knew that someday I'd become the woman who wears a suit like this.

Today is that day.

I've spent the last week developing a media strategy for the Thomas Morton situation. Steph and I call it our "Executive Strategic Plan for Covering Our Butts."

The strategy is to overwhelm Morton and the public with evidence of the manipulation of the Ameritocracy system. That way we can kick him out cleanly, while also explaining what happened and ensuring the public that it won't happen again. But it turns out that producing that evidence is taking longer than expected, so here I am, alone at The Q Hotel in Los Angeles, prepping for the biggest three days of my life without Steph by my side.

She stayed in Santa Clarissa to run the office and finish the document we'll present to the public, but the rally is just two days away and the last thing we want is to raise questions by postponing the scheduled events.

The candidates will arrive any minute and, now that I have an outfit, I dress quickly, tying my hair up in a French twist and sliding on my three-inch heels just as there's a knock at my door.

Beverly Johnson and Orin Gottlieb arrive first, chatting like old friends as they walk in because they recognized one another on the flight and shared a taxi to the hotel.

Gottlieb is shorter than I expected, just a few inches taller than me, but he takes up a lot of space in his black suit, speaking loudly and constantly moving his arms. Johnson's striking red hair flows halfway down her back, and she's wearing a simple apron-style dress that looks a size too small.

After a quick greeting, they head to the buffet set up along the window in the living room of the suite.

Next to arrive is Tanner Futch, who wears a stenciled shirt, bolo tie, and work jeans. "Pleased to meet you, lady," he says with a deep bow.

I'm about to ask him not to call me "lady" when a group of people get off the elevator at the end of the hall.

Thomas Morton, Justine Hall, and Marlon Dixon.

I notice Morton first because I've been dreading our first meeting and, unconsciously, I've been on the lookout. He's in his typical brown suit, stylish but not too stylish. Like the other candidates, he's chosen clothing that matches his brand, rather than dressing up or dressing differently for the occasion.

I shake Morton's hand with as much confidence as I can, hoping not to let on what I know. For today, I need to pretend as though everything is normal.

"Hello, Ms. Rhodes." He shakes my hand. "Thank you for creating Ameritocracy." He says it in the same monotone I've grown used to from watching his videos, and his eyes are vacant and bored.

"You're welcome," I say. "It's nice to have you here."

He must have booted up his "stump speech" program on the elevator, because next he says, "America needs new ideas, new options, and new presidential candidates. Ameritocracy has helped deliver those candidates to the American people."

I'm about to tell him that he can save the speech for the cameras when Marlon Dixon slides in and pats me on the back, "Ms. Rhodes! The woman herself, praise God. So great to see you again."

I smile and pat him on the back as he walks past. His shoulders are broad and he's almost bursting out of his white linen jacket, like he's spent extra time in the gym since he took our office by storm a couple months ago.

Morton follows him in, and I shake hands with Justine Hall, the most surprising of the bunch. Online, she looks attractive, but not overly so. Like a woman who spends little to no time on her appearance. Nothing wrong with that, of course. If I had a city to run, every day would be a ponytail day.

Today her black hair is shiny and straight, hanging just below her shoulders and framing her face, which glows bronze. Her red lips match her sleek pants. Her dove-gray blouse perfectly fits her tall, lean body.

Hall walks gracefully into the suite as Destiny O'Neill and Charles Blass stroll off the elevator. They are without a doubt the oddest couple in the top ten, but they chat amicably. For one crazy moment, I imagine them on a presidential ticket together, a seventy-five year old Communist professor and a gun-toting sex-kitten YouTube star.

Only in America.

Today, O'Neill is in a blue trucker hat with white lettering that reads "Starf*cker," her bosom barely concealed under her white tank top and orange hunting vest. Blass wears his trademark Russian hat and wrinkled corduroy jacket, walking with a cane, looking every bit the part of an old man lost in the park.

I greet them quickly and point them to the buffet, where they continue to talk like any two colleagues meeting at a professional conference.

On the flight to L.A., I decided that the two candidates most likely to be late were Cecilia Mason and Wendy Kahananui, and they proved me right.

After I spend fifteen minutes pecking at the fruit platter, engaging in small talk, and enduring awkward silences, they emerge together through the open door. Wendy Kahananui strides right up to me wearing a flowing white dress, apologizes profusely for her tardiness and explains that her flight from Prague was delayed.

Cecilia Mason—the only billionaire in the group—marches past me like I'm the maid, offering no explanation at all. She pours a glass of orange juice and surveys the suite. I can't tell whether the disdain on her face is for the other candidates or the accommodations.

The room quiets as everyone notices at once that the top ten candidates are present. Awkward glances are exchanged before all eyes land on me. I say nothing.

Of course it's Futch who breaks the silence. "That's it, right? We're the ten?"

"We're expecting one more," I say.

I watch my candidates to gauge reaction, then say, "Our eleventh-ranked candidate will be here as well, as backup. She won't appear on stage unless someone gets sick or...or something."

Cecilia Mason steps to the center of the room. "In the theater we call that an 'understudy'."

Tanner Futch looks her up and down. "You were an actress?"

Mason smiles at Futch condescendingly, like she can't believe she's in the same room with someone like him. "The correct term is the gender-neutral 'actor.' Female performers prefer it. And I personally *fund* three off-Broadway theaters."

"Well *zippity-doo-dah*," Futch says. "Aren't you something!"

Just then, Maria Ortiz Morales walks in, limping slightly on her prosthetic leg. She's wearing a crisp white skirt suit that, I'm guessing, is supposed to remind people of her Navy uniform. She has what I'd call a *handsome* face. Proportional, angular, but not especially soft, with deep brown eyes and brown hair pulled back in a ponytail.

I survey the crowd of would-be politicians, who slip back to talking amongst themselves. Futch chats with Beverly Johnson in the corner, filling the room with occasional bursts of raucous laughter. Gottlieb has sidled up to Cecilia Mason and, from what I can hear, is arguing with her about individual rights versus group rights.

Justine Hall sits on a couch, sipping a cup of black coffee. Wendy Kahananui stares at her phone as Marlon Dixon cheerfully assaults Maria Ortiz Morales with a boisterous greeting. By the window, Charles Blass tries to convince Destiny O'Neill that true communism has never been tested.

The whole scene is unreal.

The last time I had this feeling was when Steph set me up with a dude named Byron who worked in the accounting department at Door Knockers. Byron and I chatted online and texted for about two weeks before meeting. Online he came across as funny, confident, even charming. But as we sat together at a sushi bar, I was confronted with the real person, and the whole thing felt odd. Like he was supposed to exist only in my phone, on my laptop screen, because that's where I'd formed my first impression of him. It's not that he wasn't funny or confident or charming in person, it's just that he was *different*. Different than what I expected. We didn't have a second date.

Meeting my candidates in the flesh is much different than watching their videos, reading their statements, or talking with them on the phone. Watching them chat amongst themselves, the gravity of the moment hits me. If things go according to plan, I'll soon be giving one of these eleven people—or another candidate who takes their spot—millions of dollars to run for president.

I swallow hard, fingering a brass button on my suit, then move to the buffet table, catching a glance at myself in one of the mirrors. Despite feeling out of place at my own meeting, I look like my normal self. Except now "my normal self" does stuff like this.

"Welcome," I say, loud enough to quiet the chatter in the room. "The eleven of you represent the hope of the American people. Hope that we can take back our democracy from special interests, stagnation, and corruption."

As I say this last part, I make sure my gaze doesn't stray to Thomas Morton, fearing that I'll give him a searing glare without intending to.

"This morning will give us time to go over the schedule for today and tomorrow, and discuss the next eight months of the competition. It will also give you time to get to know one another and ask me any questions you may have. Please notice that no one is in this room besides the eleven of you, and me. No photographers, no other staff. I want this to be an open, honest discussion."

I pause, looking from candidate to candidate. I have their full attention, and the fact relaxes me. "First, the schedule. Tomorrow at one o'clock is our first public event. Reporters, TV crews, and the American voters will be watching. Please arrive at the conference room at least fifteen minutes early. You'll each have three minutes to give opening statements before questions. You all received the seating chart and schedule from the front desk when you checked in, right?"

Everyone nods, and Marlon Dixon waves the white folder over his head.

"Good. That event will end at three. The rest of the afternoon will be an informal time to meet with Ameritocracy fans and reporters without any official structure. I suggest you make yourselves available. At seven p.m., we'll have a two-hour meet and greet, where drinks and *hors d'oeuvres* will be served. At this point, I'd like to briefly lay out the rest of the contest schedule, then we'll do questions."

The more I speak, the more I realize that *I* represent their hope just as much as *they* represent mine. In the two-party system, none of these people have a chance to become president and, though it's still a long shot for each of them, they see me as the woman who gave them a shot.

"As you know, candidate enrollment doesn't end for three months, February fifteenth, to be exact, but—"

"Good!" It's Tanner Futch's voice from the back of the room. "Bring on the competition!"

Beverly Johnson, who seems to be taking on a mothering role with Futch, shushes him, and I ignore the comment. "After this weekend, the contest will have three main events. The first is March first, when we cut the field to twenty-five candidates. That's Super Tuesday for Democrats and Republicans. I assume most of you will make that cut, though there's no guarantee."

"Let it be so!" shouts Marlon Dixon.

"A month after Super Tuesday, April first, we will cut the field to ten. So that's a date to keep in mind. At least one of you, and possibly more, will exit Ameritocracy at that point."

I pause, waiting for more comments, but they are quiet. Most look around the room, probably sizing up the competition as they contemplate the field being cut to ten.

"Just as the Democrats and Republicans are narrowing their fields in their respective primaries, we'll be narrowing ours. At that time, we expect the top candidates to receive a surge in votes, since voters will have the option of re-voting once lower-ranked candidates are eliminated. Between April first and June first, we will have two debates, eliminating two candidates after each debate. In the first debate, questions will be taken directly from voters and candidates will respond via livestream. The second debate will be in person, at a location to be determined.

"That'll leave us with six candidates going into our final debate, which takes place on July Fourth in Washington D.C. It will be streamed live on Facebook and our site, but if I do my job well, networks will pick it up."

Everyone's eyes are on me and I imagine they are picturing themselves making it through the various rounds of eliminations to take their places on the final debate stage.

"The morning after the July Fourth debate, final voting will open, and will close exactly twenty-four hours later. A winner will be announced live, also on the stage, at nine p.m. Eastern on July sixth. We will design the event on July sixth—typical political stuff with red, white and blue balloons, cocktails, and so on."

"Can I choose my own music when I win?" Wendy Kahananui asks, smiling. "Sorry, just trying to inject a little humor into the room. I can actually *feel* the ambition and anxiety in the air."

A few of the candidates chuckle, but Kahananui is right. My guess is that hearing how the competition will progress is forcing them to contemplate what happens if they lose. Or, perhaps more terrifying, if they win.

I smile back at her. "I don't see why you can't bring your own music. The July sixth event is not the official start of your campaign. It's an Ameritocracy event, and we assume the winner will want to throw a campaign launch party as well."

"Yes, I will!" Tanner Futch's loud voice bellows, and gets laughs out of about half of the candidates. The ice is breaking, a welcome development. The more at ease the candidates are, the better they will come off on tomorrow's stage.

"That's basically it," I say. "Questions?"

To my surprise, Beverly Johnson's hand shoots up first. "How much money has been raised? For the winning candidate, I mean."

I anticipated this question. "Total donations for the victory fund are a little over three million, which includes the chunk set aside from Mr. Colton's initial donation. Keep in mind, those donations are non-refundable, not tied to a particular candidate. Users can't ask for their money back if their favorite candidate doesn't make the final cut, or doesn't win. Also, we expect that number to increase at least fivefold by the final debate. Possibly much more."

Johnson frowns at the floor. "Even with a fivefold increase, that's only fifteen million, less than a sixth of what the Democrats and Republicans will have."

"True," I reply, startled that she's disappointed by *only* fifteen million. "Could be more, but we expect the winning candidate will be able to raise additional money *after* the contest ends. Our data shows that sixty percent of our active users have not yet made a donation, and our guess is that some are waiting to see if their candidate wins, and plan to donate directly to the campaign when that happens."

Justine Hall's voice cuts through the room with quiet precision. "And fifteen million is enough to win. If used correctly."

"She's right," Orin Gottlieb says. Then he smirks and adds, "About this, that is. Still hasn't got a clue about free markets, though."

They lock eyes and Justine forces a tight smile.

"Seriously," Gottlieb continues. "She won Denver with ten percent of the war chest of her opponents. I respect achievement, even in someone...well. I respect achievement."

"He's right." Despite the insult, Hall's voice is steady. "About my campaign anyway. But the entire point of this campaign is that money isn't the point. The Ameritocracy candidate will have a platform like no third party or independent since John Anderson, and that kind of exposure and attention can change a lot of minds."

"Nobody since Ross Perot, you mean," I hear Futch mutter.

"Getting attention is about more than money," Destiny O'Neill chimes in. "It's about sex. It's about controversy. I can get ten times the free media of any Democrat or Republican. TV stations will cover my speeches like the Super Bowl."

The conversation is getting away from me. "I'd like to think it's about more than sex, but I agree that the celebrity Ameritocracy will create for the winning candidate will be worth millions in free ad time."

Thomas Morton has been standing silently in the corner the whole time. He meets my eye and, though I open my mouth to speak, he beats me to it. "What happens if you don't like the winning candidate?"

I'm taken aback. "I, I—"

"Can you ensure," he continues, "that you'll keep the playing field level all the way through?"

The balls on this guy. I consider outing him in front of everyone, kicking him out of the room and handing his spot to Maria Ortiz Morales. Instead, I lock eyes with him and say, "Absolutely."

"I've been wondering that as well," Cecilia Mason says. "We're putting a lot of faith in you."

"I was gonna ask the same thing," Futch says. "Though even I was gonna put it a little nicer than that. What happens if you don't like the winner?"

His tone isn't accusatory, but his words are.

"I was actually going to ask that as well," Dixon asks.

It takes everything I have not to glare at Morton. "If you're playing by the rules, the winner will be the winner."

"But you could easily find a technicality to knock us out of the contest," Futch says. "Look, I know you don't agree with my views, little lady, but I have every right to—"

Morales whips around to face him—*very* quickly for a middle-aged woman with a prosthetic leg—and I wouldn't want to face down the look she's got in her eye. "That's the last time you're going to call her 'little lady.' Got it?"

Futch flashes a broad grin, happy to elicit a reaction from Morales.

"And while you're shutting up," Morales says, "quit with your conspiracy theorizing. You're not going to get eliminated just because Mia, like any sane person, abhors you."

"Just wondering." Futch holds up both hands as if to plead his innocence.

"Okay," I say, "let me put this to bed once and for all. My staff and I are one hundred percent committed to neutrality. It's *why* we created the platform to begin with."

"So we have your word," Cecilia Mason asks. "The winner will be the winner, no matter who it is?"

"Yes!" I say it as strongly as I can, though I'm a bit annoyed that this is even a question. I take a glass of water from the buffet table, drink half, then set it on the table. "Here's the deal. The competition is on the level, one hundred percent. If anyone doesn't like the terms and conditions, there's the exit." I stab my finger toward the door and look around the room. No one moves. "Okay, then, so how about we focus on the event?"

"No need to kick us out of the room," Futch laughs. "We were just asking."

As he says it, the tension in the room drops. Abrasive though he might be, the guy can land a comedy beat, and he knows how to be disarming.

For weeks, I've worried about the reactions the media and our voters will have to the Thomas Morton news, but now, even though we're moving on, I'm just as worried about the reactions of the people in front of me.

[20]

When my meeting with the candidates ends, I send them off to work on their opening statements and grab my phone, hoping for a text from Steph. And there it is.

Steph: *On the noon flight into LAX. Bringing Ben. We've got it. You know what to do.*

I do a little happy dance around the room before replying.

Me: *I'll start leaking it. Post-it?*

Steph: *Malcolm picked him up this morning.*

Me: *Good.*

Steph: *Peter is on the plane.*

Me: *What plane?*

Steph: *This plane. Now. I'm looking at his designer shoes poking out from his seat in first class. I'm twenty rows back in economy.*

Me: *Did you talk to him?*

Steph: *No.*

Me: *Why's he on the plane?*

Steph: *Hold on lemme use my psychic powers, oh wait...*

Me: *Sorry. So you'll be here when?*

Steph: *5ish.*

It's time to kick Morton out of the competition, and my next move is to arrange a room for the press conference, which is easy enough because we have rooms reserved for events starting tomorrow.

I book a room for six p.m. and move to phase two, finalizing the rollout of the story. I update the press release and send it to one of our interns back at the office with detailed instructions about how and when to release it, with a reminder to say nothing to anyone before then. For a week I've been living in terror that an intern will brag on social media about how they've got super-special inside info, but so far it hasn't happened.

The plan is to release the statement at five minutes to six on our website and forums. We'll also email it to our mailing list and plaster it across social media. We want our fans to hear our version of events before anyone else's.

One of the golden rules of PR is to control the story as long as possible, and for me that means getting as many reporters and TV stations to the announcement as I can. That's phase three of my plan. If the news networks cover the announcement live, people's first knowledge of the scandal will come from my mouth—and with *my* spin. By beating the press to the negative story, we'll limit their ability to shade it in ways that make us look bad. In this case, I want to limit the number of "See, I told you Ameritocracy wouldn't work" stories. Of course, all sorts of bad pieces can and will be written, but it's the best we can do.

For the next three hours, I pace the suite, texting journalists, calling secretaries at newspapers and TV stations to beg for phone numbers, and giving quotes to a few blogs I hope will get pieces up soon. I tell them I have a major announcement about Ameritocracy, one that will shake up the race and bring a new candidate into the top ten.

But I'm not telling them everything.

After exhausting every journalistic avenue I can, I flop onto the couch and call Bird at *The Barker*. I tell myself that it's to ask whether he has any reporters in L.A. he can send to the press conference, but I already know he doesn't. I think I just need to hear a friendly voice.

I stretch out on the couch as the phone rings and, as I'm about to hang up, I hear a voice, but not the one I expect. "Calling to ask for your job back?"

It's Alex Vane, my old boss.

"I, uhhh, I—"

"Just kidding, Mia. Bird is here, in my office. You're on speak-erphone."

"Hi, Mia!" Bird says. "We hear you're in L.A. for your first big rally."

"Sorry we're not sending a reporter," Alex says, "we're just gonna piggyback on everyone else's reporting and chime in with some postgame analysis."

"How's it going down there, anyway?" Bird asks.

"Fine," I say.

I don't know what to say next because it's just so good to hear their voices. The last time I spoke with them, I felt small—worried I'd disappoint them, worried about leaving them in the lurch, and afraid they'd be mad at me for quitting. More than that, I was afraid I'd fail.

Now I'm afraid again. Turns out that's the real reason I called. "Alex," I say. "Remember when you gave that press conference?"

"I've given a hundred of them."

"The one after *The Barker* got sued for libel?"

"Which time?"

"You got sued more than once?"

"Half dozen times at least," he says, "but some of them might have been before you were here. What are you getting at?"

I press my feet into the arm of the couch. "I'm about to kick a candidate out of the competition and I'm scared as hell."

"Who? Why?" Bird asks.

I pull the phone away from my face when my screen lights up with a new text.

Steph: *B there in 10. Meet in lobby?*

Me: *K.*

"Mia, you there?" Bird asks. "What's going on?"

"Sorry," I say. "I have to go. But Alex, in one paragraph or less, give me the best advice, the best pep talk you can about breaking bad news to the public with a dozen TV cameras aimed at your face."

When he was a beat reporter, Alex was known for being able to compose whole news stories off the top of his head, often while standing at a payphone in New York City or, later, in the back of a taxi on his cellphone. And even though he hasn't been a real reporter in years, he still has the gift of being able to summarize things in a way I find comforting.

"What's going on?" He sounds concerned.

"I'd tell you, but I really do have to go. Turn on the TV in about an hour and you'll find out. Not sure which news networks will be covering it live. I doubt CNN will but I know the video will be tweeted out in a million directions. Alex, please, I need some reassurance here. Best advice."

"Okay, lemme think. Quick question. You say you're gonna announce something bad. Is it catastrophic, Ameritocracy-ending bad, or just bad?"

"Just bad. I hope."

"Alright, pep talk program loading and...go." He pauses for a moment. I know from experience that he enjoys the moment right before he gets to answer a big question. He gets a little smirk on his face, half arrogance, half pleasure at the sheer act of communication. As full of himself as he can sometimes be, he genuinely enjoys helping people.

"People want to believe in Ameritocracy," he begins. "They want to believe in you. And, to a great extent, they already do. I come from the school of journalists who don't admit they vote, who try to remain neutral. And you know I've never been a political guy. But you've inspired me, you've forced me to take action. You've changed me. And I'm one of millions of Americans who feel this way. Tomorrow morning—no matter the fallout from this announcement—you can announce that Alex Vane is donating a million dollars cash to Ameritocracy, and that four other media executives will be joining him with a million each. I'll convince them tonight. If bad stories are weighing down the news cycle, change the subject with the announcement of another five million dollars in donations. Announce that we believe in Ameritocracy. We believe in Mia Rhodes."

He pauses, and I'm speechless. Alex has the clout to convince four others to donate a million each, but I had no idea until this moment that he had any intention of doing so. In fact, I'm not sure if *he* knew he had any intention of doing so. Alex is the kind of guy who could have decided to donate a million bucks halfway through his speech just because it sounded good.

But I know once it's been said, it will be done. "Thanks, Alex."

"And if that doesn't work," he adds, "spin the living hell out of the story. People love Ameritocracy, and they'll forgive an honest mistake. They trust you more than they trust the press, so be tough and don't let reporters give you any crap."

"I have to go," I say. "But thank you."

"Go get 'em, Mia," Bird says.

"Oh, and...guys. Have some political analysts *and* some tech analysts ready to write about this. And if you have anyone who knows Eastern Europe, wake them up." Offering them a head start on the story is the least I can do.

"You got this," Alex adds, and, for the first time, I think he's right.

~

An hour later, I stand behind a small podium in a corner of the conference room. A large banner behind me reads: *Ameritocracy: Democracy Reborn.*

We held a slogan contest on social media in October. The winner received a round trip vacation for two to Washington D.C. to watch our final debate. We got over a thousand submissions and only settled on our choice after a week of debate. Among our finalists were:

Ameritocracy: By the People—For the People

Ameritocracy: The Best Thing to Happen to Democracy Since 1787

Ameritocracy: Democracy Upgraded

Ameritocracy: Power Back to the People

Steph preferred *The Best Thing to Happen to Democracy Since 1787*, but I convinced her that too few people know that the Constitution was ratified in 1787.

About a dozen reporters sit patiently before me, notebooks and recorders out. Behind the reporters, three local TV crews are set up, cameras trained on me. Behind the TV crews, Steph and Benjamin are watching.

Steph holds a stack of blue folders that contain detailed information about how the hack went down, how we fixed it, and what steps we've taken to ensure it never happens again.

Moments ago, Benjamin texted final notice to Brianna, our white-hat hacker back at the office. When I begin speaking, she'll initiate the set of actions she and Benjamin set up to eliminate Thomas Morton from the competition. At the same time, Steph will hit send on the emails she composed on the flight to L.A. One to Thomas Morton, informing him of his expulsion, one to the FBI, and one to each of the other top ten candidates.

Now, the presentation falls to me.

"Welcome," I begin, "and thanks for coming. I'll read a brief statement, then take questions."

I expect hands to shoot up all over the room and reporters to start shouting questions, but as much as I'd like to be as tall and glamorous as CJ Cregg, this isn't an episode of *The West Wing*.

"A month ago, members of our staff detected abnormal voting behavior on the Ameritocracy2020.org website. We investigated immediately, and brought in a team of cyber security experts to assist us. Over the last four weeks, we have determined definitively that hackers in Ukraine and Cyprus have attempted to manipulate our voting system by creating fake users and controlling their profiles from computers located within those two countries."

A camera clicks. I scan the room, clearing my throat, wondering who still uses an old-fashioned camera with a shutter.

"Using what's known as a botnet, controlled via servers located on multiple Indian reservations within the United States, these foreign actors propelled one candidate to the top spot in our competition. That candidate is Thomas Morton."

"As of five minutes ago, Mr. Morton has been stripped of all votes and eliminated from the competition. Mr. Morton, and his backers in the Ukraine, have been defeated." A hand shoots up in the front row, but I ignore it. The last two lines were designed as the sound bite we want news stations to run with. If I'm reading the room right, it got a strong response.

"Through extensive data analysis and cyber forensics," I continue, "we have determined that Mr. Morton *knew* of the efforts to manipulate our voting system. We have provided the FBI with all the technical details of the hack, and are making those available to you as well. Ms. Blackmon will hand that out."

I gesture to Steph, who begins walking from reporter to reporter, giving each a ninety-page packet that contains more proof than most news organizations will ever need.

"We have also uncovered evidence that Mr. Morton violated the financial terms of Ameritocracy, terms he agreed to when he registered. These violations include accepting money from members of the Ukrainian oligarchy in order to pay for travel that supported his campaign, and providing false financial documents to Ameritocracy. Evidence of these violations can also be found in the packets."

I scan the room again, planning who I'll call on first. "There are just three other things I'd like to add. First, this was a single candidate. Our team has been working around the clock. We've found no evidence that any other candidates were affected, other than losing potential votes and ranking.

"Second, though we will issue statements if and when we find out more information about a possible motive, we expect the FBI will be looking into this for some time. At this point, our best guess is that members of the Ukrainian oligarchy got wind of Ameritocracy and when they saw it was viable, funded Mr. Morton and created the fake votes in his favor as a way to get a toehold in the American political system."

More hands shoot up, but I'm determined to get through this. "And third, I'd like to personally apologize to any genuine Thomas Morton voters out there. It's not your fault he engaged in this fraud. We hope you will study the remaining candidates and find someone else to support. Finally, I'd like to announce that all plans for the first Ameritocracy rally will go forward—*as planned*—tomorrow. Maria Ortiz Morales, who until moments ago was our eleventh-ranked candidate, will take the place of Thomas Morton. With that, I'll take some questions."

Hands shoot up, and I point at an older gentleman who covers politics for the *San Francisco Chronicle*. "Why is the FBI involved?" he asks. "Given that Ameritocracy isn't an official or sanctioned U.S. election."

"I should be clear: the FBI has only recently been informed, but hacking is still hacking. The FBI investigates hacking efforts that originate on foreign soil."

He shakes his head at my answer, but I'm moving on. "Moira," I say, pointing at a young woman from an alternative L.A. weekly who's called me for quotes at least a dozen times.

"Over the last few months, Ameritocracy has grown in popularity at an amazing rate. But in light of this admission that your system was massively compromised, how can voters be sure that the system is fair, that the votes are on the level?"

I stop myself from wincing. I just know she already has the phrase "massively compromised" written down in her notebook, that I'll be reading it a lot in the near future. "In the packets we handed out, you'll find complete bios of our cyber security team, including Benjamin Singh and Brianna Layton. Their expertise speaks for itself. And despite this intrusion, we're confident the voting is now one hundred percent secure. In fact, *because* of this nasty little scheme, we've tightened security. Our voting system is now more secure than most state governments."

She looks skeptical, and I do my best to channel the confidence of Alex Vane. "In less than a month, they thwarted one of the most sophisticated hacking attempts that's ever taken place. They've done something governments have failed to do in the past. Read the information. Study it before you report. Our voting is now completely secure, and we'll put the expertise of our team up against anyone on earth."

I say the last few lines with an air of finality and look around the room. I'm learning that, when you have a room—when you really have them—you can feel it. And I can tell that I have at least half of them.

The easy story, the story most of the reporters in the room wanted to write at the beginning, was: *Ameritocracy was hacked. It's technologically vulnerable, and the whole idea can't work.* But I think I convinced many of them to write a different story.

By now they all know the story has broken online, that it's being discussed on Twitter at the speed of light. Instead of writing a *dumb website can't work* story, some will have to start learning about the Ukrainian oligarchy so they can write about that.

I take questions for another hour until the air has left the room. I've done all I can. The only thing left to do is wait to see how the public, and our candidates, react.

[21]

Since the press conference ended, Steph and I have conducted an all-out media offensive. Answering calls, texts, and emails, replying to Tweets and blog posts, and directing our staff and interns to spin the living hell out of the story.

It's working.

Since it's Saturday, the national network news isn't airing, but all the cable channels have covered the press conference, showing snippets and, to my immeasurable delight, using the soundbite I provided during the Q and A. One of the reasons we took so long to announce the hack was to put together overwhelming evidence, partially because we wanted to be certain, but also to help our coverage.

We knew the hack would get tons of coverage, but also that none of the news networks, and very few TV organizations, would understand the technical details. But we counted on them, as journalists, to hesitate lest they get the details wrong. We placed them in the position of having to take our word for it, of parroting the conclusion we drew—that Ameritocracy is now secure. *We* know that conclusion is correct, but the trick was getting *them* to say it.

We're getting our share of bad coverage, too. At least fifty blog pieces have gone up with headlines like, "Ameritocracy Falters" and "Site That Hacked Democracy, Hacked." Most mention in the first paragraph that the problem has been solved and many even use my phrase: "more secure than most state governments." If it gets them talking about the security of the voting system, so much the better.

A couple articles even present the hack as proof Ameritocracy has passed its first major test. That's even better spin than we came up with.

Debates rage on our message boards, on Twitter, and pretty much everywhere else people have opinions about public events. And though it's too early to tell for sure, it looks like most people are siding with us.

Legitimate Morton voters are pissed, others feel cheated. But there aren't many of them, which starkly illustrates the entire problem. He didn't have many real voters. Steph handled one of the messiest tasks while I was on the podium: fielding a call from Thomas Morton himself.

All in all, Steph, Benjamin and I are in good spirits when we stagger into the hotel restaurant for a late dinner, determined to take a break from the news and eat a meal in a civilized fashion.

"Tell me again what Morton said," I say after we order.

Our drinks arrive. White wine for me, red for Steph and Benjamin, who are splitting a bottle of an Oregon pinot noir, despite Benjamin's initial attempt to order a Bud Light.

Steph has already told me the story twice, but it's a celebration and there's nothing better than tales of foes vanquished and victories secured.

She cracks a wide smile. "I answered the phone knowing it was him, but I didn't let on. Then he's like, 'Is this Stephanie

Blackmon?' And I'm like, 'It is.'" She takes a long sip of her wine, then continues, doing her best to impersonate Morton's dry, monotone speaking style. "Then he says, 'This is Thomas Morton, former candidate on Ameritocracy2020.org. I am calling to acknowledge receipt of your email, and to inform you that, though I had no knowledge of any attempts on anyone's part to cast false votes, I accept that I have been eliminated from your political competition.'"

"Why do you think he said that?" I ask. "I mean, why do you think he took it lying down?"

"Dude doesn't seem like much of a fighter, does he?" Benjamin asks.

"No," I say, "but I guess I expected him to...I don't know, at least seem a little mad."

"From what we gathered," Benjamin says, "he is basically owned outright by three Ukrainian bankers. It's possible he was being blackmailed. He—"

"Yeah," Steph interjects, "we doubt he even wanted to be in this thing in the first place. I'm half-surprised he didn't say 'Thanks for getting me out of this in a way that's not my fault.'"

"There's a good chance they knew we were on to them over the last few days," Benjamin says. "So they may have prepped for it."

"How would they have known?" I ask.

"When Brianna set up the code to delete all the fake accounts, she triggered a script that may have informed them."

"Tell me again how the call ended?" I ask Steph.

"So, after he says he accepts his elimination, he gets to the point of the call. Sounds like he's pleading with me, like a little boy, and for the first time he sounds like a person. Says, 'Ms. Blackmon, *please* don't drag my name, or my family's name, through the mud any more than you must. I, I never wanted it to end up like this.' His voice cracked and, if I thought he was capable of human tears, I'd have thought he was crying."

~

When we finish dinner, the restaurant is nearly empty. It's almost midnight, and only a few stragglers remain at the bar, watching ESPN or Saturday Night Live on one of the flatscreens mounted above rows of colorful liquor bottles.

Benjamin and Steph stand at the same time, exchanging a look I know means something I don't want to think about. "We're tired," Steph says.

"Yeah, gotta hit the sack," Benjamin adds.

"Right," I say. "Is that what the kids are calling it these days?"

Steph swigs the last of her wine. "See you in the morning. We're meeting at six sharp, right?"

"In my suite."

"You wanna ride the elevator up with us? We're not on the top floor like fancy old you, but, y'know."

"Nah, I'll finish my wine."

I try to banish any thoughts of the two of them "hitting the sack" by staring up at the TV. All the channels are on commercial, so I glance around the bar, letting my eyes go soft, enjoying the quiet. I'm beyond tired, having made it through the evening on coffee and adrenaline.

"I was wondering when they'd leave." It's a voice from the direction of the bar.

Peter's voice.

I shake my head, forcing my eyes back into focus, but at first I don't see him. After a confused moment, he emerges from behind a pillar at the corner of the bar, not more than ten feet from me.

"How long have you been there?" I ask, standing.

"Half an hour. Not that I don't like Steph or Benjamin, but there's something I wanted to share just with you. And the timing is perfect." He pulls out a barstool. "Have a drink with me?"

"Okay." I sit next to him. "But what did you want to share with me?"

"Should be happening soon."

I look around the bar, which is dark and nearly deserted. The lobby of the hotel, which I can see far down a hallway, is sparsely staffed and quiet.

He nods up to the TV over the bar. It's on a commercial for cat food.

"What?" I ask, confused. I can't tell if I'm missing something obvious because I'm tired, or if he's being obscure on purpose.

"Remember DB?"

I want to say, "No, I forgot the *movie star* you brought into my bedroom." Instead I say, "Yeah."

"He's on SNL tonight and, unless he's messing with me, so are you."

Peter gets the attention of the bartender and asks him to change the channel on the TV in front of us. And just like that, there's David Benson, handsome as ever, introducing the musical act.

"Are you serious?" I ask.

"I don't know the details, but yeah."

"When?"

"Toward the end."

"Which is—"

"Show ends in fifteen minutes so..."

"Are you *serious*? What are they gonna—"

"I don't know. I really don't. He texted me a couple hours ago and said when he got there to rehearse, they had a sketch about Ameritocracy."

"Prove it!" I demand, but he's already scrolling through his phone.

He's not lying. The text from DB says there's an Ameritocracy sketch that might get cut but might air at the end of the show.

A waiter clears the table we ate at, and I head back to it and grab my glass of wine before he takes it.

"What do you think they'll say?" I ask, sitting back at the bar.

"You know it doesn't matter, right?"

"It's just that—"

"Mia. You know it *doesn't matter,* right?"

His repetition of the phrase makes me stop and look at him. He's got that same all-knowing smile on his face but, for the first time, I don't wonder what it means. "You're saying that the simple fact that they're doing a sketch means we made it?"

"More than that." He takes a long sip from a champagne flute, filled with his signature Red Bull. "It means *you* made it. You absolutely killed it at the press conference today. I don't think you know how big this is going to get. How big it's already gotten. I know you don't think you belong in this world, but you do."

"I *do* have a suite on the top floor," I say.

"Actually, *I* have the one on the top floor."

"What?"

"There's a suite they don't rent out to the public. I'm in it."

Of course he is. "Okay, well, fine."

Just then, I hear applause and hooting from the TV speakers. I glance up at the screen, where a cast member walks out in a blue-and-white checked dress. I know it's supposed to be me because she's wearing a red wig that looks like a neon version of my hair. Plus, she's carrying a basket with a laptop in it. The dress and basket suggest we're in for a *Wizard of Oz* spoof.

"I'm searching for my long-lost father!" says Fake-Mia. "Or

democracy! Y'know, whichever. And I know I'll find it with better technology. After all, I'm in color now instead of black-and-white! I have to do something new, something different. Something...millennial. That's it! I'll elect the President of the Internet!"

I should be freaking out right now, but I'm not. The mainstay of weekend comedy just opened with a joke about my father, and based on everything I know about myself, I should want to hole up in bed for a week. Instead. I feel like they can't touch me.

Up until now, whenever I felt exposed I borrowed the confidence of others—often Steph's, sometimes Alex's. I mimicked their self-assurance, wore it like a costume.

Now I feel naked. But naked in a way that brings power, like there's nothing left to lose, and I'm just me.

On the screen, parody versions of Tanner Futch, Marlon Dixon, and Destiny O'Neill compete for Fake-Mia's attention as she explains that, as President of the Internet, they will be responsible for moderating Facebook comments, reading all of Twitter, and appointing the Secretary of Cat Videos.

"Sadly," Fake-Mia says, "I fear that America won't elect *any* of you president."

"Why?" all three candidates ask at once.

"Because you, Destiny O'Neill, have no brain, you, Tanner Futch, have no heart, and you, Marlon Dixon..." Fake-Mia trails off awkwardly.

Fake-Dixon shrugs in resignation. "I know, it's the black thing."

Next, David Benson enters the picture and he's playing Peter Colton as The Wizard of Silicon Valley. His hair is dyed black and he's wearing Peter's trademark black suit and carrying an oversized novelty check for five million dollars.

"What the?" the real Peter says.

"He didn't tell you he was playing you?"

"Nope. I don't walk like that, do I?"

"Shhh, I want to hear this." I put a hand on his arm to shush him, then leave it there.

Onscreen, Fake-Peter is cackling, "I'm the Wizard. I own everything around here!"

"You mean the internet?" Fake-Mia asks in dismay.

"Well, fifty-one percent of it."

He goes on to say that he has just what these poor candidates need: advertising! He hangs large cardboard ads around the three candidates' necks. Fake-Dixon's ad reads MALE ENHANCEMENT DISCOUNT PRICES, and he objects that women might not respond well to that message.

Fake-Peter points to Fake-Mia and says, "Watch this," then flips the sign. The other side reads CLICK HERE FOR INSTANT WEIGHT LOSS.

Fake-Mia reads the sign and taps it like she's clicking an online ad. "You really are a wizard!" she shouts. "But can you help me find my long-lost...uh, democracy?"

Fake-Peter smiles devilishly. "Don't you see? You've had the power of democracy all along!"

"You mean...democracy is inside me?"

"Why sure! It's inside all of us! All you have to do is click your mouse three times and say, 'I agree to all terms and conditions.'"

I smile and ask the bartender to turn the sound off.

Peter looks surprised. "Don't you want to see how it ends?"

"I don't need to," I shrug, and it's true.

I was just parodied on Saturday Night Live, and it doesn't bother me a bit. I consider that for a moment, doing my best to let it sink in.

Peter turns, and I take his hand. "That smile, the one you always do. I think I understand it now." I squeeze his hand, sliding my other hand onto his knee. "It's a smile that comes when you've done something. Created something no one can take away from you. When it doesn't matter what anyone says about you because you know you're doing what you're meant to do."

He squeezes my hand and gives me what I can only describe as a hungry look. "That's true," he says. "And you know what? You're smiling that way right now."

I lean forward and kiss him, much more gracefully than I did in the car in front of his mansion. "You said you're on the top floor, right?"

"Yeah, you need a special elevator key to get up there."

"So, what are we waiting for?"

Hours later, I wake and study the stars through the skylight over the king-sized bed. Peter has rolled over with the blanket tucked under him, leaving my legs and feet exposed and cool.

The sex was good, better than expected. I guess I assumed that a handsome billionaire wouldn't make an effort in bed. I was wrong. From the way he took off my heels, to the way he kissed my neck, to the way he made sure I was satisfied multiple times, he was an attentive lover.

I've only had three serious boyfriends, and with each of them I got the feeling they wanted me to be something in bed that I wasn't. Maybe it was them, or maybe I imagined it, but I always felt like I came up short. Like I couldn't be something they needed—or wanted—me to be. But at the same time, they weren't what *I* wanted, weren't what *I* needed.

With Peter I felt fully myself, strong and in command, despite the fact that the whole situation still felt unreal.

I think to grab my phone to see how the press conference is

being covered by the morning papers, which have probably already added their front page stories to their websites.

But, just like at the bar, I feel somehow above it. Like I've moved to a place beyond the day-to-day twists and turns of press coverage, that I've moved beyond crisis mode. Not that there won't be crises anymore, but I've come to a place where I can step back and see the forest, rather than stumble from tree to tree.

I press my cold feet into Peter's warm calves, which are muscular but relaxed. He stirs, but doesn't wake. Even more than the sex, I take this as a good sign for our relationship.

As I doze off, I imagine taking the stage, flanked by my top-ten candidates, and I feel no a trace of anxiety.

I wake to a series of phone chirps and a harsh light pouring through a crack in the curtains. I roll over slowly, and then it hits me. Yes, I slept with Peter Colton last night, and I'm still in his bed. But Peter is gone.

I sit up and grab my phone as it chirps again.

Steph: *Destiny O'Neill quit. Where are you?*

I have another dozen texts and six missed calls. It's already seven in the morning. A lot has happened overnight.

I throw on my clothes and tap a reply to Steph.

Me: *Meet me in my suite in five.*

Steph: *Already here. Been banging on the door.*

Me: *Be right there.*

Exiting the bedroom, I see Peter, dressed in pajamas and a black silk robe, drinking orange juice on the balcony. He walks inside when he sees me. "Morning, sleepy head." He leans in and kisses me on the cheek. "Big night."

"You heard about Destiny O'Neill?"

His face pinches and I fear I may have hurt his pride. "No. What? I mean us."

"Oh, you mean Saturday Night Live?"

"That too, but no, I mean *us*."

I give his hand a firm squeeze, pull him in and kiss him hard. "I gotta go. There's a Destiny O'Neill thing. But, yeah. *Us* was real nice."

～

Steph is on her cell phone, waiting at the door to my suite, but glances up just long enough to frown at me.

"Goodbye," she says into the phone as I make it to the door.

"Who was that?" I ask.

"Who was *that*? Where *were* you?"

"Peter's room."

"You didn't."

"I did."

Steph follows me into the living room and hands me a cup of coffee as I sit on the couch. "You look like you need this more than I do."

I take a swig. "I do. Thank you."

"We have a situation, but I've been handling it. First, you gotta tell all. How was it?"

"C'mon," I say, "tell me what happened with Destiny O'Neill."

"It's not every day you get some with a billionaire who looks like the model in a Rolex ad. Give me the ten-second version or I'm not telling you what happened."

"You know I can just check my email, right?"

She raises an imploring eyebrow.

"Fine. It was amazing. We watched the SNL sketch together. Turns out he was at the bar while we ate with Benjamin. I felt, I don't know how to put it, strong and vulnerable at the same time."

"The sex, Mia. How was the sex?"

"Remember my last boyfriend, Aaron?"

"That was like a year ago, but yeah."

"With him it often felt like he wasn't really there with *me*, like I could have been any woman."

"Like he was using you for sex? Oh, heavens! When has a man ever done that?"

"Not exactly that, but like he just had no idea who I was, what I needed."

"And?"

"Let's just say that Peter does not share Aaron's limitations."

"Ooooh, damn! I *knew* it."

"You promised to tell me what happened with Destiny."

"Fine, fine. Here." Steph hands me her phone, which is open to an email from a company called American Made Television Productions. "Read it."

It's a press release, dated today, issued on AMTVP letterhead.

For immediate release

Hollywood, CA

One of America's most popular and engaging personalities will be digging into the issues facing real Americans in the new AMTVP production, American Destiny, *a ten-episode reality series slated to begin filming on February 1st, 2020.*

Meet Destiny O'Neill: an idealistic, sensual Internet sensation who wants to open up the country to new possibilities. A staunch Second Amendment supporter, Ms. O'Neill is as serious as she is sexy, and her new show will send her across the country to talk to real Americans and engage in a series of wild awareness-raising stunts that will change the way people talk about the issues that matter.

AMTVP CEO Michelle Brierson is excited about the partnership. "Destiny O'Neill has been known to Americans for years for her inimitable voice on important social and political issues through her Instagram account, and her YouTube channel. Lately, she's become widely recognized as one of the top candidates on the reality political competi-

tion, Ameritocracy. American Destiny *will mark her first foray into television, and AMTVP couldn't be happier with the partnership."*

Filming of the first season is expected to last two months, and discussions are already underway for distribution with a range of cable stations.

The rest of the press release is a long bio of Destiny O'Neill and a shorter history of AMTVP and their many accomplishments, including their top-rated show, *Death Pickers*, a reality show about a team of Americans who traveled to Indonesia in search of the rarest flower on earth, the Corpse Flower. The team didn't find the flower, but one cast member nearly died from a violent strain of the flu and two others hooked up in the mud during a monsoon, so the show was a hit.

I hand the phone back to Steph. "She parlayed Ameritocracy into her own show?"

"Yup. She deleted her account on the site around five a.m., while you were on your booty call."

"So were you," I say, half-panicked that we're a candidate short, but half thrilled to see Destiny O'Neill out of the competition. "Wait, she didn't even let us know?"

"Maybe she emailed you, but she didn't email me or call the office."

"So after we quadrupled her fame, she let us know she was dropping out by having her production company email a press release. Classy."

"You're surprised?"

"I'm pissed." I walk a lap around the couch, fuming. "You know they're announcing it now to capitalize on the PR of the rally. She's trying to steal our thunder."

"Exactly. She's doing a live event at a shooting range at one o'clock today."

"The exact time the rally starts."

"Gotta hand it to her. She's smart. As much as I hate what she stands for, I'm not even mad at her. She's getting hers."

"I'm mad enough for both of us," I say. "We're gonna look like fools with nine candidates up there. Not only did she plan this to steal our media coverage, she did it late on purpose so we couldn't replace her."

"Already taken care of that."

"What's the plan? Maria Ortiz Morales was our backup for Morton. We don't have another backup in town."

"Not yet, but we have one on a plane right now."

"Who?"

A wry smile crosses Steph's face. "Your favorite."

"Axum?"

Steph nods. "Reached him in D.C. this morning. He said I just barely caught him on his way out the door. He's on a plane right now. Robert Mast is already in town for a speech at UCLA, but he said he could make it here with two hours' notice."

I look at the clock on my phone. It's eight a.m., five hours before the rally starts. "Will Axum be here on time?"

"Kinda depends on L.A. traffic, but I think so."

I walk a couple quick laps around the couch, glancing out the window at the hazy Los Angeles skyline. My mind goes in ten directions at once, and I eliminate them one by one, trying to focus in on what needs to be done for the rally.

Then something occurs to me. "Wait, you called Mast, too?"

"Technically he's twelfth, but I wanted a backup in case Axum gets delayed or something. Plus, c'mon, he'll be in the top ten soon. We both know that."

"Well, maybe," I say, "but right now he's twelfth, and I don't want him to think he can cut in line just because he bought some TV ads. I still can't believe he did that, but I guess it doesn't matter. We're getting Axum. Should I ask what the fallout from the Morton announcement was overnight? Have you read much of the coverage?"

"I read all the coverage I could get my hands on last night, and all the big papers ran pieces this morning."

"Give me the summary."

Steph taps her phone, then stands and hands it to me. "This WaPo piece kind of sums up the sentiment that's out there."

I glance down at the article, which is actually a *Washington Post* editorial. I look up at Steph, who's smiling. "Our first major Op-Ed?"

"Yup, and it's not half bad."

Ameritocracy Clears a Hurdle, But Does it Matter?

By Rachel Abramowitz

While conventional wisdom has dismissed it as an irrelevant fly around the tail of American politics, Ameritocracy may have just become a bee.

The online political competition that started over three years ago, but only began gaining traction after a $5 million donation from billionaire Peter Colton four months ago, announced yesterday that its voting system had been hacked. Candidate Thomas Morton—former ambassador to the Ukraine and, for months, their leading candidate— was eliminated in a sudden announcement backed up by reams of data compiled by Ameritocracy's impressive team of techies.

Many in the press are writing of Ameritocracy's vulnerability today, some even pointing to hacking as the potentially fatal flaw for the site. And we agree, to an extent.

Even though America's national voting systems remain inconsistent and vulnerable, the fact that American elections are run locally actually makes them more difficult to hack. So Ameritocracy must do more—much more—to protect itself from future digital disruption.

The way it handled this attack was impressive. Overcoming a sophisticated hack is no easy task, and they proved up to it.

More than that, the founder of Ameritocracy, Mia Rhodes,

displayed the ideals she founded Ameritocracy on as she took questions for over an hour, exhausting the reporters in the room. She herself is modeling the ideals of transparency that Ameritocracy set out to bring to American politics, and for that she should be commended.

Only time will tell whether a viable candidate will emerge from what until recently was a hodge-podge of misfits and fringe thinkers. But, for today at least, Ameritocracy appears to have cleared its first major hurdle.

I finish reading and hand the phone back to Steph, who's grinning from ear to ear.

"Not bad, huh?" she says.

"Not bad," I agree.

[23]

The conference room is packed, and I wonder whether Avery Axum got lost at LAX. I turn to Dale, one of the three interns who took the flight down with Steph this morning. "You're *sure* his flight got in on time?"

"Sure." Dale's squeaky voice makes me feel old. He holds up his phone as if to indicate that he checked it.

"And we're sure he doesn't have a cell phone?"

"Yup, he's one of the seven people left in the country without one."

I'm starting to freak out a little. "Keep checking," I say, unsure of what I want him to check.

I walk to the side of the room and ascend the five steps to the stage, where my nine other candidates sit. Modeling our stage after the Democratic and Republican primary debates raging around the country, we decided to seat our two top candidates in the center, the rankings of the candidates dropping further from the center. Three podiums have been set up before the candidates, so no one has to walk far to reach to a microphone when it's their turn to speak.

With Thomas Morton eliminated, Marlon Dixon is now

number one, and he sits center-left, next to Tanner Futch, our number two candidate, who sits center-right.

To Dixon's left sit our candidates ranked third, fifth, seventh, and ninth: Cecilia Mason, Orin Gottlieb, Wendy Kahananui, and Maria Ortiz Morales. To Futch's right sit our candidates ranked fourth, sixth, and eighth: Justine Hall, Charles Blass, and Beverly Johnson. To Beverly Johnson's right, there's an empty chair intended for Avery Axum.

The room is just as I imagined it, and I smile at the row of possible donors in front of the stage. Behind them, bored-looking journalists chat amongst themselves or tap at their phones. Behind the journalists, one thousand voters and fans of the site fill the conference room.

I walk from candidate to candidate, asking if they need anything and telling them that we'll start in a few minutes. Most just smile and nod, either nervous or busy with notes for their opening statements.

Wendy Kahananui sits with her eyes closed, apparently deep in meditation, but she turns quickly as I step behind her, as though she sensed me. "Mia, there's something that didn't get said upstairs, that just came up in my meditation."

"A question?"

"Gratitude. I want to say 'thank you.' Regardless of who wins, you've done an amazing thing for us, and for the world. I usually can't see the future, but, regardless of whether one of us wins in 2020, I expect great things from you. You've already reminded the world there are ways to be involved in politics that aren't cynical and spiritually debilitating."

"Thank you." I glance at the clock. It's one on the dot. We can hold off for another couple minutes.

When I reach Marlon Dixon's seat, he looks up with his usual big-hearted smile. "No need to comfort me, Ms. Rhodes. I was born for this."

I smile back because I love his confidence, and I know he's right. Of the nine people on stage, Dixon is the one I expect to get the biggest bump from an event like this. Possibly Gottlieb or Futch as well, because they're both compelling speakers, though as far from Dixon politically as one can get.

Behind the TV crews, a few of the producers stare at their watches, anxious to get going. I'm anxious, too. A late start isn't a good way to get cable news to break into their programming to cover the rally.

A slow stream of late arrivals have been coming into the hall for the last few minutes, and I take one final glance at the door, thinking I better just get started. Then I feel a tap on my shoulder.

Behind me, Dale stands with Avery Axum. "He waited for a taxi," Dale says, shaking his head in utter bafflement. "No phone to order an Uber."

Axum wears tan slacks, a blue shirt, and a brown blazer. His hair is mussed and he looks confused, like he's not certain where he is.

"Welcome," I say.

"Thanks, and please accept my most sincere apologies for my tardiness. It's all just a little..."

I follow his eyes as he scans the crowd.

"Overwhelming?" I ask.

"I did not expect to end up here. My students practically forced me to join the competition, and two of them had to help me enter my information on the website. I—"

"I'd love to hear the story," I say, guiding him to his chair, "but we really need to get going."

Before I leave, Axum clasps my hands in his. "By the way, *thank you* for the invitation."

I smile at him, then make my way to the center podium and step onto a riser that was set up just for me. "Ladies and gentlemen, we're going to get started...Ladies and gentlemen...As you see, our tenth candidate just arrived and we're going to get started."

The chatter slowly quiets as I survey the hall.

A few rows from the front, dressed down and trying to look inconspicuous, is Peter. Next to him, dressed up and trying not to spring out of her seat and wave to me, is my mother. She's in her best dress, a poofy purple-and-black thing she got for a wedding a few years ago, and her graying hair is up and recently styled. She stands out a bit from the casually-dressed crowd around her, but I know that today is a very big deal for her.

In front of my mother is David Benson, who's wearing dark sunglasses, a Cubs hat pulled low, and a brown jacket with the collar pulled up around his cheeks. He must have flown in from New York as soon as SNL ended last night, and he's trying not to be recognized. I feel a shiver of some unnameable emotion go through me—the hottest movie star in the world is hiding his face because he'd rather people pay attention to my project than to him.

I lock eyes with Steph, who stands in the back of the room, then look at my notes. "Thank you all for coming. Ameritocracy began as an idea during the 2016 presidential election campaign. Like many of you, I was dismayed at the partisanship, the cynicism, the hypocrisy, and the negativity. Like many of you, I was dismayed at the failure of the media to cover issues, to provide a platform for substantive debate. But mostly, I watched the debates and asked myself, is this the best we can do?"

I make a sweeping gesture across the stage to my left, then my right. "I think you'll agree as you get to know our top candidates, the answer is a resounding 'No.' We can do much better."

It wasn't intended as an applause line, but claps rise from the back of the room and slowly catch on. Soon, the entire room, minus the journalists, is applauding. Some politely, some enthusiastically. Even though I realize the applause is for the candidates, the genuine gratitude of the audience moves me.

"I know you all want to get to know the candidates better, but first I want to encourage you to visit Ameritocracy2020.org. There you will find hundreds of other candidates, and it's not too late to register and vote. If you're inspired by the dedication and intelligence you see on stage this afternoon, if you're inspired by the idea that there must be a third option in the 2020 election, please consider donating."

I let the word "donating" hang in the air, then say, "And with that, let me introduce our moderator. Gwen Winters has been a political journalist in Washington D.C. for over twenty years, and currently hosts *D.C. Today*, which airs Sunday mornings at ten. She's also the author of *Campaign Season*, a rollicking memoir of her year covering the 2012 election."

I cast a look behind me, where Gwen has been waiting patiently. She's a stately woman with long blonde hair and a look that says, "I know more about this stuff than anyone in the room."

And she does. It's why Steph and I worked so hard to get her.

To the audience, I say, "Please welcome Gwen Winters."

The audience applauds as Gwen takes my place and subtly slides the riser out of her way. At almost six feet tall, she doesn't need it. I ease away, standing against the wall to the front left of the stage, near enough that I can head back up if a need arises, but also in a good position to see the whole room.

"Thank you, Ms. Rhodes, and welcome to everyone here this afternoon and watching around the world. Welcome to the first-ever Ameritocracy rally. Today, you'll have an opportunity to meet the candidates and to hear them respond to *your* questions. Though I'll be the one asking them, I have drawn from questions taken from the Ameritocracy Forum, from email submissions, and from the questions the audience submitted over the last hour. But I know you're not here to listen to me, so without further ado, let's meet the candidates. Each candidate will have three minutes to introduce himself or herself, and I ask that you hold your applause for the full thirty minutes it will take to hear from all ten of them."

Pointing toward the back of the conference room, she continues, "As a reminder to the candidates, the large clock on the wall will count down your time, flashing at thirty seconds with a warning to wrap it up. And, please keep in mind, there will be *no* interruptions when other candidates are speaking. For anyone who's watched recent primary debates, this *should* be a welcome change."

Soft laughter fills the hall as people recall the wild west shitshows that most mainstream political debates have become.

"The order for opening statements was determined by random drawing. Ms. Johnson, you're up first. You have three minutes."

Beverly Johnson, who's about my height, has to adjust a riser in front of her podium, and even then must tilt the microphone down. I feel her pain. "Thanks, Ms. Winters. And thank you all for being here today. I'm a little surprised to be here myself. I know a few folks have cracked jokes about me, saying that I'm running as a full-time mom, but tonight my husband's putting the kids to bed because I'm making a speech in Los Angeles. Oh, and since I know you're watching, hi, Leo, and hi, kids. Listen to your dad and be good for him."

That's a solid laugh line, and she lets it land.

"It still seems strange to me that I'm actually running for president, and sometimes I have my doubts. But every time I wonder why I'm doing this, I run into the same answer: I can't *not* run for president. Someone will be sworn in on January 20th, 2021, and I think it ought to be someone with some basic common sense. We've tried a lot of men without any, and I'm sorry, but it's just not working very well.

"The simplest political rule I know is a quote I read, I don't recall who it's by. 'Before you tear down a fence, find out why it was put up in the first place.' There are a lot of people whose high-minded ideals have them running around in all directions, tearing down fences left and right, tearing down laws and values and social contracts, and none of them seem to be checking out why those things were there in the first place.

"But you know who these big idealists always seem to forget? The ones who get left out of their grand schemes for remaking society? That's right, our children. *Our children.*

"Any parent will tell you their children are their highest priority, but politicians always seem to have something that's more important. I've worked and sacrificed for my children. I've baked I-don't-know-how-many brownies and cookies and tarts for bake sales to raise money for school activities, and you know what? *I'm tired of it!*

"There's always plenty of money when some weapons maker comes up with a new airplane the Air Force doesn't even want, isn't there? Tax giveaways for billionaires deducting yacht maintenance? No problem, just add it to the national debt! But when it's time to pay for schools, to pay for children's health care, to help parents spend more time with their children during the most precious and critical time of their lives? Then all of a sudden they can't afford it. Well you know what? There's a word for that, but it's not one I'll say on camera.

"If you believe, as I do, that our children are our future and our highest purpose, then this is your chance to put your money where your mouth is. We need a president who will put parents before politicians, and if no one else is going to, then I guess I'll have to be that president."

Some applause breaks out as she finishes, and Gwen Winters leans in close to her mic to get a volume bump as she says, "Please hold your applause until all the speakers have finished, or we won't have time for questions." When the applause drops, she continues. "Mr. Axum, you're next, and your time begins now."

Axum steps to the podium and clears his throat a little too loudly. "Is this thing on?"

A few chuckles and a few calls of "Yes!" come from the audience, and he smiles like the old man in a Werther's Original commercial. Despite being by far the least-prepared person on stage, he seems unflustered.

"Thank you. And thank you, Ms. Winters. I have a great deal of respect for your work. And thanks to Mia Rhodes, without whom none of us would be here."

The gaze of audience shifts to me, and, as they begin to applaud, Gwen Winters squashes it. "Again, to respect everyone's three minutes, please hold all applause until the end."

"Okay," Axum says, "but she *deserves* our thanks." After a long pause, he continues. "I didn't want to register for Ameritocracy. I didn't want to be president. I'm *still* not so sure about it. I've worked for three of them, and, let me tell you, it's not an enviable job. Long hours, excruciating decisions. Life or death decisions you think you want to make until you actually have to make them. I've seen the look in the eyes of three presidents, two Republicans and one Democrat. And I learned quickly that the look was the same."

He speaks slowly, each word chosen carefully, as you'd expect from a lawyer turned professor.

"The look was fear. And that's why I never ran for office. Despite teaching my students that public service is a great calling, and encouraging them to use the law to serve the greater good, I hid out in academia. And when my students told me about Ms. Rhodes's project, I dismissed it as an interesting idea that would likely go nowhere.

"Only after a month of haranguing by some of my more insistent students did I allow myself to be registered. Now, you can see my various positions and videos online, but there's only one point I want to make today, and it has to do with the idea of America itself.

"In 1787, as America debated the ratification of the U.S. Constitution, James Madison wrote a remarkable document, an essay we now call Federalist Number Ten. I'm *sure* you've all read it."

Mild laughter fills the room, and he gives it a moment.

"In it," he continues, "he argued against a two-party system. Continuing the work of Alexander Hamilton from Federalist Paper Nine, Madison defined faction as 'a number of citizens, whether amounting to a minority or majority of the whole, who are united and actuated by some common impulse of passion, or of interest, adverse to the rights of other citizens, or to the permanent and aggregate interests of the community.' Factions, he believed, were caused by inequality, largely economic inequality. If left to run amok, they could destroy the nation. The nation just then being born.

"Madison saw two ways to guard against faction. The first was to restrict liberty. This, of course was not desirable. The second was to force equality. To create a homogenous society, thereby eliminating divisive factions. This too was nonsensical because the government cannot be in the business of guaranteeing equal outcomes. 'The latent causes of faction are thus sown in the nature of man,' he wrote. *'Sown in the nature of man.'* The only option, as far as Madison was concerned, was to design a government to control the divisive *effects* of faction. That's how American democracy was born.

"For the last two hundred thirty-two years, America has

struggled to balance our desire for liberty and our desire for equality. Lately, the tension between these two desires has come close to tearing the country apart. Look around, watch your TV, or scroll through your phone, and you will likely agree with me.

"But it's not hopeless. We have political parties that are sometimes well-meaning, sometimes corrupt, but almost always mired in partisan politics. At their best, though, at their core, Republicans favor liberty over equality. And, at *their* best, at *their* core, Democrats favor equality over liberty. Neither side is inherently right, and our whole political system can be understood as a push and pull between these two poles."

He shifts his eyes to the clock, which is blinking red. "Personally, I lean toward liberty in most cases. And I see that I'm out of time, so I'll conclude by saying this: should I be chosen to represent Ameritocracy in the general election, the work of my campaign will be to pragmatically strike a balance between liberty and equality, the two fundamental yearnings of the American political spirit."

"Thank you, Professor Axum," Gwen says. "Third up—again by random drawing, is Tanner Futch."

Futch steps to the podium in full radio mode, exuding a deliberate manic energy. Unsurprisingly, his mic control is much better than Axum's. "Thanks, Gwen, and thanks, Professor, for that little history lesson. It sounded nice, but I, for one, don't have a damn idea what that means for real Americans.

"The fact is, real Americans used to have it pretty good. An honest guy could get an honest job and provide for his family. He didn't have to worry that he'd get mugged walking down the street. He didn't have to worry that the government was tapping his phone. He didn't have to worry about not being able to put food on his family's table. That stuff happened over in Russia, sure, but back then, you could still say with pride, 'I'm an American' and have it *mean* something!

"And now look around you. All those honest jobs are gone, shipped off to Mexico or China. All those honest families are broken up, eaten up inside by drugs and weakened morality. Today, all over the country, you've got honest hardworking Americans who no longer know how they're going to put food on the table, something that would have been unthinkable once. And they want to know why. They want to know how all that got taken away from them.

"Real Americans deserve to know why their jobs are being taken from them by immigration and automation, real Americans who have seen their once-united society torn apart by the radical leftists, radical feminists, radical Islam, and a global financial conspiracy to destroy this once-great nation."

He laughs to himself, and it's too well-rehearsed to look rehearsed. To Tanner Futch, this is a performance, and the red-faced exasperation is part of it. He pulls out a red bandana and wipes his brow. "Well, someone said I can't go a full minute without saying the C-word...no, not *that* C-word, I mean *conspiracy*...and according to that clock I just proved them wrong. I made it ninety seconds.

"They like to make fun of me for using that word. They call me crazy or paranoid, just like they call you ignorant or racist. But you know what? So be it.

"They called me a conspiracy theorist when I said the CIA runs most of the media, then I taught them about Operation Mockingbird. They called me a conspiracy theorist when I said that a cabal of international banking elites actually runs America and most of the world. But every day we uncover more about The Bilderberg Group and the World Economic Forums. Their attempts to murder American sovereignty and create a world government. They called me a conspiracy theorist when I said that four out of five mass shootings are false flags perpetrated by our own government to justify the dismantling of the

Second Amendment. And on our website right now—
TheTruthShouter.com—we've provided the proof. Las Vegas,
San Bernardino, all the way back to Sandy Hook."

His words come quickly, growing louder as he gains steam,
and when he pauses he practically gasps for air, the effect being
that either he's a raving madman or he's willing to use his last
breath to bring out the truth.

"Don't believe. Go look it the hell up, people! My motto is—"

"Mr. Futch, that's time." The clock blinks zeroes and Gwen
has interrupted him.

"I'm sorry, but no, you let the old man go on, and I—"

"Mr. Futch."

"My motto, for my campaign and for America itself is: *Don't
defend. Attack.* Attack the lies, shout the truth! Get your damn
country back! It's what I've fought to do to become the leading
voice in true conservative politics, and it's what I'll do as
president!"

"Thank you, Mr. Futch." Always the professional, Gwen says
this with the same respect she'd show an old lady crossing the
street. "Justine Hall, you have three minutes."

Stepping to the podium gracefully, Justine Hall tilts her
microphone down and eyes the room. "Those are going to be
tough acts to follow," she says, smiling. "My name is Justine Hall
and I'm the mayor of Denver, in the great state of Colorado.
Borrowing Professor Axum's formulation, I'd say I fall on the
side of equality more often than not, but I'm sure the questions
will allow me to explain where I stand on many of the issues of
the day. I want to take this opportunity to introduce myself to
you all."

The timid woman from the early videos is gone. She's been
well coached or she's found a genuine place of comfort from
which to speak. "My mother was a nurse for thirty years in the
suburbs outside Denver. My father was the first black POTUS.

No, not the President Of The United States. The professional wrestler, POTUS, the Legal Eagle."

She's used this opening line before, and it's a good one because it grabs everyone's attention while introducing her background and making the audience laugh at the same time.

"That's right. My dad wrestled for fourteen years and is a three-time MWA champion. That's Midwest Wrestling Alliance for those of you who never got a chance to see him drop his patented Elbow of Justice from the top rope."

Another round of laughter from the audience shows that Justine Hall has read the crowd perfectly. The people in the room are serious Ameritocracy fans, and probably already know where she stands politically. She's using her time to get them to *like* her.

"From an early age," she continues, raising her voice, "my calling was the church, the church my mother went to dutifully and, occasionally, dragged my father to. In our neighborhood, the church was the one place everyone got along, where white folks and black folks came together, and where a little half-Japanese, half-Black girl could feel at home. I grew up there and planned to attend seminary after high school.

"But when my dad returned home with a broken tailbone after one suplex too many, I opted to stay in Denver, attend community college, and work with the homeless and drug-addicted. I became a minister in the Unitarian church, and I was able to help lots of folks who needed help. I know I haven't got the Reverend Dixon's style—who does?—but I believe he and I have had a lot of the same experiences ministering to people going through bad times.

"Like Mr. Axum and, I assume, Mr. Futch as well, I never intended to go into politics. I ran for mayor of Denver because I wanted to bring practical solutions to real problems, and to do so unencumbered by the expectations of large donors or special interest groups. Look at my record and I believe you will agree that we've succeeded in Denver.

"Give me the chance, and I'll do the same for America. Truth is, I'm more of a doer than a talker, unlike some of the men who went before me, so I'll just say this: I believe in getting things done. You can have the purest motives or the highest ideals, but none of it means a thing if you can't get things done." There's a light smattering of applause at that, even when Gwen shoots the audience a stern look.

"Thank you, Ms. Hall," Gwen says smoothly. "Reverend Dixon, you have the floor."

Dixon rises, adjusts his jacket, and steps to the podium. He looks over the crowd with a practiced eye, and opens up in full voice. "It's an honor and a privilege to be here addressing all of you, and I thank the Lord every day for the life I've been given, and the opportunities I have to change lives in His service. But the Lord didn't do it all on His own! I am—we should *all* be— deeply grateful to Ms. Mia Rhodes for her vision, her hard work, and everything she's done to make this day happen!"

Despite Gwen's admonition, another round of applause starts, this one growing louder and louder, shaking the room. All eyes shift toward me and I can feel my face redden. I smile broadly, uncontrollably, fighting back tears.

Gwen steps forward to cut off the applause, but Dixon gives her his disarming grin, a grin that says *hey, just let it go, the audience needs this*. A man in the crowd shouts, "Thank you, Mia," and I burst into tears, still smiling like I've just won the presidential election myself. All of a sudden, the other nine candidates stand and begin clapping.

Even a few of the journalists are clapping now, and the moment hits me.

Hits me so hard I can't breathe.

As the thunderous echo of genuine gratitude fills the hall, I realize that these people aren't just fans of the candidates or the site. They're fans of me. They think I did something amazing, something they believe in and want to be part of.

Me. The office manager who adopts cats by accident and has struggled through the last four months, barely able to keep her head above water. They think I'm a hero.

As the applause dies down and eyes shift back to the stage, I'm beaming.

Dixon continues, voice rising and falling hypnotically. "This rally here today should have been impossible. A real alternative to the two-party system? No such thing, we've been told! Can't be done, we've been told! And yet, look around you, here we are! So we need to start changing our minds about what is and is not possible!

"Now, I don't know if you've heard, but I happen to be a Christian." That gets a decent laugh, and he lets it fade before he continues. "That means I believe in the greatest miracle in history: that God Almighty came to earth and walked among us as a man. That He came to bring us His greatest gift: the unconditional love and forgiveness that is His, and that can be ours. And how did we respond to that gift?" His voice falls, low and serious and dripping with pain. "We stoned Him. We whipped Him. And we crucified Him.

"That day two thousand years ago showed us the basic conflict that still defines us today. The spirit of God that dwells in us cries out for that love and that forgiveness. And our fallen nature tells us to hate, to fear, to torture and kill. We all face that choice every day, in a hundred ways, between what's right and what's wrong. And it sure doesn't help when every crazy dude with a website claims he's got God on his side!"

Another laugh, more nervous this time. Dixon's laying bare a lot of people's fears. "God, though, made it very clear whose side he's on. When He came to earth, He was not born as a king, as a soldier, as a rich man. He came to us as a poor child in a small corner of a vast and oppressive empire. That is who God wanted us to listen to, to care about. The forgotten, the poor, the helpless children. He told us again and again, 'what you do unto the least of my children, you have done unto Me!' Not the greatest, not the richest, the Lord tells us He is to be found among the *least!*

"Every day in my ministry, I see cruelty and neglect toward those people of God. I see men and women languishing in prison unjustly, people trapped in poverty without hope, people tortured and killed for no reason, because not enough has changed in two thousand years! And people ask me, Reverend, how can this be? How can a rich nation tolerate such poverty? How can a free nation keep so many in chains? How can politicians wear a cross on their lapel and still vote to torture and kill their own people? I tell them the same thing: because that nature within us has not changed, and a nation willing to kill a child in the womb is willing to do *anything.*"

The thirty-second warning flashes, and his eyes flicker to it for an instant. "We know, deep within us, what is right and what is wrong. We all hear the voice of God in our innermost souls. And if we choose, as a people, to let that voice guide our actions, we can bring His love, His mercy, His forgiveness, and His Kingdom to this nation! Thank you. Thank you all for taking the time to listen, and may your best conscience guide you when you vote."

Much of the audience applauds as Dixon takes his seat and Gwen Winters moves back to the microphone. Charles Blass is up next, but I'm beginning to tune out.

I haven't seen much here that I haven't already seen in their videos or position papers. For me, the important thing about this event isn't the speeches.

I don't agree with half of what's being said on stage. I don't know if one of the ten candidates in front of me will become president, but for the first time in a long time I feel satisfied.

Satisfied that the conversation is happening. A conversation free of partisanship, free of hypocrisy and lies.

I have no idea where this conversation will end, but I'm happy it has begun.

Later that night, Steph and I meet back in my suite for a quick glass of wine before the cocktail reception, where we'll introduce donors, fans, and journalists to the candidates.

I set my laptop on top of the entertainment console. "Music?"

"Yeah, we need to unwind for a minute. That was...incredible. I've waited my whole life to hear politics talked about like that. Real people with real ideas. Even the *shitty* ideas at least didn't sound boring. Well, except your boy Axum. He's boring as hell, but he's for real. You were right about that."

While she speaks, I plug my laptop into the sound system, which has six speakers mounted in the corners of the room, then open it up to find a playlist.

The moment the Wi-Fi connects, a few dozen emails download, and I give them a quick scan, determined not to get bogged down in any bad news right now. I'm still riding high from the success of the rally.

In the middle of the batch of emails, there's one from Malcolm, who, as far as I can remember, has never emailed me. The subject reads: *Congratulations.*

Despite the fact that you left me with a terrorist cat who attempted to eat my Marvin Gaye LPs, I made you a little something.

Below the message is a link to a YouTube playlist.

Steph walks up behind me. "What is it?"

"Malcolm sent us a congratulatory playlist. He did remixes of a bunch of patriotic songs. The Ray Charles version of 'America the Beautiful,' the guitar version of 'The Star Spangled Banner' that Hendrix did at Woodstock. Tom Petty's 'American Girl.' It's got like ten songs."

"Ooooh, he made you a mixtape. When I was in high school, it meant one thing when a boy made you a mixtape."

I roll my eyes. "It's a playlist, and you're a filthy-minded woman. He's just congratulating me."

"Right. Yeah. That's it. Sure."

"C'mon, he knows I'm with Peter."

"Does he?"

I think for a moment. "I'm not sure."

"Well then?"

I start the playlist, which begins with a 90s-style chunky hip-hop mix of the Woody Guthrie classic, "This Land is Your Land." Following Steph to the couch, I kick my shoes off and swing my feet up onto the coffee table.

We sit quietly, listening as the beat slows and transitions seamlessly into Elvis Presley's "American Trilogy," slowed down and backed by dozens of layers of epic synth.

Steph sips her wine, eyeing me over the glass. "You don't remember making mixtapes for your crush?"

"I never did that."

"Well, most people did."

"They did?"

"When you can't say how you feel, you get someone to say it for you. Someone famous, with a better voice and a better team of writers."

"You think Malcolm's flirting?"

"If he is, he's doing a good job. This playlist is fire."

Elvis's voice fills the room. The moment is just about perfect, but, of course, it's interrupted by a text. But it's not my phone chirping. It's Steph's.

"What is it?" I ask, noticing the shocked look on her face.

"David Benson just entered Ameritocracy."

"What do you mean?"

"Just what I said. *The* David Benson, star of the *Atlantis* movies, friend of Peter Colton, and all-around stud who stood in your bedroom a few weeks ago, is now a candidate."

"Who texted you?"

"Benjamin. He's on the site right now."

"He's serious?"

"That guy doesn't know how to joke."

I leap off the couch and open up our homepage on my computer, and there he is. He's got a full profile page and, of course, a handsome photo. I open Twitter and find that DB is tweeting about his candidacy from his verified Twitter account.

Sitting back on the couch, I take a long drink of wine and stare blankly at Steph.

"Pace yourself," she says. "We have a long night coming up."

"I know, but...David Benson."

"He's smart, handsome, and famous."

"I never thought that an actual, real celebrity would enter. It's gonna—"

"Shake things up?"

"That's putting it mildly," I say. "When we re-open the voting after the rally, he's gonna be number one with a bullet."

"Maybe, but you know what?"

"What?"

"David Benson is a problem for tomorrow. Right now we're celebrating success, listening to Elvis, and enjoying the night. In a few minutes, we'll be wining and dining a bunch of rich donors, famous journalists, and our candidates. Just enjoy it."

The Elvis song ends, and a wild banjo-fiddle tune takes up, backed by a throbbing bassline and some jagged yowls. I don't recognize it, but it kinda kicks ass.

"I love this song," Steph says. "Dolly Parton's version of 'My Country Tis Of Thee'."

Just as I'm beginning to enjoy it, my phone rings, and Bird's name shows up on the caller ID. "Hey there, calling to critique my performance on TV? I haven't watched it back yet."

"You did great. You *were* great. But most importantly, you *looked* great."

I laugh. "Seriously, did the cameras catch me crying? I bet my face got all red."

"No," he says, "But we all noticed around the office when your face popped up on six different TVs. I like what you did with your hair, by the way. You looked like Nicole Kidman—good Nicole, not *Eyes Wide Shut* Nicole."

I smile into the phone. Even a thousand miles away, I can count on Bird to notice my hair. "Except I'm half a foot shorter."

"You were gorgeous. And you *looked* tall."

"They gave me a riser to stand on. But thanks, Bird. I'd ask how things are going at *The Barker,* but I've gotta get ready for a party."

"Cool cool, but I didn't just call to tell you that you looked gorgeous. Check your texts. I'm sending you something right now."

I pull my phone away from my ear. "Not here yet."

"Be patient."

"What is it?"

"Something you're gonna want to see. You know FiveThirty-Eight, right?"

"Of course I do."

Taylor Swift's cover of Tom Petty's "American Girl" comes on, sped up and transformed into a distorted, EDM frenzy. Then Petty's original starts cutting into the mix, turning the track into a dialogue between the two versions.

"They're doing a thing about you that's gonna run tonight," Bird says. "They called Alex to get a quote, and Alex passed them along to me. I gave them all sorts of great—flattering—stuff about you, but, more importantly, I got them to send me what they're working on."

"How'd you do that?"

"Reporter owed me a favor and I promised not to tell anyone. But I screenshotted it."

My phone chirps with a new text, and I switch the call to speakerphone so I can read and talk at the same time. "Steph, come over here," I call across the room.

"Steph's there?" Bird asks. "Tell her congratulations. I think I caught a shot of her on TV."

Steph sidles up next to me. "Thanks, Bird. But why're you bothering Mia now? She's got Peter and a million reporters and ten presidential candidates waiting for her downstairs."

"I forgot," Bird said, "she's *famous* now. Parodied on SNL. Soon she'll be on Oprah, or whatever the modern day equivalent is."

"There isn't one," Steph says.

I read the text, a photo of a headline and the opening paragraph from the FiveThirtyEight story. "You say this is gonna run when?" I ask Bird.

"It's gonna be on their homepage later tonight. Multiple stories, including all sorts of polling data."

"What's it say?" Steph asks.

I hold up the phone so she can read the headline. "Holy hell!" she says. "They wrote that?"

"They did," Bird says.

I hang up with Bird and grab my wine from the coffee table, then walk back to Steph and read the story again:

2020 Now a Three-Way Race

With the success of today's rally, a lackluster field of Democrats and Republicans eviscerating each other in the primaries, and a brand that seems to resonate with the American people, the theoretical winner of the Ameritocracy competition is now polling at 20% in a three-way race against a generic Democrat or Republican. With 28% supporting a generic Republican, 26% a generic Democrat, and 26% undecided, FiveThirtyEight will be modeling the 2020 presidential campaign as a three-way race going forward.

Steph and I exchange a look. We both know exactly how big this is.

"Thanks for coming to California," I say. "None of this would have happened without you."

"I know," she says. "But we don't have time for self-congratulations. We have to get down to that party. You ready?"

"Gimme five minutes," I say, sliding on my lucky T-straps. I stand to give her a short hug and a smile. "I'll be right down."

At the door, she pauses. "Tonight's gonna be big. Tomorrow's gonna be bigger once news of David Benson goes wide. We're gonna get more votes than the Democratic and Republican primaries combined. The finale is in eight months."

"And those months are gonna be bonkers."

"Bananas."

"Crazy."

"So, you ready?" she asks again, but this time she doesn't wait for me to answer. Instead, she spins on her heels and walks out. Within minutes, she'll be chatting in French to a potential donor, glass of pinot noir in hand.

Back at my laptop, I restart the "American Girl" cover, cranking the volume until the windows shake. I walk to the balcony and gaze over the city, pondering Steph's question.

Los Angeles is a carpet of lights all the way to the horizon, and the cars pass below, a gentle rushing sound like faraway waves. *What does it feel like to be ready?* I wonder.

Ready for the explosion in coverage Ameritocracy will get from the rally. And from David Benson's entry into the competition.

Ready for the increased scrutiny this will bring to me, and most likely to my past. To my father.

Ready for what's developing with Peter, and ready for it to become public.

The track fades out. I walk back into the suite, close my laptop, and head for the door. As I step out into the hall, I decide that "ready" isn't a feeling that exists. It's just what's left in the absence of doubt.

I'm ready.

I am.

Thanks for reading!

I came up with the idea for Ameritocracy in the summer of 2016. Like Mia, I was dismayed at the level of political discourse in the country, and yearned for a fantasy world free of hypocrisy and political speech.

At first, I envisioned the story as a single novella, maybe 150 pages. But as I explored the idea, it grew into a trilogy. Books 2 and 3 are already in the works, and Book 2 is now available for pre-order.

Ameritocracy, Book Two: OFF MESSAGE
(February 15, 2018)

Ameritocracy, Book Three: ECHO CHAMBER
(Spring, 2018)

Now, some thanks...

I worked closely on this book with my brother, Noah Brand, and my wife, Amanda Allen. When we decided to expand Ameritocracy into a trilogy, the three of us worked together in Portland to create new characters and scenes. Though I do the bulk of the writing, many of the cleverest ideas come from them.

Noah also wrote some of the funniest lines in this book, and pored over my drafts multiple times, making improvements each time. Many times I messaged him with a request like, "See what I'm getting at in that line on page 34? Make it funnier." And he always did.

As always, my wife Amanda deserves something more than thanks. In addition to the specific improvements she makes to all my books, she supports my writing tirelessly and enthusiastically. Without her, I'd still be "planning" to write my first novel.

I also want to thank my dad, Robert W. Fuller, whose interest in politics and media inspired my own.

Special thanks to my team of "Just in Time" readers: Chet Sandberg, Nancy Swanton, Chris Rhodus, and Bonnie Dale Keck. Their help in the final weeks made this a much better book.

I spend a lot of time studying the American political landscape. I couldn't do this without the wonderful journalists, bloggers, and podcasters doing their best to make sense of the world in confusing times. Thanks to all of them.

And to the readers who enjoy my books, thanks!

A.C. Fuller

SPECIAL THANKS

I owe a great debt to Chet Sandberg, who offered invaluable feedback before this book came out. I tend to be wordy in my early drafts, and Chet stepped in toward the end to suggest thousands of small cuts that made the book more readable.

Remember Alex Vane, Mia's boss at *The Barker*? He's got his own series. I call them The Alex Vane Media Thrillers, and if you enjoyed *Open Primary*, I think you'll love them.

The Cutline
(An Alex Vane Novella)
Available *free*, and only though my website
The Anonymous Source
(An Alex Vane Media Thriller, Book 1)
The Inverted Pyramid
(An Alex Vane Media Thriller, Book 2)
The Mockingbird Drive
(An Alex Vane Media Thriller, Book 3)
The Shadow File
(An Alex Vane Media Thriller, Book 4)
***

Or get books 1-3 together in the boxed set
The Alex Vane Media Thrillers: 1-3

ABOUT THE AUTHOR

Once a journalist in New York, A.C. Fuller now writes stories at the intersection of media, politics, and technology. He also teaches writing workshops around the country and internationally.

Before he began writing full time, he was an adjunct professor of journalism at NYU and an English teacher at Northwest Indian College.

He now lives with his wife, two children, and two dogs near Seattle. For a free copy of one of A.C.'s books, check out: www.acfuller.com/readerclub.

And he loves hearing from readers.
www.acfuller.com
ac@acfuller.com

Made in the USA
Columbia, SC
13 January 2018